26 Hours in Paris

Books by Demi Alex

The International Affairs Series

26 Hours in Paris

Four Nights at Sea
(coming in December)

26 Hours in Paris

Demi Alex

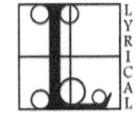

LYRICAL PRESS
Kensington Publishing Corp.
www.kensingtonbooks.com

LYRICAL PRESS BOOKS are published by

Kensington Publishing Corp.
119 West 40th Street
New York, NY 10018

First Electronic Edition: June 2016
eISBN-13: 978-1-60183-599-4
eISBN-10: 1-60183-599-X

First Print Edition: June 2016
ISBN-13: 978-1-60183-600-7
ISBN-10: 1-60183-600-7

Printed in the United States of America

With love for my Florida sisters.

Acknowledgments

Heather Graham, Traci Hall, Karen Kendall, Kathleen Pickering, and Bonnie Vanak; thank you for the encouragement to reach through it all.

You're the best!

Chapter One

One article selected. One author featured. One friend disappointed.

Kathryn Taylor groaned, dropped her head onto the mahogany conference table, buried it beneath folded arms, and freaking hid. The best opportunity to advance her career had presented itself in the form of a bloody, word-wrangled catfight.

"That's right, ladies. This is your chance. We're going to feature the winning article in the Valentine's issue," Paul repeated, a smug grin on his good-looking face. "The selected piece will join 'Aphrodisiac Foods from Around the World' and 'How to Say I Love You in Twenty Languages' in *City Wings'* Valentine's edition. Our readers devour anything and everything having to do with international desires. It's a way to escape the daily grind and dream of possibilities. Who would have thought New Yorkers were so romantic?"

Determined to keep the migraine at bay, Kathryn rubbed her fingers across her forehead and pressed her thumb against her temple. Paul was playing games with her damn life. Her future. She wanted to grab him by the shoulders and shake some sense into the man— preferably until he conceded and allowed them to do a dual perspective piece. That way, neither Kathryn nor Charlene, better known as Charlie, would lose out.

It simply wasn't fair to compete with a best friend. She'd worked so hard for a second chance at a writing career, and in spite of the threatening headache, perhaps even heartache, she still wanted the byline.

Kat was a damn good journalist, as was Charlie. She'd worked her ass off and done her time, as had Charlie. But, shit. Kathryn wanted her byline so bad, she could practically see the ink on the paper as their boss proposed the assignment. She had to enter the arena and fight for her career.

"Get out there. Do your research," Paul said, raising his arm and circling his hand above his head. "Lasso someone that makes your body hum, and write about the perfect place to find love, ladies."

"Seriously, Paul? Lasso someone that makes our bodies hum?" Kat rolled her eyes. Like those kinds of men were easy to find. With the same amount of exaggeration Paul had exhibited, Kathryn swept her arm through the air and landed the back of her hand across her forehead. "Wait. Hold on a minute. Wait . . . wait. I'm seeing a handsome man, in a far-off and romantic place, sweeping me off my feet."

Actually, she could envision someone, someone in a far-off place, sweeping her off her feet—in her dreams. But no one in New York fit the bill or compared to that distant someone.

"Paris is romantic," Kathryn admitted in a low voice.

She and Charlie had already exhausted the typical channels to meet the right men. The kind of guys most women dreamed of were an alien species and simply didn't inhabit their universe. However, she needed to find a man, just one, and fast. She had an article to write and a byline to claim. Feelings of guilt over besting a bestie would have to wait. She tamped down the objection in her gut, and let her creative ideas take flight. It was time to visit the ideal location to find love.

"I think we can take a small detour from the publication's travel angle on this. Why can't a woman find love in her neighborhood, and *then* sail off to a foreign and exotic land with the love of her life?" Charlie asked. Paler than usual, the other woman twirled a nervous finger into a renegade blond wisp, and just happened to skim over the e-cig stuck in her hair bun. She pulled it loose and looked at it with great longing.

"If it's done properly, I can see it working. However, any featured lovers must take off in the end for a foreign destination." Paul leaned back on his chair and tapped his fingers on the wood. Kat had known him way too long not to recognize the wheels of triumph turning in his mind. "There is a pragmatic benefit, too. If we concentrate on finding love locally, more of our readers will relate to the accessibility of that goal and can dream of escaping to a romantic place with their loves."

"Exactly," Charlie added, her posture relaxing a bit. "The dating scene has evolved so much over the past few years. There's always the chance of meeting someone at a bar or a club. Online sites host a bunch of events in this city. And let's not forget the old-fashioned way of being introduced by common friends."

"Great options," Kathryn said, looking up from the notes she'd scribbled on her legal pad. Her friend and rival had given in to temptation and was taking a long drag on the pink contraption, eyes tightly shut. "Earth to Charlie." Kathryn snapped her fingers and waited for her friend to look at her. "How are those local options working for you?"

Charlie's pretty shoulders dropped a few inches as she exhaled the vanilla-scented vapor. "Not fair. Maybe it's been bad timing for me. I really haven't tried too hard. It's been difficult to trust anyone since my divorce, so maybe I'm the problem and the scene is just fine."

Their boss cleared his throat and held up a hand to stop the personal reflection. They all knew Charlie's self-criticism would end in a door needing new hinges or something.

"You're not the problem, Charlie," Paul said, covering the blonde's hand with his own. His dickhead persona took a backseat for a moment. "Your asshole ex is. So let's take jerks like him out of the equation for the benefit of this piece." Paul could be a decent guy—he was just a pain in the butt the rest of the time. "And don't forget what I said about vaping on the premises."

"Okay, okay," Charlie agreed with a forlorn sigh before she offered them a small smile and put the e-cig back in her bun. "I don't know why I thought to quit vaping now."

Damn, Kathryn's heart ached for her friend, it really did, but they were on opposite ends of the spectrum when it came to beliefs in romance. Charlie believed a happily-ever-after kind of love existed and completed you. Kathryn was practical. She knew that romance could make life fun, if it didn't complicate your life and ruin your career. But love was an added benefit, not the driving force, in one's life.

"Listen, babe, with idiots like your ex showing up all over the city, it's best to try a new place," Kathryn offered. Travel and escape had always seemed like the right venue for romance. No long-term expectations meant no long-term disappointments.

"Somewhere far away and ultra-romantic. Think about it. Paris. City of Lights. City of Love." She made a sweeping gesture across the air and then came to a dead stop for dramatic purpose. She held up a finger and waggled it with significant intent. "Not to mention the endless supply of foreign, specifically French, men that are schooled in the art of sex from a very young age."

"Cute." Charlie actually giggled. "Let's stereotype a nation of men to get a good feature. Why don't we add making love on the banks of the Seine as a favorite hobby while we're at it?"

"Sounds good to me," Paul said. "Maybe I should tag along for the research?"

"Good thing you're the publisher and head honcho of this place." Kathryn leaned across the table and landed a playful fist on Paul's upper arm. "If you didn't have so much influence over me and I didn't like you the way I do, you'd be facing a lawsuit. Besides, January is too cold for outdoor sex in Paris. Is it even legal?"

"Whatever, Kittykat," Paul replied, laughing at the inside joke. "You owe me and you know it. So when I collect—"

"This is a very incestuous organization," Charlie said, pointing from Paul to Kathryn to the door. "Between you two and the accounting department, a tree house should be the official headquarters of *City Wings*. You're all too tight."

"And you've chosen to live with one of us," Paul reminded her.

"That's because Kathryn begged me to let her share Grammy's closet of an old apartment."

"True. It's the only way I could afford to live two blocks from Central Park. I thank you for your generous spirit, Miss Innocent-in-All-of-This," Kathryn said. "Now let's concentrate and get back to work for a few minutes. We need to write about finding love and about how not to end up like old spinsters—with no cats." She glanced at Paul. "Grandma's building doesn't allow pets."

He laughed, tossed his pencil in the air, and caught it before it hit the mahogany. "Let's hear the rest of this expensive trip you're planning."

Charlie cleared her throat and held up a hand. "I honestly feel it's best if we feature local romance opportunities, and doing it that way, it won't strain the budget—for us or for the readers." She shifted in her seat and turned away from Paul. "There are plenty of eligible men right here. Kathryn, you met that construction manager at happy hour last month. He was nice. So we have proof that nice guys do exist around here."

Fine. She was right. The guy had been nice, but Kat had ended it just before Christmas. He hadn't been able to hold her attention for more than three dates and one romp between the sheets. It seemed like no man could. Maybe she needed to lower her standards? Maybe the desire for more than a single good conversation topic was unrealistic? Or maybe she shouldn't expect earth-shattering orgasms, or even one orgasm, with a partner?

"I never said it was impossible to find a man around the block," Kathryn countered, deciding not to settle and still hoping for the elusive "O" in her sex life. "But finding love in the most romantic place on earth is much more exciting. Imagine gliding beneath an old bridge in a tiny rowboat, and gazing up at all those padlocks of love for inspiration."

"You know the padlocks have been cut off, right?" Charlie pointed out.

"And why not a luxury yacht instead of a rowboat?" Paul added.

Kathryn waved them off and continued. "How could a romantic dinner at the Eiffel Tower, with the city lights at your feet, twinkling like a room full of candles, not fuel amorous sensations?" She paused and glanced from Paul to Charlie. Paul adjusted the crotch of his slacks and stretched his legs while Charlie stared dreamily at nothing in specific and licked her lips. "And let's not forget the allure of a mysterious stranger in a whirlwind affair that will have readers packing their suitcases for Paris by the time they flip to the last page. Maybe we'll even get an ad from the Paris Tourist Board?"

"We're looking for love, not sexy interludes," Charlie insisted, a spark lighting her eyes with a new idea. "Sexy interludes. But. Fine. Okay. Got it." She placed her palms flat on the table and stood. "If we're really looking for the perfect place to find love, why not a cruise ship? It's textbook romance. What about one designated for singles? Passengers board with an agenda. Just think how much fun we'll have writing about a cruise, Kathryn."

"Nope. There is no 'we.' You can sail away on a Love Boat, and Kathryn will fly off and take her chances in Paris." Paul spread his fingers over the hard surface of the table, seemingly content with his decision to keep them on opposite ends of the world.

"Why do *I* need to go to Paris?" Kathryn asked, rubbing her temple with more force. "I'll be looking over my shoulder for him at every turn. What if I bump into him? What happens then?"

"You mean, how do you research the perfect place to find love when love finds you?" Paul folded his muscled arms over his chest and leaned back in his seat. "You could even have a true Parisian show you around all the hot spots. Why is that so bad, Kittykat?"

"Because Marko is not an option. He's loaded, cultured, and out of my league." Even worse, he'd insist on introducing her to his family like he had that Christmas years ago. "I've worked real hard to establish myself as a competent professional. It would kill me to have the mighty Renards look down on me."

"Why would they look down on you?" Paul asked. "You're being ridiculous."

"You could never understand, Paul. You're rich and entitled, cut from the same cloth as Marko. I'm a girl from Long Island that had to take online classes for eighteen months to finish my last semester and get my degree, all while keeping my dad's aluminum-siding business afloat to save my childhood home. Could you picture a woman in Marko's family with chipped nail polish and callouses on her palms?"

"Marko stayed by your side. You were the one that ran away from him." Paul's jaw was set, but his gaze was full of compassion. He'd seen what her father's passing had done to her and her mother, and he'd also been there for her in that difficult time. She hadn't turned away from him. The difference was that Paul was her friend. Marko was her soul mate.

Charlie cleared her throat. "I've heard about Marko, but no one has ever elaborated on who he is to you."

"Marko is a very good friend from school. One of my best friends," Paul explained. "He and Kat were joined at the hip from the moment they met. They did everything together. At first, they kept telling themselves they were only friends, but when they finally got their act together and hooked up, our Kittykat glowed like the brightest stars."

"We didn't—" Kathryn tried, but failed to correct her friend.

"Whatever," Paul said, waving her off. "They thought they were having a secret affair in Kat's senior year, but when her dad was in that horrible accident and passed away, she understandably shut down and retreated into a shell. No matter what we did, me, Justin, and even Marko, she wouldn't come back to us. I know it was a hellish situation for her, but I've never seen a man so tortured as Marko was at that time."

"What do mean, Marko was tortured?" Charlie asked.

"Marko is a take-charge kind of guy. He gets things done. Seeing the woman he loved suffer and not being allowed to help was torture for a man like him," Paul explained.

Kat hadn't had a choice. She couldn't have allowed Marko to change all his plans because of her. If he had, he would've resented her forever. It wasn't meant to be. "I'll take the cruise. Charlie can have Paris. She's more cultured and in tune with high society."

"No. Charlie won't do well on an eight-hour flight. You've always wanted to see Paris. No more objections."

Paul was right. Paris had been a dream of hers forever. And what were the chances of running into Marko at a tourist attraction? "Fine. Paris is perfect."

"Good. Time for you ladies to bring out the claws and get down to work. You each have your assignment. Your expense accounts will be adjusted and ready to go by noon. See Justin for the details. Get me your stories by next Wednesday. I'll decide which one gets published in the Valentine's issue."

"On what criteria will the winner be chosen?" Kathryn asked.

"Whatever I want," he said with a smile and a shrug. "I'm the boss." He stood, pretended to tip an invisible hat, and strolled out of the room muttering something about beautiful women pulling off their bikini tops and wiping mud from their faces.

Chapter Two

A two-thousand-dollar expense account barely covered an airline ticket from JFK to Charles De Gaulle. Kathryn's travel dates were too near for any special deals, so the prices were astronomical. She didn't care. She was getting her byline via Paris.

"Kathryn." Charlie's head appeared from the other side of the cubicle's divider. "Paul is a total ass. A nice ass, but still an ass. He's doing this on purpose."

"Tell me something I don't know." Kathryn continued her Internet search. "And what's so new about what he's doing?"

"He's making us compete against each other, and he's enjoying it. Did you hear the crap about mud and bikinis he muttered as he walked out of the conference room?"

"I sure did," Kathryn replied, reluctantly floating on the reality of seeing Paris. Her mind hesitated, but her body sang with joy. She was freaking going to Paris! "Though, I'd like to put a different twist on it. Like, he was fantasizing about a vacation of his own where mud-splattered women stepped out from the ring to seduce him. Either way, who cares? We can do it."

Charlie's chair rolled close and her chin rested on Kathryn's shoulder. "We have less than a week and won't be able to bounce ideas off each other. He wants us to present, in person, a complete feature on Wednesday, like elementary students presenting a book report to the class."

"It doesn't matter. This is our chance at a byline," Kat said, scrolling down the options on her screen.

"He's asking too much. Look at the prices for those flights. How are you supposed to research Paris on the budget he allocated?" Charlie let out an exaggerated grunt and touched a finger to the screen. "That's not how a publisher should act. For him, it's divide-and-conquer Neanderthal stuff."

"Sexy Neanderthal stuff." Kathryn laughed, pushing her friend's finger away. If it were anyone but her childhood friend doing this to them, she'd be outraged and searching for legal counsel. "He likes to take things to extremes."

"Tell me about it. That's part of his sex appeal," Charlie whispered, an obvious longing in her voice. "Too bad he's gay. I'd let him take me anyway he wanted . . . any day. It's been forever since I've had Neanderthal sex. Actually, any sex."

"I've told you he's not gay," Kathryn said. She had absolute proof. Paul had been her first lover, and he'd been a real good first, at that. They'd simply decided to stay friends, friends with occasional benefits, until Justin had come into their lives. Justin had been the game changer and the reason for Paul to enter a committed relationship. Staying friends, with occasional benefits, wasn't an option after that change in status. They were friends . . . period.

"It really doesn't matter. This isn't a short on the opening of a new hotel or the latest drink trend at the hottest ski resort.. This is the chance we've been working our butts off all year for, Charlie. We want our own bylines." Kathryn worried her lower lip as she considered how to word her thoughts without alienating her friend, but she knew what had to be said. "Get out there and write the best freaking feature you can. I know I will. Paul may have thrown us into a mud fight, but you can count on me for anything. I'm still here for you . . . or rather, I'll be in Paris and there for you."

Kathryn clicked select on an outbound flight option, and opened a second window on her screen. "I'm using the train to get from the airport to the center of the city." She'd make every last penny count. "Besides, public transportation will give me a true sense of the city and its residents. If I can make this work on a small budget, any woman can."

"Just ask him to increase your expense account," Charlie said. "He'd do anything for you, and you know it."

"No way. That's what Sir Paul wants. More control for the control freak." She wouldn't give him the satisfaction of pointing out that readers of all income levels needed to relate to the feature. He'd already hinted that finding love in Paris was a stretch for most working people. Expensive or not, it didn't change the facts. Paris was the perfect place for love.

She shrugged off the needling voice of reason in her head. Men didn't get the fairy-tale aspect of seeking love, and Paul wouldn't hesitate to push her buttons and let Charlie's idea win. More importantly, she wasn't about to give another inch of control. She needed to name the terms in her life in order to remain semi-sane.

"I'm not asking him for an extra dime."

"Suit yourself." Charlie chuckled, then rolled back into her cubicle. "I'm under budget with this last-minute special on Lovers Sail Tours. Reserved my cabin on the sixth deck. I'll be eating lobster and drinking margaritas all weekend."

"At least some guy won't make you pay for dinner on the first date. Food is all-inclusive on a cruise. But—if you're going to put out, make sure he buys the drinks."

They both laughed. However, they both knew such disappointment with dates was what had kept them single and living as roommates in Charlie's grandmother's closet.

"Screw woman's lib. We want knights in shining armor and wicked pirates to star in our fantasies," she insisted. Kathryn rarely made it past the awkward first date, but maybe some sexy French man would make her want to. She'd let him cook for her in his artist's studio. They would dance on a balcony, overlooking the city, and make love until the sun rose.

Fine. She'd settle for a stroll in the museum and a glass of wine at some bistro.

She had never been to Paris, so she needed to do a bit of sightseeing in order to write about the most romantic place to fall in love. She logged into her bank account, did a quick calculation of the following month's fiscal essentials such as rent, electric, and subway card. The tension in her shoulders released once she figured there was a bit over five hundred dollars left. Rather than a standard room in one of the arrondissements the magazine's budget allowed for, she had enough cash for a hotel room on the Left Bank.

Flying out on Thursday would get her to Paris on Friday morning. She had the option of returning either Saturday or Sunday afternoon. They'd both give her enough time to write her article and present it on Wednesday. Time wasn't the issue. Funding was.

"I'm going to take a Seine river cruise and a second tour via bus to see the remainder of city," she informed her friend behind the divider. "Well, that's assuming I can get it all jammed into one day of sightseeing. Hotels in Paris are as expensive as they are in Manhattan." She really liked the one that was catty-corner from the Notre Dame, but moving the dates around by a day altered the bottom line drastically. The airfare was way cheaper when she stayed for a single night.

She shrugged. The shorter trip allowed her more time to polish her work and make the "presentation" deadline.

"If anyone can get it done, it's you," Charlie replied.

Damn, Kathryn was blessed with good friends. She loved them all. Even Paul, the control freak.

Back to Paris.

As far as meals went . . . well, food was overrated anyway.

She called the number on the back of her credit card, and while she entered the account information, she pulled a box of protein bars from her desk drawer and stuffed it in her borrowed designer tote. Having a trust-fund roomie had great benefits—even if Charlie didn't access the money to live off of, she had gorgeous goodies to borrow. Once again, relief danced on her spirits when the bank recording announced she had enough room on her line of credit to eat *and* buy a new outfit.

Tapping her feet beneath her desk, she navigated between the open windows on her laptop and clicked BUY on each screen.

"I'm going to Paris," she breathed in a singsong manner, reserving her airfare and the room, and purchasing both tours. She sent the details to the printer, gathered her stuff, and then peeked over the divider at Charlie and announced she was off to Bloomies for a drop-dead sexy new look.

"I'm also here for you, my friend. Just don't call me collect." Charlie winked and blew her an exaggerated kiss before looking over her shoulder. With the coast clear, she snagged her e-cig from her hair. "By the way, choose the right dress and F-me boots for your trip. You never know who you may meet in Paris. Let loose. Enjoy the ride."

If only.

Kat waved away the puffs of scented vapor. "Don't get caught with that again. It's company policy. We won't be able to afford Grammy's apartment on my salary alone."

Charlie rolled her eyes. "Okay, Mom. Please don't tell Dad. I wouldn't want him to spank me."

"I'll see you at home," Kathryn replied, laughing as she walked to the printer to collect her documents. And as for letting loose, there was only one man she'd want to let loose with. It just so happened she'd let him loose. Their goals didn't mesh. Time had expired on that option.

"You calling him?" Justin stepped out of his office and sidled up behind her. A woman couldn't have a moment with her own thoughts in her own office when she worked with three of her best friends. Paul's Justin, her Justin, with all his mathematical genius, was *City Wing's* accounting department.

"No." Kathryn refused to meet his gaze, crossing her arms beneath her chest and waiting for the printer to finish. Justin had shared one too many martinis with Kathryn, and he knew her too well to believe that she wouldn't melt at the sight of Marko Renard. "No way."

"Why not?"

"Because," she replied, pretending she was too absorbed in the printouts about the Eiffel Tower to give the question more merit, "this is about work. I need to prove that people find love in Paris, not recapture a lost possibility. I've worked my ass off to get to where I am. I'm not screwing it up by spinning my wheels over something, someone, that's never going to happen."

"Right," Justin replied, leaning over her shoulder and bringing his mouth next to Kathryn's ear, at least pretending to keep their exchange on a professional level for the others in the room. "If that's how you really feel, you need to get laid by a real man and let the overseas god go. Your man from the past is the reason nobody else is enough for you. You know you're measuring these poor guys against a dream guy. Let him go, or invite him back."

"Past," Kathryn said, regret swelling in her chest. "It didn't work then. It's not going to work now."

"He emailed you—"

"Stop, Justin. This isn't about me and Marko. It really isn't. Plus, we're just friends." It didn't matter how she felt, because she knew she loved him, had always loved him, and would probably always love him. What mattered was that there was an ocean between them. "We've always been friends and will always *be friends*."

"Always?"

Damn, that was too many always in one thought.

Full disclosure was not part of her relationship contract with Justin. She wasn't going there. No need to share everything. After all, in the two years she'd been that close with Marko, there had only been a few weeks of complete surrender. Glorious and earth-shattering weeks. Then, her world had gone black.

They had crossed their best friend line, but she'd never acknowledged what it had meant aloud and she hadn't let him speak of it after the worst Christmas of her life. Her fairy tale had crashed the night her father had passed, and what she wanted had no longer mattered. Kathryn had needed to be there for her mom. Nothing else.

Marko had stayed at her side, but at her insistence, they'd reverted to best friends in those dark days. She'd needed him as her friend. Her rock. He'd been there. She hadn't permitted a romantic future together. The only thing she'd allowed was a predetermined date for a reunion—if they were both still single.

She had been shocked when she'd received his email on their should-have/could-have-been reunion date. While still in school, they'd set a time to reconnect seven years in the future, but she'd never dreamed he would remember their pact. She'd actually gone to the Empire State Building that Wednesday before Thanksgiving with every intention of meeting with him if he showed, but she hadn't stayed. Feeling stupid, she'd turned and run. She hadn't been able to take the risk. Apparently, according to Paul and Justin, Marko had remembered. He'd been waiting.

"A romantic relationship with Marko is out of the question. I just need to put myself out in the dating world. I'm ready for a man that will be *here* for me and rock my world."

"Who said it has to be a relationship? Why not a tryst? Give the man a chance."

She gave Justin her best out-of-bounds look and shook her head.

"Fine." He raised his hands, palms forward, in a sign of surrender. "But you know what they say about those French men?"

She crossed her arms over her chest and shifted her balance. "Best lovers?"

"*Oui.* French men have mastered the art of flirtation, and they try much harder than most, especially when you're playing hard to get. Don't think you'll get away with a simple 'No, thank you' with a real Frenchman. To a French guy, a response like that just means you're considering his proposition." Justin cupped her chin and raised her face. He dropped a kiss on the tip of her nose. "Not to mention those hot Italians. They're known to be irresistible and very determined."

"Got that covered." She raised her left hand and wiggled her ring finger. The cubic solitaire she kept in the top drawer of her desk for unwanted happy hour advances reflected the light and shadows bouncing off the walls in the small space. "It may work against my research, but I'll pack it just in case I need it."

Justin laughed. "A ring on your finger means you already have another man's stamp of approval and are worthy of his efforts, so he'll try even harder."

"That's fine," she said, shrugging in resignation. "I deserve some sweet talking and a nice tumble between the sheets."

"You certainly do." Justin placed a sincere kiss on her cheek. "Good luck, sweetie, because you deserve so much more than one day. What you need is an amazing lover for many days. Either way, pack the new black teddy and those sexy kitten heels. I can't wait to see that morning-after glow on your beautiful face."

"Thanks," she said, hugging the man who, in her college rebellion days, had held her hair away from her face on more occasions than she could remember, and trying to recall when she'd told him about the teddy. "Love you."

"Love you more."

She knew he cared. Really cared. They'd been the best of friends since their sophomore year, and they weren't timid on calling each other's bluff, so she didn't mind Justin pointing out the obvious. After all, he'd been there during her Marko roller coaster.

She couldn't help but sigh. Justin had intentionally hit the nail on the head. Marko, her Frenchman with an Italian mother, had proved to be more than hard to resist. She loved the whispered French words and the Italian endearments from his lips. She could still hear him calling her *bella*, and she could feel the tingles spread over her skin at the thought. But after much soul searching and internal turmoil, she'd let him go. They belonged to two different worlds. Years had passed since she had resolved to move on. She simply hadn't accomplished that task yet.

"I already have the best friends a girl could ask for. Now to find my main squeeze."

"Who will give you all the orgasms you want," Justin finished.

"Exactly." Kathryn went up on her toes and gave him a quick peck. "Keep an eye on Charlie while I'm gone. I have a feeling she's going to back down from her trip. She's going to need support."

Chapter Three

"Can you please stand to the side for a moment?" The female gate agent winked and smiled conspiratorially, then gestured for Kathryn to move to her right. "Your seat has been changed. We need to print the new boarding pass."

"No problem." Deciding to send *au revoir* messages to her friends and check Facebook, Kathryn retrieved her phone and connected to the terminal's free Wi-Fi. With a huge grin, she read over a dozen wishes for a good trip on her timeline, and then she got to Justin's post of a picture of the Eiffel Tower wrapped in black lace and laughed aloud.

He'd practically detailed a schedule on her public page, including links to museum passes, Yelp café reviews, and the best lingerie shops in Paris.

You're a huge stinker! she thumb-typed, shaking her head like a nut. Looks like a personal 'Kat Does Paris' ad on my page.

But you love me. Have fun, sweetheart! Hope he calls.

So did she . . . sort of . . . but she wasn't getting her hopes up. Don't think he has my number.

You never know ;)

Well, you posted all that stuff last night, and he hasn't reached out yet. He's probably planning a weekend rendezvous with a bimbette and won't even be in town.

Jealous?

No.

Give him a chance. If not, find a different one. Get laid in Paris. <3 U

<3 U 2!

"Mademoiselle, you're ready to board." The young woman held out the new boarding pass and waited for Kathryn to approach. "You're going to love first class. Enjoy."

What?

First class?

"Thank you," she replied, and then quickly headed through the jet bridge before they decided to change her seat again. Somehow, her measly expense account had morphed into the most luxurious and fancy cubicle-style accommodation.

"Yes," she breathed, tossing her overnight bag into her very own personal space. "Personal space," she repeated aloud and dropped onto the soft leather. She propped her feet on the ottoman thingy, and played with the little television screen. This was going to be one fine flight.

An attendant appeared with a bottle of mineral water, and then offered Kathryn an alcoholic drink before takeoff. Tempted to take the edge off her flight jitters, but aware of her deadline and tight schedule in Paris, she accepted the water and opted to wait for dinner to indulge in some wine.

Just as soon as she got some rest, this was going to be the trip of her lifetime.

She hated the idea of wasting the first-class experience on sleep, but she hadn't slept since she'd booked her flight. She was exhausted. A quick peek in her compact mirror showed dark circles had taken residence under her red-rimmed eyes. With that visual, she knew she was beyond exhausted, which explained why she was having a hard time remembering which train to take to which station and even the name of her hotel. Adrenaline had kept her functioning, but it wasn't enough. If she wanted to maximize her trip, she would have to sleep on the plane.

She pulled a travel book from her bag, pushed the extra undies and black teddy back under her laptop, rearranged the only other outfit, also black, and then stowed the borrowed Louis in the proper compartment. Fluffing a pillow and laying a soft blanket on the seat, she decided on a quick nap before dinner and a review of her schedule afterward.

Plan set, she settled in her seat and buckled her belt. She pulled it tight across her middle and leaned back against the headrest.

"Bonjour, mon amie."

Kathryn looked to her left and saw the dark bedroom eyes that belonged to the deep masculine greeting. Damn, this ride was getting better by the minute.

"Hello," she said, observing the lazy manner in which his eyes lowered and his lips smiled. Heat flushed her face, and tingles crawled where his gaze trailed. How the heck had he managed to get such a rise from her body without a single touch?

"I am very pleased you are my travel neighbor," he said in a distinct French accent, then stepped across the aisle and into her very *personal* space, leaned down, and kissed each of her cheeks in turn. "I am Cyril."

"Hi," she breathed. "Kathryn."

"Beautiful," he replied and stepped back. That was when she noticed the gold band on his left ring finger. Charming Cyril was married.

Disappointed, but remembering the French flirting etiquette she'd read about, she smiled and pulled the blanket up over her shoulders. He was being nice and appreciative. French men did that. It didn't mean he wanted a crazy love affair with her ... well, maybe just a crazy affair. And that was okay. More than okay. When she'd boarded the plane, she'd climbed over the fence she'd built around herself, and she was ready for new experiences. Cyril was good practice.

"First time you travel to Paris?"

"Yes." Her fingers tapped a quick staccato over her tummy. "Is it obvious?"

"Of course, my dear. But your nervousness is very endearing." He sat and stretched his long legs. "You will love Paris. It is very much like you. Beautiful, sexy, and intriguing."

She couldn't help but hiccup a small laugh. "Thank you." Her face grew hot again, but she refused to become flustered and shut down. "I'm a writer. A magazine reporter. I'm preparing a piece on why Paris is the perfect place to find love."

"Very, very true." Cyril nodded enthusiastically. "I have had much success in finding love in Paris. Of course, I have also had many years there. I was born and raised in our amorous city. My first love found me beneath Pont Marie." A big smile colored his handsome face in memory.

She sensed she was missing the significance of the location. "Is that an 'extra' pretty bridge?"

"It is pretty, but my first love introduced me to a sensual custom on that afternoon. It is said that when you stand beneath the bridge, you should kiss the one standing beside you. Josette tipped up my chin and lowered her sweet mouth before she explained why she had kissed me. I fell in love with the first sweep of her tongue over my lips."

"Aww, that's so romantic." Kathryn hugged her middle and curled her feet beneath her bum. "It's a perfect first kiss."

"It was. Josette taught me so much before her fiancé returned that weekend. I had to stop visiting her because he was much older, and bigger, than I was. I couldn't compete with a university student."

"How old were you?"

"Fourteen. A good age to experience first love."

"And Josette?"

"I did not ask and she never said. But she was more mature than I." He reached across the aisle and, with a tender finger, swept her hair off her forehead. "With your big brown eyes, long waves, and full lips, you resemble my Josette."

Surprisingly, she didn't recoil from his touch. She actually enjoyed it and hoped he'd linger a bit longer. Kathryn was amazed at how natural it was to speak with such a man. "Thank you."

"I wish you find all you seek in our lovely city," he said, as the aircraft pushed back from the gate.

"I believe I will," Kathryn said, and grasped the armrests.

"You will," he agreed, taking a business card from his case and writing something on the back. "When you do, bring him here." He pointed to the address he'd written and handed her the card. "At the door, show Jacques my card. Tell him I have invited you and that you are my guest."

"What is this?" Kathryn asked.

"It is a surprise. One of Paris's hidden gems," he explained, adding a quick wink. "Perhaps we will meet again."

She tucked the card between the pages of her book and didn't pursue the invitation any further. The plane was moving. Feeling the power of the engines beneath her seat, she worried her lower lip. Paris may be an adventure, but a plane leaving solid ground had her stomach clenching into a tight knot.

"Cyril, I have a question," she said, brushing her hand over his and waiting only long enough for a tilt of his head. "No funny business. I see that you're married and all. I'm just nervous during take-offs and landings. Would you mind if I hold your hand while we takeoff?"

"It would be my pleasure," he replied, closing large fingers over her clenched fist and making little circles on the back of her hand. Comfort and warmth filled her, and she closed her eyes, breathing deep like the *Conquer Your Fears* podcast had instructed.

The smell of fresh brewing coffee woke her. She looked to the left and found Cyril reading a French newspaper.

"*Bonjour, ma chérie.* Did you sleep well?"

She stretched in her bed and managed to cover a yawn as she nodded. "I didn't realize I'd fallen asleep," she added, licking her parched lips. "That was a smooth takeoff."

"Yes, you were asleep before we reached cruising altitude. I adjusted your seat to a bed when the seat-belt light went off. You were tired and needed to rest." He offered her a butter cookie, but she refused. "I also asked the attendant not to wake you for dinner, but they will be bringing breakfast soon."

"Breakfast?" She'd slept for hours. She wasn't ready for Paris. Had no idea which train to take. Which station her hotel was at. Nothing. Bypassing the material at her side, she stood and reached for her laptop. "We have Internet access, right?"

"Yes, but we will be landing in a little over an hour."

"I just need to check on a few things." She lifted the computer's lid and pressed the power button. Connecting within moments, she quickly checked her social networks, and then opened the notes she'd made on her arrival transportation.

A text displayed on her screen.

Buongiorno, bella.

Her contacts showed only a phone number. No name. She recognized the New York area code.

Did you sleep well?

She glanced at Cyril, but he was engrossed in his reading. Besides, she hadn't given him her new number, and the original message had been in Italian, not French.

She typed out three consecutive question marks.

It's been so long that you don't recognize the number?

Kathryn mentally recited the number and held her breath. She knew it. She'd known it very well. But she'd had no idea Marko had kept it all these years.

Hi. How'd you get my cell number? I've changed it since we last spoke.

It wouldn't be difficult to find, bella, but I didn't. I'm sending the message to your email address. ☺ How is the flight?

Great. I slept for most of it.

Were they really doing this, messaging like it was an everyday occurrence? And how had he known she'd just woken up?

Kathryn ran her fingers through her hair, once again unbuckled her seat belt, and looked around the cabin. She stood, placed the laptop on her seat, and searched passenger faces for the man who lit the fire in her belly and set her heart on overdrive.

Cyril looked up and smiled. "We can call for the attendant if you want coffee."

She shook her head, but didn't move. He wasn't anywhere on the plane—not that she could see. A new message sounded.

Kat, are you still there?

She dropped back to her seat.

Yes. Where are you?

Waiting for you.

I'm coming for work. I'll only be there for a day, and I have a lot of research to do for an article. This isn't a vacation.

I'll see you when you clear customs.

She stared at the computer screen. Waited. Realized she was holding her breath and exhaled.

Marko was waiting for her in Paris. It had been years since she'd last seen him. Would he recognize her? What did he look like? Well, she actually had an idea of what he looked like, but she wasn't sure how recent the company photo on the website was.

Every time she'd known he was coming to New York, she'd hibernated in her apartment, ensuring there would be no chance meeting. She couldn't risk having to say good-bye to him again. It hurt too much.

Kathryn bent at the waist and stared at the floor between her knees. Why did he love his career and country more than he loved her? It could never work. He was a European boardroom shark, and she was a New York bohemian. She crossed her hands over the back of her head and moaned.

"*Ma chérie*? Are you feeling ill?" Cyril asked.

"No," she breathed and straightened. "I need coffee."

With cold fingers wrapped around her coffee cup, she continued staring at the screen. The lack of new messages kept her preoccupied, and she didn't bother to check the train schedules. She knew that once she was in Paris, she was with Marko. Period. She wouldn't be able to control her schedule, and for the first time in her life, she didn't mind the idea. She craved seeing him, hearing his voice, and smelling his scent. She missed him so much. She sipped, stared, and sipped some more. As for work, having a real Parisian showing her the best places in the city to fall in love would be a great angle. Yes. She'd enjoy time with Marko. She'd let loose. It was only for a day, so the pain of leaving him again couldn't be as bad.

"Excuse me, *mademoiselle*. We need to stow the laptop for landing," said the flight attendant who had appeared beside her.

Kathryn's hand trembled as she hit the power button and lowered the cover. She returned her beloved MacBook to her tote and handed it to the attendant.

"No worries." Cyril reached for her. "I will hold your hand during landing."

Chapter Four

If he didn't stop pacing, Marko Renard would wear a groove in the marble flooring of the arrivals hall. Kat's plane had landed, but he hadn't seen any New York passengers exit yet. She was probably still at immigration.

He stuffed his hands in his trouser pockets and willed the electric door to open and Kat to walk out. He missed her. From the first moment he'd seen her, he always missed her when she wasn't by his side.

Whether knowingly or not, she had come to him and she was finally on his turf. If she wanted to learn why Paris was the ideal place to fall in love, he was going to show her exactly that. His Kat had put her life on hold way too long. She'd more than met her responsibilities to her family. It was time for her. Her and Marko.

Marko was no longer a young man who didn't want to overstep his bounds, nor did he worry about making wrong life choices. He wanted her. He was going to have her. She would be at his side. His lover. His confidant. His everything. Just the fact that she'd mentioned Paris as the perfect place for love proved the point he'd argued for years. There wasn't a chance in hell he'd let her get away this time.

A loud groan escaped his throat, so he immediately apologized for startling the older woman standing beside him and moved to a different viewpoint.

Marko typed a quick group message to his college friends: I owe you.

Big time, came Justin's reply.

Make it count, Paul added.

The door slid open again, and he searched over the heads of the other people waiting at the railing.

There she was. Standing behind the yellow line, the most attractive woman he'd seen in ages crossed her arms beneath her chest and tapped a booted toe with impatience. He couldn't help but smile. Long dark hair, tousled and framing her gorgeous face, mocked his fingers for a feel, and the adorable pout of her sensual lips stirred the lower region of his anatomy.

Fuck. He was a grown man sporting a hard-on in the waiting area of an airport. He stifled yet another groan. Dressed in sleek black, his free-spirited girl was business tailored and ultra-sexy. How had she grown more beautiful?

Marko frowned, noticing how the smooth Frenchman kissed her cheek and guided her ahead of him. It wasn't until she waved her fingers in a dainty farewell and left her travel companion that Marko managed to unclench his fist. No matter how, she was coming to him.

Impatient, he pushed to the railing and didn't look away from the door. It opened again. Walking toward the agent, she looked past the exit and met Marko's gaze. He lifted a hand over his head. Her eyes grew big. Her small hand flitted over her chest. Then, finally, she smiled.

He waved and motioned for her to walk toward the right. He couldn't move quickly enough, and he wanted to argue with the guard at the gate who stopped her. Instead, he waited, opening his arms and folding her into his embrace when she finally stepped past the barrier and back into his life. He buried his face in her hair and inhaled her sweet scent.

Kat was with him.

Her breath warmed his neck and her heart beat against his chest. Marko moved his hands up her arms and cupped her face; then, without a verbal greeting, he took her full lips in a proper hello.

As he'd expected, at first touch, she tensed. Then her mouth softened beneath his, welcomed the coupling, and invited him to take more. He did exactly that, tasting her essence and breathing his intent against her soft acceptance.

"*Ciao, bella.*" He cupped her face, kissed the tip of her nose, and dropped his forehead to hers. He felt her smile beneath his fingertips and sighed.

"That's quite a welcome for a best friend," she breathed against his lips, her voice a little shakier than he was certain she intended. "Even for an Italian-speaking Frenchman."

"Kat, you're in Paris. On my territory. We're playing by my rules now. We are not simply best friends." His words burned so damn true that they singed his soul. There was no room to ignore the reality between them.

"I'm only here for a day," she whispered.

"Make no mistake," he pressed, taking a small step back and tipping her chin to look at her beautiful dark eyes. "I've been very patient and understanding. I've waited for you, because I want all of you. Every last bit. I won't settle for only a friend."

Her breath hitched and her pupils dilated, filling with yearning and desire. The slowest seconds of his life stretched between them as he waited for a response.

Six long years earlier, it had torn him apart to do the right thing and put her needs first. There was no doubt that he loved her and wanted her by his side, but her grief had consumed her. He'd given her time and space because she'd needed to cope with her father's sudden death. He'd stepped back into the role of her best friend. When he'd graduated and revisited the possibility of Kat joining him in Europe, she'd rejected the option. She hadn't been able to consider a relationship past friendship. The only thing Kat had wanted was to stay with her mother and heal. The tragic accident had cost both women so much, and they'd needed each other.

At first, he'd remained as close as possible, but he had honored her requests and hadn't pushed her back into a romantic relationship. Eventually, she'd insisted on personal space and turned away from him. He had believed there was no choice but to continue with his professional plans. When he visited New York, she was never available. It hurt, but he focused on being patient and making his own accomplishments before he would insist on making her see what was truly between them. Their type of connection was not typical.

Time had passed though. There would be no limit to their relationship. Kat stood inches from him, and he could no longer deny himself. His need was too great. It couldn't be appeased.

He brushed his knuckles down her cheek, and saw the moment she admitted the truth to herself.

"Yes," she whispered.

The distance between them disappeared. He claimed her mouth, her acceptance, and didn't break away until the last bit of oxygen had been spent. A tiny moan escaped her lips when he pulled away. He smiled.

"You're so beautiful, *bella*." He needed one more kiss before releasing his hold. It was selfish, he knew, but he couldn't resist. "Thank you for coming."

Kat held his gaze, telling him with a look what she didn't say with words. She was glad she'd come. She'd needed to come.

He lifted her bags, not appreciating how much weight she'd been carrying, and slung them over his shoulder. "Am I correct in assuming this is all you have?"

"Yes," she replied, searching his eyes. "I don't need much. When I made the arrangements, I calculated that if I took the RER to and from the city, I'd have twenty-four hours in Paris. So, the clothes I need are in the carry-on with my laptop."

"Twenty six—since there's no need for the train. I'll make sure you won't need clothes for the added two hours."

Heat sparked in her eyes. She'd missed him, too.

"We have a whole day together. Where to first, *bella*? The apartment to rest and freshen up or—" Her tongue wet her lips and Marko's body reacted. He wasn't taking her home so she could get ready to leave and go sightseeing. Once he had her to himself, he planned to keep her that way, and in his bed, as long as possible. "It's still early. Let's start with some breakfast. *Chocolat chaud?*"

"We have time to spare? Don't you have meetings or something?"

"I cleared my schedule for the day. I'm completely available to you. You can tell me all about your research."

Kathryn touched the chiseled line of his jaw, and forced herself to breathe. The years had been so freaking good to him. His hair was dark and combed back from his strong forehead. The planes of his face had settled into a very masculine profile and taut muscles filled his tall frame, but thankfully, his intoxicating fresh scent had remained.

"Thank you," she said, trailing her fingers down his broad shoulder and reveling in the feel of his hard muscles. "Sounds perfect."

Screw the wall she'd built around her heart. She'd jumped over it before she'd left JFK. Making the decision to be with him, even if only for a day, released the fist squeezing her insides. What was a broken heart in the midst of everything he offered?

Scared but unable to resist, she conceded to what she truly desired, added a time limit, and pasted on a sultry smile. She could do this.

Glad for the added height her new boots afforded, she stretched the remaining inches to his mouth and placed her lips on his. "I'm so looking forward to spending time with you, my not-just-a-friend person," she whispered.

"*Moi aussi*," he replied, wrapping his arm around her waist and once again pulling her against his warmth. He possessed her mouth in a long, slow, and addictive kiss, leaving no room for retreat, only a craving for more of what he offered.

Her body hummed and her mind grew fuzzy. Heat seeped through her coat and warmed her chest, causing her nipples to pebble and strain against the lace bra she wore. Marko's obvious need pushed at her belly. She ached for him to take her and show her exactly how much he'd missed her. Kathryn had dreamed of him, of being his, and if she didn't accept his terms, she knew she would regret it for the rest of her life. She had one day with the man of her heart in a city of love.

There was nothing she wanted more than to mix business with pleasure this time out. She'd have her twenty-six hours in Paris.

Unable to quench the thirst, her tongue swept through his mouth, and she lost herself in his kiss, alone in the sea of people at Arrivals. Her legs went weak, and he held her upright and crushed her against him.

"You get your twenty-four hours in Paris. The additional two are all mine." He pulled back and looked at her, a wicked pledge in his dark eyes. "I promise those will be the best two hours of our lives."

Moisture pooled at her core and she squeezed her thighs tight. Marko always kept his promises.

"Let's get this day started," he said, tucking her against his side and moving toward the exit.

Chapter Five

Damp cold whipped past Kathryn's coat, and she shuddered as she moved closer to Marko. He set his body against the wind, shielding her from the chill, and raised a long arm for an approaching Mercedes.

The driver immediately brought the vehicle to where they stood and exited the car, but Marko waved him off and reached for the door himself. He helped her inside, unbuttoned his coat, and followed behind her. She scooted to the seat on the far side, admiring the smooth way his body folded into the luxury car. The man sent a different kind of shiver through her body.

"Come here," he said, holding open the dark wool and gathering her against his side. "You'll be warm in a few minutes." He instructed the driver in French, and a stream of hot air surged from the vents. The privacy partition rose, and he curved a large arm around her.

She didn't speak; rather, she snuggled against him, folded her hands, and fit them beneath his suit jacket and on his chest. Dropping a kiss atop her head, he tightened his hold.

"Today was one of the coldest mornings of the season. I'm afraid it's because of the wind chill." With one hand, he rubbed up and down the length of her back, warming her. With the other, he covered her clasped hands and held them over his heart. "They're forecasting a warm-up by noon. The wind is supposed to die down and the sun will be strong. It's the perfect day to take in the sights. Are you comfortable now?"

"I'm good," she replied. "And I'm not worried about later. Anytime you're around, I'm warm."

"Really?" There was a note of surprise in his voice. "Why is that, *bella*?"

"I think your body temperature naturally runs high." She closed her eyes and inhaled his familiar scent. She was mentally transported back to a fall night on the beach, before exams. "Whenever I was cold, I'd snuggle against you and instantly get warm."

They'd been cramming for midterms when they'd decided on a late-night visit to the ocean as a study break. Sitting on a low wall, they'd talked and drunk coffee from Styrofoam cups. The wind had picked up and spurred Kat to rummage through the trunk of the car for a sweatshirt. She'd pulled it on and returned to find Marko sitting on the sand, patting the space between his outstretched legs.

"Come here," he'd said. *Same words, same sentiment.* He'd taken off the sweater he always ended up giving her when she was cold and added it to her layers. Then, settling her between his legs, he'd pulled her against his chest, wrapped his arms over her body, and fit his hands in the pockets of her sweatshirt . . . beneath his sweater.

Kathryn sighed and opened her eyes. "I still have the sweater. It's a bit tattered and frayed on the sleeves, but it still looks good." She'd swear it even still smelled like him.

He chuckled and rubbed the back of her hand. "It always looked better on you than on me." His lips brushed her forehead. "I liked seeing it on you," he added, placing a finger beneath her chin and turning her face up toward his. "I liked everything about you. I still do."

The cold was no longer an issue. Heat tingled inside of her and her heart raced. "We shared the best of times and some pretty tough ones," she said. "You were always there for me when I needed you. I never thanked you for that. I don't think I could have gotten through that Christmas in the hospital if it wasn't for you. To this day, I hate hospitals. Every short beep I hear reminds me of the machines that breathed for my dad. Every antiseptic smell turns my stomach. If it wasn't for you, I would have fallen apart."

"You didn't," he insisted. "You were incredibly brave. You took care of your mother, and you both made it past those dark days. Your father would have been very proud of you."

"Thank you," she said, pushing the heel of her palm into her tummy. "You were my strength." She fell silent and, once the sadness passed, a smile curved her lips. "We also had great times together. Late nights in the library, walks on the quad, Thursday-night parties. They were special. Do you remember?"

"I remember," he said. "We even watched the nightly news snuggled against each other on your bed, with your sweet body testing my control every time."

"Well, we did have some times when we gave in to the temptation," she reminded him. "Those were the best days of my life. I wouldn't change a minute of our past—"

"I would. I wouldn't have let—"

She placed a finger over his lips and shook her head. "I loved every minute I spent with you." Being with him had been as natural as breathing. "You were this stuck-up and all-knowing grad student that got under my skin from the start. The way you were so opinionated and had something to say about every policy or change we came across. The way you made me feel when you looked at me and smiled. How you appeared each time I needed you. Everything."

"I recall a rather argumentative and very liberal undergrad egging me on."

She laughed, remembering how fun it had been to tease him and play with him. "I knew that, beyond any doubt, I could count on your support and friendship. I really value that." She feathered her fingers over his jaw and smiled, truly regretting that she'd never fit into his privileged life. Despite Marko's insistence to introduce her to his family, she'd never felt comfortable with the idea. She simply didn't bring enough to the table to have his parents accept her. And he was real tight with his family. "But even with such a special past, I need to stay in the present. I've worked hard to overcome obstacles and finally embark on a dream career. I'm in Paris. I'm with you. I simply want to savor today. I really want today, Marko."

"I want you. You," he said, a challenge in his gaze. "All of you."

She recognized the look. Anticipation fluttered in her belly and her breasts grew heavy with need. She wasn't the girl on the beach who had shied away from the same challenge in the past. She was a woman who knew exactly what she wanted. She wanted Marko Renard.

"I want you, too," she replied, angling her face for a kiss.

"Dieu merci," Marko breathed, cupping her nape and lowering his lips. It hadn't been his intention to ravage her in the car, but he wasn't about to wait a second longer to claim her. He tangled his fingers in the dark, silky strands of her hair and held her tight. The

woman's moan was his undoing. He knew it. And he welcomed it with the zeal of a starved man sitting down to a feast.

He worked each button of her coat until the heavy material fell open. "Are you warm enough?"

"Very," she replied, undoing his tie, then dropping her hands to his belt buckle.

Pleased to find the black sheath disrupted by her show of arousal at the nipples, he smiled. "I like the outfit. Too bad it's not going to last for long."

He pulled her onto his lap, and in a fluid motion pushed the dress up past her hips so she could straddle him with ease. There was so much of her he wanted to experience, to worship, and he wanted it all immediately.

Lace garters held sheer stockings, and a black silk triangle covered the apex at the top of her gorgeous thighs. His cock ached to burrow inside her, but he insisted on pleasing her first. Holding her gaze, his hands smoothed beneath her dress and over her soft skin to her breasts. Moving his thumbs over the erect nipples in tiny circles, he waited for her to settle against his touch.

"Breathe," he commanded.

She released a breath and her body sank against him, his erection straining toward the heat she offered.

"You're so beautiful, *bella*."

She touched his face and lowered her mouth to his lips. Slowly sweeping her tongue across the seam, she tortured his control.

"I hadn't planned on taking you like this. Flowers, champagne, and a big bed had been on my mind. But that can wait," he said, pushing her coat off her shoulders and letting it fall to the floor. "You're sure it's warm enough in here?"

"At the moment, it's a heat wave." She smiled and shoved his jacket off his shoulders and freed his shirt from his pants. "Aren't you warm?"

Instinctively, his hands moved to the hem stretching across her hips and exposing the black silk he wanted gone. "Feverish," he admitted.

Marko lifted the dress over her head, marveling at the wonderful response each brush of his fingers elicited. Kissing the trail of goose bumps that surfaced, he savored the feel of her skin beneath his tongue and cherished the slow grind of her hips against his groin. Tasting her sweetness, his hunger grew. Her scent filled his senses and intoxicated his mind.

"Are you sure you're warm enough?" he asked, fighting to hold on to his last ounce of reason.

"Burning," she breathed, seemingly surfacing from a sensual haze and rising on her knees to offer him her breasts. Gorgeous, full breasts, tipped with the most tempting nipples, and promising to taste better than a gourmet meal.

His fingers gripped the curves of her hips, holding her up while she unbuttoned his trousers. She took him in her hand and stroked from the base to the tip of his cock.

"I'm healthy and I'm protected," she said, meeting his gaze. "Do we need anything else?"

Damn, she was an angel.

"Just you," he managed, suckling one nipple and rolling the other between his thumb and finger. "This isn't going to be slow, *bella*."

"Who said anything about slow?" she replied, peeling back the silk panties and positioning him at her entrance.

A trimmed dark crown adorned her beautiful pussy, and he ran a finger through the soft curls. She was hot as fire and dripping with need.

Tempted, but determined, he stilled her hips from descending onto him. He fisted the base of his throbbing erection and guided himself along her folds to the bundle of exquisite nerves at the top. As he circled her clit with the head of his cock, she coated him with her moisture and threw her head back to expose more of her throat. His mouth claimed the delicious skin, and his excitement swelled at the thought of his mark on her neck.

"Don't come before I ask you to. Hold it, Kat. First, I'll have your pleasure, then you'll have me."

His fingers replaced his erection, and he spread her swollen folds to gain more access. He loved the sound of the strained whimpers coming from her lips and the way a pretty pink blush spread over her body, but mostly he rejoiced in the pleading gaze she gave him.

Kat rode his hand, grinding against the heel of his palm and sighing with ecstasy when he pushed first one, then a second, finger into her tight channel. He stretched and prepared her, reaching for that special spot that had her panting for release. The manner in which her tongue wet her lips almost had him losing his patience, but the frenzy of need in her expression maintained his resolve to feel her unravel more than once. There was no way he'd be able to hold back if she came undone around his cock. The simple thought had it weeping for deep contact.

"Tell me," he rasped, stroking deep inside her. "Tell me you're mine."

"Yours," she breathed, squirming close, and breathing heavy. "All yours."

"Come," he commanded, sliding a third finger inside her and urging a climax with his final thrust.

Her pussy convulsed and cream coated his hand as her orgasm claimed her and she called his name. She collapsed against his chest.

He drew her against him and kissed her shoulder, closing his eyes and fitting his hand between them to position his cock at her opening. "Now, we do it again. Together this time."

He lifted off the seat and buried himself in her heaven. He stilled, balls deep, held her down against him, and allowed her time to adjust as he took her mouth and was lost.

Each thrust had him swelling a little more, and he reached deeper and harder until her breath grew erratic and her pussy gripped him with volatile pressure.

"I can't hold this one," she cried, looking into his eyes, and then letting her head drop back as her climax grew and her control slipped.

He caressed the top of her womb, and when she cried out with pleasure, he filled her with a blessed release.

Marko dropped his face to the curve of Kat's neck, and breathed in the essence of his angel.

Entangled in each other's arms, they rode in sated silence on the motorway until the driver rang Marko's phone and announced they were ten minutes out.

Resting his chin on her head, he rubbed her back. "We still on for Les Deux Magots, or would you rather we go home first?"

She looked up and smiled. "Are you kidding? I'm starving."

He laughed and lifted her off his lap, gently depositing her on the seat beside him. "And you want to be where Hemingway and Picasso once sat."

"Exactly," she said, reaching into the tote for her makeup bag.

"No need," he said, cupping her face and tracing his thumb over her kiss-swollen lips. "You are so beautiful the way you are."

She tossed the bag back into her tote and leaned down for her dress.

"Let me," he said, taking the dress from her hands and dropping a soft kiss on her lips. "Welcome to Paris, *bella*."

Chapter Six

Dressed and composed, Kat accepted Marko's hand and stepped from the privacy of the car. She welcomed his possessive hold when he closed his fingers over hers and folded his arm behind his lower back, keeping her snug against him as she turned and admired architecture and history she'd pictured in her mind's eye for years.

She listened to his authoritative tone instructing the driver in French, but wasn't in the least bit concerned about what he said. Marko would take care of everything and she could actually take in the splendor that surrounded them. She could enjoy the experience without worries. The realization that she'd left Kathryn behind and accepted the remaining twenty-five hours as Marko's Kat filled her with a sense of empowerment, strength, freedom, and joy. She inhaled the cool air and smiled. Before her stood the oldest church in Paris.

"I've dreamed of this place," she said aloud, snaking her hands around him and leaning her chin on his broad shoulder. "This is really it. The bustling spirit and grandeur of Saint-Germain-des-Prés."

"Up until a few centuries ago, the Abbey owned the majority of land on the Left Bank. Right to the Seine. It's survived fire, war, and so much more. As you know, artists and intellectuals from all walks of life have always flocked to Paris. This is where your Hemingway and Picasso gathered in the cafés. These are the streets you had pictured on your walls in school," he said, gathering her in his embrace and pointing beyond the massive boulevard and tourist traffic.

"Can we walk from here to the Seine after breakfast?"

"Absolutely," he replied, raising her hand to his lips and kissing her palm. "Anything you want, *bella*." He turned for the infamous café with the white and green canopy, her hand once again tucked against his warm body. "You'll love the old bookstores and quaint shops."

Kat moved toward a table beneath a propane heater, but Marko insisted the glass-enclosed terrace afforded the same views and wouldn't disappoint. He led her past the café patrons sitting outside.

"It offers needed shelter from the wind," he explained.

Without an objection, she followed and sat at a small table in the corner. They didn't speak, simply sat together and looked out the window at the pedestrian traffic. It took no time for a middle-aged waiter to approach and take their order with brisk efficiency. Marko ordered their drinks and suggested an omelet for her. She agreed and the waiter jotted the order on a tiny pad, gave a curt nod, then maneuvered over the suitcase at the neighboring table with an explicit phrase on his narrow lips.

"He doesn't seem to enjoy his job," Kat observed.

"Not necessarily so," Marko laughed. "It's just his way of acknowledging the tourists. That attitude is as expected as the lighting of the Eiffel Tower at night."

"I guess," she replied, watching the other waiters interact with patrons. They weren't rude or nasty; however, they all wore blasé expressions on their faces.

Marko pulled his chair beside hers and rested his arm across her back. Awareness prickled up her spine as his fingers caressed her nape.

"I'm guessing you've been in contact with Paul and Justin," she said. "Did they update you on my whole itinerary?"

"Yes," he replied, meeting her gaze, clearly unabashed with the admission, but pulling away for the first time since they'd met in the terminal. His jaw set hard, he dropped his arm from the back of her chair. "Why didn't you come to the Empire State Building as we'd agreed?"

Tears stung her eyes, but she blinked them away and worried her lower lip. She couldn't find the words to express why, but she had to be honest. "I went early," she whispered. "I couldn't stay."

"Why?" He leaned forward, but didn't reach for her.

She replayed the night in her mind. Every thought. Every hope. Every picture she'd seen of him over the years. They lived in two different universes, and fate had chosen very different paths for them. Every morning he woke in a posh home or a luxury hotel in any corner of the world. On almost every morning of her mundane life, she woke on a futon, in a shared rental, in the same state she'd always lived in.

"It wouldn't work," she breathed, and managed to glance into his dark eyes. "I couldn't stay and deal with it if you showed up. Even more, I didn't know what I'd do if you didn't. I did what you accused me of doing after my father died. I ran away."

"From me," he said, catching a solitary tear that escaped from the corner of her eye. "From us."

Nodding, she dropped her shoulders and clasped her hands in her lap. She tried to swallow the knot lodged in her throat. Tried to miss the disappointment in his face, but she couldn't lie to herself or to him. She owed him that much. "I'm sorry, Marko. I couldn't face the possibility of an us and the hurt that would follow."

Their drinks arrived at that very moment. They fell silent.

"I'll let that go for now. I share in the responsibility for us being apart all this time. We made our choices. Our choices have made us." His chest expanded, and he reached for her intertwined hands and pulled them into his own lap. "I have a few important decisions to make in the next few days. Tomorrow will be very telling. I'm scheduled to meet with a New York–based firm for a position in Manhattan. I also have a few offers in Europe to consider. Once we've caught up, I'd like your input. Your opinion means everything to me."

Kat licked her lips and nodded. "Anything I can do to help, I will."

"There's one thing that will help. Only one. And since we are together right now, I won't allow a single doubt to come between us. You've agreed to the next twenty-four hours together. I won't let you run. There's no choice. Understand?"

She understood. She didn't have any desire to run. She wouldn't grow old regretting that she'd walked away from the best day of her life. "I don't want to run."

"Good," he said, sweeping his thumb over her cheek and wiping away the tears. He gave her lips a quick kiss. "I'm happy you're here, and I'm so proud that you're finally following your dreams. Tell me about the research you need to do."

Taking a deep breath, she accepted the olive branch he'd offered and returned to the moment. "The guy who was supposed to write the Valentine's Day feature left *City Wings* on a rather sour note. Actually, Paul kicked him out on his ass when he found questionable expenses on his corporate card and deleted his proposal for a story. He's history. The douchebag's spot is up for grabs, and so is the byline."

"So Paul gave you the assignment?"

"Not quite." She leaned back and waited for the waiter to place her omelet on the table. "This looks heavenly."

Marko smiled and spooned whipped cream on her hot chocolate. "Go on."

"In typical Paul fashion, he pitted my story idea against Charlie's proposal. That's my roommate and best girlfriend. She's been there for over two years, has a point to prove to her family, and also wants her own byline more than anything else. Paul wants a catfight. He thinks that we each want it so bad that we'll turn on each other."

"I doubt that, sweetheart." He laughed and shook his head. "That's just Paul." He adjusted her plate and cut into her eggs. Forking a mouthful, he presented it and waited for her to accept.

She closed her lips around the small bite, and didn't question the ease with which she'd reverted to speaking to and confiding in the man who was destined to break her heart. Instead, she gave in to the feeling. Damn, she deserved some happiness.

"Anyway, he's not getting the fight. I told Charlie to write the best feature she can, because that's exactly what I'm going to do."

"Hence, your Paris research."

"Exactly," she replied, sipping the hot chocolate and licking the whipped cream off her upper lip. "I have a list of all the best places to fall in love. I also made a schedule." She retrieved her folder and placed it in the center of the small table.

She continued eating while he flipped through the stapled sheets. Each grin, smirk, or shake of his head had her perching on the edge of her seat. He didn't look up until he'd reviewed the whole file and anticipation was pushing at her calm.

"Well?"

"Impressive list." He cocked his head in an amused tilt. "If we start right now, we'll be done two minutes before *City Wings* hits the stands. I'm sorry, Kat. You either need to remain in Paris for much longer or return to the city for weeks to cover that list. It's impossible to see all those places in one day."

"You promised," she reminded him. "You can do whatever you set your mind to. Are you backing out on me, Marko Renard?"

"No, sweetheart." He smiled and touched her chin. "I'm absolutely doing what I've set my mind to. As far as your research, we've started with the perfect spot. Not to fall in love with Paris—but to find love in Paris."

She wrinkled her nose, but let him guide her to look past the window and at the pedestrians outside.

"I introduce to you the sidewalk café. These are the places to see and be seen, to meet new and old people, and to fuel your heart's desires for any adventure. Whether a tourist trap or a local gathering spot, large or small, expensive or affordable, a Parisian café is at the core of all relationships."

"I see."

There was a young couple snuggled together at a table beneath the same heater she'd spied earlier. They fed each other a decadent-looking chocolate cake and shared long kisses between bites. A grandmother played with a baby, while a younger version of the woman motioned a young man to the table and offered him a chair to join them. Two men laughed as they exchanged animated stories. An older couple shared a cup of tea in silence, but with hands intertwined beneath the table.

"I like the café angle," she announced. "It's romantic."

"It may be romantic, but it's not an angle. It's a way of life." He looked over her head and nodded to someone. "Now what about the bridges?"

"There are so many. At first, I wanted to see the Pont des Arts and envision all the lovers who had left locks there through time, but a man I met on the plane mentioned a different bridge that piqued my interest."

With a grimace, he held up a finger and requested she hold the thought. Kat turned to see a messenger approach them. Dressed rather fashionably for someone who made his living on a bicycle, the young man greeted them, then handed her a luxurious black and silver shopping bag.

Marko thanked the deliveryman, and placed a bill in his hand as he returned the signed slip. The other fellow gave a slight bow and tipped an imaginary hat. "*Adieu.*"

"So which bridge intrigued you?" Marko asked, taking the bag from her hands and pulling on the silver tie.

"The Pont Marie. He . . ."

Marko produced a red cashmere wrap. He fit the oversized garment around her shoulders and arranged the way it flowed down her body.

Swaddled in pure luxury, she raised the soft material against her cheek. "Thank you. I love it."

"You're welcome." He rolled the edge between his fingers. "It was a self-serving gift. At least you'll be warm while we stroll through Paris. Tell me, why Pont Marie?"

"Cyril, the man on the plane, said it was the first place he fell in love because an older girl kissed him beneath the bridge as legend requires."

"Okay. That one is easy," he said, a shadow crossing his handsome features. He reached for his espresso and looked at her with a bright twinkle playing in his eyes. "We'll have an afternoon picnic there."

"Not fair. You've taken over planning the whole schedule." It was a fail of a scolding. Marko was efficient and complete in everything he did, and she had no reason for concern. Just because she was relieved didn't mean she couldn't protest for fun's sake. "Please remember it's *my* research, dear friend."

"Kat, I haven't seen you or spent any time with you in over five years. You no longer hold a friend card over me." He sipped the remainder of his coffee. "You agreed to my terms. Therefore, I arrange the schedule. I keep you warm, and I make all our plans. I assure you will have the material for your article. You don't argue."

"Sounds like I'm supposed to surrender my will and do everything you want."

No verbal reply. He raised a dark brow and cocked his head.

"You're serious?"

"I am." He tucked a stray lock behind her ear and caressed the side of her neck. "Let me spoil you, Kat. Allow me to make decisions and plans."

Her insides went soft and a molten pleasure spread through her chest. It would be such an indulgence to let go.

"For once in your life," he continued in a soft voice, "live in the moment and don't worry. Relax and enjoy. Trust me to take care of you and all your needs."

"I do trust you," she said, studying his expression and wanting more than anything to simply be with him. "Okay. No more arguments from me."

He sealed the agreement with a coffee-flavored kiss. "Good choice," he said. "Eat up. You need your energy for the day." He pulled a small piece of bread off a baguette and popped it in his mouth while she finished her eggs and followed his advice. She relaxed into the moment.

"Why the grin?" Kat asked, heat sparking her insides at his expression.

"I'm thinking of how the cashmere will keep you covered and warm when we visit the highlights on your list. But mostly, I'm imagining how it will feel against your bare skin when you cry my name as I make you come, at the location of my choice. " He stretched out his hand and turned up his palm. "Give me your panties."

Chapter Seven

He knew what she needed.

He knew what she needed.

He knew what she needed, and Marko repeated it over and over in his head.

Holding his hand steady, he looked into her eyes and waited. Kat resumed breathing and her luscious lips softened. He could see the argument brewing in her mind with each pass of her teeth over her lower lip. She needed to be pushed.

Once upon a time, he'd chosen the patient and understanding path. He'd listened to her concerns and had given them credence. Unfortunately, it was caution that had ruled their paths after his wrong handling of the situation. Kat's hesitation had kept them apart when he could have settled her family's financial situation, if only she'd allowed him to help. If he could have made payments on the home until she graduated or paid off the remaining mortgage for her, she would have been free to follow her dream of grad school in Europe—at his side. Rather, the stubborn woman had insisted on doing it all herself. Without him.

Without him was no longer an option. He'd tried it her way, but he knew what he wanted. Past, present, and future. He wanted her. She needed a push. He was going to push.

"Would you prefer to stand so I could remove them myself?"

She shook her head and her fingers went white around the edges of the wrap. With a nervous glance around the café, she clearly weighed the chances of being seen, but the flush on her face revealed that the possibility excited her. "I'm doing it. I was just trying to remember if the thong was over or under the garters."

"Over. *I remember*," he said in a steely tone. He wriggled his fingers to show his impatience, and he smiled inwardly when she squirmed in her seat, her dainty hands disappearing beneath the cashmere.

Marko worked to maintain a calm and collected façade while his heart pounded in his chest and excitement buzzed in his ears. He'd give Kat all she needed and, in the process, he'd fulfill her every desire and fantasy. There was no misinterpreting her expression of yearning to relinquish control. He was the man for this woman, and he'd grant her every wish.

With her gaze sealed to his, she placed a shaky fist in his hand and slowly opened her fingers. Warm with her heat, the silk seared a trail from his palm to his cock. "Are you wet?"

Wide-eyed, she nodded.

"Nice," he replied, fitting her offering into a pocket inside his suit. He placed his palm on her left knee, finding it clamped tight against the other. He grinned and leaned closer, brushing his lips just below her ear. "Relax your knees, Kat."

She let out a small breath, but did as he instructed.

Slow and deliberate, he smoothed his hand up her sheer stockings to the soft flesh of her upper thighs. Her muscles tensed beneath his fingers, and a small moan escaped her lips. She looked only at him.

"Wider," he said, rounding his hand over the curve of her smooth flesh and sliding higher on her thigh.

Heat radiated between her legs. His fingers skimmed her bare skin, and waves of her desire rolled beneath his fingertips. He slowly caressed the length of her inner thigh, fighting the need to move higher and bury himself in her warmth.

Yet another moan from her lips, and he returned up her thigh and feathered a rewarding touch over her sweet heat.

"Does it please you to know the couple sitting beyond that window is watching the glorious flush on your face deepen?"

For the first time since she'd handed over her panties, she broke eye contact and looked at the two young men sitting outside on the terrace. Their attractive features included knowing grins, as their arms crossed at table height. Each of their hands cupped the other's excited bulge.

One of the men angled his coat so his partner had enough privacy from the patrons on the street, but not from Kat's view. He lowered his partner's zipper, revealed a thick erection, and fisted his lover's shaft. The other man's hand joined him, and they pumped quick and hard in perfect unison.

She squeezed her thighs together and writhed in her seat.

"Time for us to go," Marko announced with a chuckle. He withdrew his hand and spread his fingers to either side of her knees, bringing them together. "The plan doesn't include being arrested for public sex or indecent exposure at a popular café and spending time apart, no matter how much I want to strip you and take you on this very table."

Marko secured the cashmere wrap over her coat, tucked Kat's hand through his arm, and started toward the left—in the opposite direction of the way she'd stepped.

"I lead," he reminded her.

She shrugged and laced her hand through his arm. With her free hand, she adjusted her coat. He touched a hand over his chest, savoring the knowledge of the treasure his pocket contained. She'd responded beautifully to his command.

Marko set a comfortable pace, and with a few more foxing turns on quaint cobblestone roads and narrow lanes, they were almost to the river before he spoke again. "I don't think I've ever seen you quiet for this long."

"That was crazy," Kat said, a faraway look still on her face. "How could—what will they—well, you know."

No question. Her rational mind was thinking about the logistics of the other couple's situation. He laughed. "Ah, *bella*. That's their concern, not ours. I'm sure the thrill of their exhibition died down once you left."

"Seriously?"

"Seriously," he replied, pulling her hand into his pocket to keep it warm. "Put the other hand in your coat pocket. It's still cold."

Considering her sweet astonishment, he laughed. "You haven't managed to shake that adorable 'seriously' question. I hope you never do. It always makes me smile. You act so surprised with the most basic of facts and the obvious effect you have on others. If I had been one of those men, I would have done anything to keep you transfixed so I could see the color on your cheeks. You looked so pretty watching in shocked awe."

"I *was* shocked," she insisted.

"I know," he drawled, unsuccessfully attempting to stop his laughter. "There was actual quiet at our table for more than a few minutes."

She playfully smacked his shoulder and joined in laughing. "Come on. That can't be a common occurrence. Not even in Paris."

"The effect you have on people isn't common," he replied. "You are the only woman to cause me to stumble over my own feet and lose my composure. You are breathtaking."

Once again, she'd been caught off guard. Kat didn't know how to reply. No one spoke to her like that. No one made her feel wonderful. "Thank you," she breathed.

The feel of his fingers, intertwined with hers, gave her security and strength in each step she took. She felt no need to carry a conversation, and she didn't mind where they ended up. "Everything here is so full of personality. I can't decide where to go and what to do."

"Then it's a good thing you don't need to," he replied, halting in front of an elegant accessory store and considering the window display. "You do need gloves and a hat, though."

"I'm fine," she said, then stopped with the argument when he looked at her. They had a deal. He decided. She accepted. "Okay. Thank you."

He smiled and butterflies fluttered in her tummy. Marko had a devastating smile. If he'd simply smiled his request from the start, she wouldn't have thought of objecting.

The store didn't have red cashmere. He selected a pair of exquisite gloves and a generous-shaped beret, all black cashmere, to match her coat. Marko insisted on keeping every bit of her covered and warm. Well, almost every bit. As they exited the boutique, the chill crept beneath her coat and up her legs to her center. The cold caress reminded her exactly where her panties were, and moisture spread over the top of her thighs.

Kat let out a long breath, butterfly sensations filling her once again. Did he know? Had she mentioned the commando fantasy during one of those long, platonic nights?

"Come here." His voice snapped her from her thoughts and she turned to look at him. Marko once again arranged the wrap tight and close to her neck. He dropped a soft kiss to her forehead, his warm lips lingering on her skin past the end of the kiss. "It's about time you're here."

Kat closed her eyes, envisioning Marko's scent gliding over her body and cocooning her in pure bliss. Nothing ever smelled as satisfying. Nothing ever touched her the same way. Damn, it was Marko. The only man she'd ever truly wanted.

"It feels wonderful to be here." *Wonderful to be with you*. She lifted her chin and looked into his dark eyes, sinking into a sea of possibilities and feeling the silly smile form on her lips. She couldn't help it. Somewhere deep inside, she wanted to sidestep reality and just live in the moment. What was that saying about not dwelling in the past?

"Where is my beautiful dreamer off to now?"

"France," she replied, no longer bothering to hide her smile. "Living in the moment."

He wrapped his arm around her shoulders, tucked her against his side, and walked. They cleared a small row of attached stone-faced homes, and all her preconceived images of the beauty of the old city unfolded before her feet. They stepped onto a wide street beside the Seine, the edges littered with the green book stands. Gorgeous views, endless river, quaint and imposing buildings, and tons of books. Perfect.

Numerous bridges, varied in architecture and design, crossed the water. The elegant and classic manicured gardens of the Tuileries, beautiful even with the harsh winter conditions, sat directly across the width of the river. The long expanse of the one-time palace, now the wondrous Louvre, stretched to the right of the gardens, with the beautiful Gothic architecture of the Notre Dame as the crown jewel in the middle of the water.

"More beautiful than I ever imagined," Kat breathed, swallowing the wonder swelling in her throat. She turned to take in the Musee d'Orsay, directly beside them and on the same bank, and then spotted the Eiffel Tower over Marko's shoulder. She walked around him, linking her fingers with his and holding his hand as she crossed the street for a view without vehicles or pedestrians. "How am I going to see it all in a day?"

"You're not," he replied. "You're going to focus on the article and the message it's supposed to reveal to your readers."

She looked up into his eyes. Finding love . . . but that wasn't due to Paris.

Chapter Eight

Marko snaked his arm across her middle and pulled her to settle against him. With her back to his chest, he held her close and fit his chin over her head. He loved they way she fit so perfectly. Loved the way it felt to have her so close. He couldn't get enough of her and he knew he was doomed when all he could think of was standing with her before him and beneath him just like that.

Kat loved him. He knew that much. He simply had a day to make her need him completely.

"The sights aren't going anywhere, sweetheart. You'll see and experience them all in time." He closed his eyes and inhaled her sweet scent. "Let's stroll over the Passerelle. Much like the Pont des Arts, it's famous for lovers' padlocks and honeymooners, but it also has some of the prettiest views of the city. We can sit and people watch, as well."

"I can't move away from this very spot. It's too gorgeous," she murmured.

Truth was, he had no desire to people watch. He wanted to watch one person . . . Kat. However, he'd do anything to give her what she wanted and what she needed.

Marko slipped his hand inside her coat, silently thanking the designer for placing the buttons far apart enough to allow the fit. Her warmth flooded his fingertips and filled his palm as he settled it beneath her chest. His cock grew hard against her, as he recalled whispered words from a long time before and erotic images filled his mind. His Kat had an exhibitionist streak. He ached to fulfill any fantasy she had of public sex, but he also knew that building anticipation would work best for Kat.

A soft moan left her lips as he brushed the underside of her breast, and she arched her back and gave him more access. Needing no further invitation, his thumb feathered her nipple and he lowered his lips to her neck. His tongue licked up the intoxicating skin, and he loved the tiny squirm of her ass against his groin as he suckled the softness of a creamy earlobe.

"I like your coat," he said, cupping her heavy breast over her dress and tracing the pebbled peak. "I like the material of your dress, too."

"It's silk," she breathed.

"You're sinfully tempting against the softness." Much like his erection strained against his trousers, her heat strained through the material. He moved his hand down her body, bunching the skirt in his fingers along the way. He didn't care if the dress was made from a potato sack or silk. It was on her. "Even more," he rasped, sounding much more in control than he was, "I love the feel of you beneath my fingers."

She dropped her head to his shoulder as he feathered a touch over the top of her mound.

"Behind us, and to the right, is the Musée d'Orsay. It briefly served as a railway station, which is very appropriate considering the foot traffic on the Left Bank."

She turned her head and looked past him at the pedestrians behind them, her shiver evident under his touch. His body shielded her small form from the people hurrying to their respective destinations, but they were there. She clearly liked that.

He kissed her flushed cheek. "Today, the museum houses masterpieces from Monet, Renoir, Degas, and Van Gogh, to name a few of the artists. Think of Monet's seascapes and how the sand would feel on your naked backside as I sink into you for sleepy sex at sunrise."

"It would feel wonderful," she said dreamily.

"Keep your eyes open, sweetheart." He nudged her head up, and grinned at the obvious effort it took for her to lift those beautiful lashes. He smoothed his palm over her belly, letting the dress cascade down her thighs and fighting the urge to keep it bunched high and run a finger through her swollen sex. "Look at the expanse of the Louvre, built originally as a palace. Today, it's one of the largest museums in the world."

What he wouldn't give to feel her melt against him. Beneath his touch. On his command. He'd circle the tiny bud of nerves and welcome the feel of her weight against his chest as he brought her pleasure. Later.

"The Louvre has exhibits from prehistoric times to the present. We won't be visiting the museum today, so enjoy it from afar, *bella*. We have different plans. I'm going to take you home and ravage the world's most delectable piece of art—your body."

Her moan played in his ears, and he felt her tremble. Satisfaction thrummed through him, confirming original thoughts on her basic needs. The quickest way to her heart, or her mind, was through her body.

"That's it, sweetheart." He grinned, then kissed behind the silver dangles framing her elegant neck. The earrings were the only jewelry she wore, and the only hint of the hippie style he so admired. "Let me hear your breath catch as you take in the Paris landmarks." He moved his hand up her tummy and over her ribs, reveling in the heat of her skin beneath his fingers.

"The Jardin des Tuileries is the perfect place for an afternoon stroll. There are two pretty ponds inside the gardens, and with the addition of a nice blanket and a picnic basket, they're the perfect place for making love to you."

"Marko, you're not playing fair," Kat groaned as she swayed rhythmically to a silent song.

"Why's that, sweetheart?"

"You're driving me crazy. Your touch is so distracting. I can't concentrate on my Paris research. All I can think of is you." Her eyes closed, dark lashes rested on her cheeks, and her head fit softly on his shoulder. "All I want is you."

Marko beamed with fulfillment and dropped a kiss over her temple. "*Très bien.*"

"No. It's not good," she said, opening her eyes and turning in his embrace. She tapped a soft finger against his jaw and met his gaze. "How am I going to manage to write this article on Paris if all I think about is you?"

"Kat, what is the premise for your article?" Reluctantly, he withdrew his hand from inside her coat and turned her to face him. He cupped her face. "What are you going to write about?"

He could see her thinking and reaching for a logical answer. Kat's rational mind was one of her greatest assets, but her conservative choices had also held her back from her true self.

"The premise is rather simple," she said. "I'm writing on why Paris is the perfect place to find love."

"Specifics, Kat. Narrow it down." He moved his thumb over her lips, parting them slightly. "Verb and noun."

"Finding love?" Her voice trembled and her pupils dilated. "The article is about finding love," she reiterated.

"Then why are you denying what you want and feel?"

She pushed against his chest and stepped out of his embrace. Turning to look out over the river, she folded her arms beneath her breasts and stood in a very defensive stance. "Because, sometimes we need to accept the circumstances for what they are. Because, one day is not going to be enough."

"That's where you're wrong," he said, refusing to let her set the terms of their relationship. He knew what she wanted, even if she wouldn't admit it . . . yet.

Marko wrapped his arms over her and held her close, waiting for her breathing to calm and her mind to settle. Words wouldn't work in his favor, so he dismissed the idea of arguing with her. He'd show her. He'd act.

"We are going to enjoy today, and you're going to get enough material to write that feature," he said. "Stop thinking so hard. The driver is waiting for us on the other bank. Let's walk over the Passerelle. Now." *Or I'll take you into the subterranean passage, claim you against the cold wall, and show you exactly how wrong you are—regardless of the consequences*, he thought. "Next destination is the Eiffel Tower." *Then my bed.* "You'll write an amazing article and have your byline." *I'm taking you.*

"Thank you," Kat said, a mix of disappointment and relief in the simple expression of gratitude.

Yes, Marko knew what she needed.

Kat squared her shoulders and stuffed both gloved hands in her pockets, pulling into herself and rebuilding the wall of protection she'd sworn to leave in the States. A sense of loss and sadness knotted in her chest, and she blinked back the sting in her eyes. Marko pulled on her right hand and took it in his, intertwining their fingers and holding her close. She let out a long breath as his body brushed hers and she realized he wasn't accepting her lame cop-out and moving away from her. He wasn't letting her go. Even if only for the day, she wouldn't deny herself. She wanted him as close as possible.

"How are your feet holding up?"

"My feet?" The question had her wrinkling her forehead. "Okay. Why?"

"Those boots," he said, smiling casually. "They're killer on the eyes, but they look hard on the feet."

"No." She chuckled at his concern. "They're actually rather comfortable."

"Too bad you're not prepared for a bike ride around Paris," he goaded, lifting a teasing brow and pointing to the area of bicycle rentals. He sidestepped the collection of bikes and made of show of tapping one of the wide seats. "We could have enjoyed a ride through the gardens and had Jean-Luc meet us with the car a little further downstream."

"I can handle it. A ride through the Tuileries sounds great," she insisted, tugging on his arm. "You forget that I'm a city girl now. Urban cycling is in my blood."

"I was referring to your dress, not your cycling abilities." His gaze traveled down her body to her toes, an appreciative smile emerging on his lips. "Not that I'm complaining, sweetheart, but I'm not sure how comfortable you'd be in that outfit."

"Or lack of," she replied, glancing at the pocket that housed her panties. "However, my coat is long enough to compensate for the missing underwear. Let's rent some bikes."

"I'll think about it once we get to the other side," he said, laughing and snaking an arm around her waist. He'd been teasing her the whole time. "Now, tell me about the island girl turning city girl. How do you like it?"

"I love it," she said, letting the bicycle option rest for a moment. "The apartment is tiny, but Charlie is the perfect roomie. We have so much in common, and we manage to be there for each other and compensate for what the other may lack. It's like one's weakness is the other's strength. Plus, we have tons of fun together."

"Charlie sounds great. Can't wait to meet her."

She stumbled on his words, her feet tripping over the uneven ground, but she didn't point out that there was an ocean between them. After she was on the plane back to New York, she probably wouldn't see Marko again for years.

"And your mother? How is she adjusting to you living in the city?"

"Mom is happily remarried and making plans to move to Florida. Three years ago, she met Ralph. It took him a full month of convincing her to go out with him, but since that first official dinner date, they've been inseparable. He's good people and good for her. I'm so happy she gave them a chance. They're so much in love." Kat looked at an older couple strolling hand in hand beside them. "I can imagine my mother and Ralph enjoying a walk over this bridge and snuggling on one of the benches, sharing a bottle of wine and a picnic."

"In that case, you need to invite them to join us next time. Even better, we can arrange for the trip to happen in June, and also invite them to join us for my parents' thirty-fifth anniversary celebration in Santorini."

She glanced over at Marko, who was watching the older couple beside them, and wondered what exactly had motivated him to make such a suggestion. After all, it wasn't as if she was a Paris resident, and she'd certainly never been introduced to his family.

"I've never met your parents."

"That's easy to rectify."

He guided her to a bench and sat on the edge. Patting his knee, he asked her to sit. She moved between his legs, wrapped her arm over his shoulders and lowered herself gently into his embrace.

"We'll change your flight, head down to the Côte d'Azur tomorrow before we go home for *ma mère's* Sunday bouillabaisse. You'll love it. My mother is an extraordinary cook, and her bouillabaisse is phenomenal. One of her best meals."

Kat studied the dark eyes of the man she loved, hesitant to ask why he suddenly wanted to take her to his home and introduce her to his parents. His parents were larger than life in her mind. Successful vineyard owners, with generations of a powerful legacy behind them, she imagined them as too good for the likes of blue-collar company.

"Do you miss Provence?"

"What's not to miss?" His aristocratic features filled with pride. No, not pride—arrogance. There was the Marko she knew. He never bothered with humility, and he always trumpeted the virtues and glory of his land.

The defined line of his jaw, the fiery gleam in his dark eyes, and even the tilt of this chin, with that chiseled dimple in the middle, all confirmed that there was nothing better in the world than his Provence.

She could see Marko, the lord of Château de M Winery, standing on the highest peak of his mountains, atop his land and his vineyards, his large muscular arm directing the plebeians below. Unfortunately, she didn't belong in the fertile fields she envisioned. They weren't her birthright. She couldn't stand beside the man who held her heart.

Kat rounded her shoulders and drew into her center, shielding herself from useless dreams. She'd never be more than a mere plebe.

"Soon, the residents will wake to that sweet scent in the mornings." The brush of his fingers at her nape, beneath the wrap and her coat, sent a physical awakening down her spine and brought her back to the conversation.

"What scent?" Kat crossed her legs at the ankles and let her feet dangle. She'd decided on a day, a single day when she wouldn't think and analyze, and she wouldn't give up any more time. Her hand skimmed over his shoulder and played at his neck. She tangled her fingers in the dark hair curling above his collar, holding tight to the moment.

"Where did that beautiful mind of yours drift off to?" Marko shook his head, his gaze searching her eyes. "You've been nodding about the impending almond blossoms and the end of winter, but you haven't heard a word."

Almond blossoms. The end of winter, the beginning of spring. "No. I heard." Almond blooms were known to smell heavenly. "I'm sure it'll be beautiful."

"So you'll come?" The tight lines on his forehead faded, and a smile broke across his face.

"Where?" She fought to rewind the conversation, but it simply wasn't in the memory files of her mind.

"Home with me."

Damn. His words slammed her psyche and had her lurching forward for balance. Her vision blurred, and moisture beaded beneath the brim of the beret. She looked down at her lap and let out a slow breath. "I can't."

"You can," he retorted, tapping her bum for her to stand. "You just won't."

Chapter Nine

How had Kat missed the whole conversation? Why had she allowed her mind to be lulled into her negative place and let the day of pure bliss slip between her fingers?

Actually, her fingers were crushed in Marko's grip. His fierce hold and quick gait confused her. Where had the accommodating man gone?

"Keep up," he commanded.

"If I walk any faster, I'll be jogging," she said, trying in vain to make her fingers squeeze his hand back. His strength prevented her hand from working, but it also made her legs work overtime. "What's gotten into you?"

"Realization of the truth," he said, very matter-of-factly, and he continued to pull her along, refusing to slow his pace.

"Okay," she panted. "Can you please explain?"

"You've agreed to put yourself in my hands for the day. Like a total sap, I accepted you setting an agenda." He glanced down at her, and she glimpsed a brief display of disappointment, or maybe it was hurt, in his eyes. "So, we're doing the freaking tourist attractions—first—and we're getting them out of the way as soon as possible. Fair warning, *bella*. I'm invoking the right to my two hours when I please. Attractions now, then I'm taking you home. Tonight, you're mine. All mine."

Marko had put his foot down and wasn't letting her get away with evasion tactics. He'd outlined what would come, and she had no doubt it would happen exactly like that.

Sensual thrills flared over her skin. She breathed deep, concentrating on the exploding sensations running through every nerve ending. Pissed and determined, Marko tossed any possibility of avoidance away. She'd agreed to the day. He called the shots.

"During my two hours, I'm going to claim every inch of your body and make you crave me as much as I hunger for you," he whispered against her ear. "In addition, I'll take my reward and color your ass so red that you won't be able to sit on an eight-hour flight without the feel of my mark burning through you."

He halted, made her stop mid-stride, and held her hard against his side while he raised his free hand in the air to summon the car. She released the breath she'd been holding and closed her eyes, remaining in the sizzling state of euphoric bliss. For one damn day, for a little over twenty hours, she'd indulge in all her fantasies.

Jean-Luc pulled the Mercedes to the curb.

"Happy?" Marko asked, yanking on the door handle and stepping aside for her to enter the vehicle.

She managed a small nod, and lowered her body into the car. It was the first time Marko's steady demeanor had cracked. The first time he hadn't waited for her approval. She'd always felt safe and secure in his care in a way she never felt with another man, but his dominant behavior set her body and soul on fire. It was as if sharing the air around him boosted her confidence in her desire for him, yet allowed her to admit her needs as a woman.

Pulling the door shut, Marko settled beside her and reached for her seat belt. He buckled it in place. "The scenic route, Jean-Luc. Miss Kathryn has a need to see Paris."

"*Oui, monsieur.*"

Hot air rushed through the vents, and the car pulled away from the curb. Within seconds, the pyramid structure marking the entrance to the Louvre loomed before them.

"I'm sure you're well read on the sights," he said, not bothering to elaborate. The amicable tour guide was gone. With his cellular phone balanced on his right knee, he wrapped his left arm around her and fit her against his side. "I need to see to a few arrangements."

"Okay," she whispered, pretending to study the scenery while struggling with the anticipation ricocheting through her body. Moisture pooled between her thighs, and she squirmed in her seat to calm the fluttering in her core. Her body was on full alert and awaiting his instruction. She tugged at the hem of her coat and tucked the wool material around her knees.

"Don't bother with modesty, sweetheart. Undo the two lower buttons on your coat," he said, typing on the touchscreen.

Her fingers fumbled with the large carved shell buttons, but she managed the simple task without glancing down. Transfixed with his profile, she was taken aback at the ease with which he issued his commands.

"Good," he added, his attention remaining on his phone as he moved his arm and rested his palm on the inside of her right knee. "Raise your dress to your hips."

Her heart hammered in her chest. The privacy divider was down. There was nothing preventing the driver from observing her every move in the mirror. Swallowing her hesitation, she scraped her teeth over her lower lip and stifled her objection. Marko didn't appear willing to discuss any other options. She lifted her butt and inched the silk over her hips.

"Very pretty." Marko hit the send button on his phone and returned it to a pocket inside his jacket.

Le paquet, s'il vous plait. The message flashed on the screen on the console to Jean-Luc's right.

"*Oui, monsieur,*" the driver replied, producing a tidy brown package once he'd stopped at a traffic light.

Marko lifted his hand and spread his fingers, as if ready to catch a baseball. Jean-Luc's green gaze flashed in the mirror, and then the driver tossed the parcel over his shoulder. Marko plucked it from the air. "*Merci.*"

Jean-Luc merely dipped his chin, returned his gaze to the road, and drove into the intersection.

Marko peeled a gold sticker from the paper bag and unfolded the neat wrapping. He looked inside the package, then unsnapped his seat belt and turned to face Kat. His dark gaze met hers and warned her not to speak.

"I can't wait to take you over my knee for being so difficult and disrespectful."

Kat's inner muscles clenched, and the dampness at her center intensified.

"The sweet scent of your excitement, and the glistening moisture between your legs shows me your need for limits and reprimands."

He slid a finger up the folds of her sex and rounded her swollen nub. "I'm tempted to take you in the car again, but you haven't earned the right for your pleasure yet."

Earned it? She deserved it. She needed it.

His thumb found her clit, while he pushed a thick finger into her channel. She dropped her head against the leather seat and closed her eyes.

"No," he scolded, removing his finger. "Open your eyes. The Arc de Triomphe is on our right. You're not missing a single landmark during this ride. Look out the window."

Kat raised her protesting lids, and watched the heavy traffic swirl around the impressive structure set in the middle of the busy round-about. The neoclassical structure was beautiful, imposing, and ab-solutely breathtaking, but the Arc de Triomphe wasn't her priority at the moment. The need to connect with Marko was. Desire burned so hot, it consumed her body and mind.

"L'Arc sits at the top of the Champs-Élysées, connecting the old Paris and the Paris of today." He slid two fingers inside her, as if fill-ing her, driving her to a physical plateau, and then leaving her hang-ing on the agonizing edge were part of the tour. He didn't pause in his speech. "As twelve avenues converge at this point, it is an unri-valed hub that proudly depicts the battles of the French citizens. The Tomb of the Unknown Soldier is also there . . . illuminated during the night."

She gasped as his finger stroked the sensitive nerves inside her. His words filtered through her mind, but the distraction of her body's buzz made it impossible to grasp those words. She heard, but couldn't listen. She stared, but couldn't see. The pressure built between her legs, and she arched off the seat and against his hand. He pumped deeper, stroked stronger, and the backdrop of the city blurred in her view.

Her muscles clenched around his fingers and a ripple of excite-ment traveled through her.

"Don't come, *bella*," Marko instructed, withdrawing his fingers but continuing the teasing of her clit. "You wanted to see the Eiffel Tower. That is our destination."

"Marko," she pleaded.

He cupped the curve of her beautiful mound, and leaned close to taste her neck. "I like your cheeks so pink. I like seeing you frustrated and battling for a climax."

"Not fair," she said, wriggling against his hold. "Why can't I come?"

"Because," he replied, fighting his own desire to feel her loss of control in his hands, "I also want you on edge. I want to see you fidget and burn until I choose to let you soar."

"Please," she insisted.

"Hearing you beg may convince me." Dark curls glistened with her juices and enticed him even more than her soft pants. He caressed her clit, rubbing erotic circles around the tight bundle of nerves and rolling it between his fingertips. Watching her eyes study him and her pupils go wide, he eventually angled his hand and rubbed the sweet spot buried deep inside her heat.

Kat's lips parted and she gulped audibly at the air. She was close. A few more strokes and she'd shatter. He lifted his hand and traced her cream over her swollen lips. He waited until her tongue swept over his fingertip and she closed her lips around it. The warmth of her mouth fueled his control and determination.

"You will come when I decide. Hold your climax."

Her soft tongue stopped moving and her teeth nipped at his finger. "Marko."

His cock jerked as she repeated his name. His name as her plea pleased him, drove his need to claim her on the spot, but he wouldn't. He wasn't changing his agenda because his erection pulsed so hard it made his ears burn.

The plan. He was sticking to the damn plan.

He reached for the package and retrieved her gift.

Panties. Black lace panties. He held them in his hand and leaned over her to keep her from seeing what he held. Lifting her right foot, he stretched the lace over her boot and let it rest at the ankle. He then fit the lace over the left boot. Hooking his fingers on either side, he slowly slid the lace up her legs, tenderly gliding over the silky stockings on his way, and stopping at the top of her thighs.

"Thank you," she said, relief evident in her voice. "I was wondering how I'd climb the tower without them."

"Lift," he said, taking the remote control butterfly from the package and placing it against the lace.

With a hand on his back, she tried to stretch and watch over his shoulders, but he easily pinned her smaller frame back against the seat. He waited.

Her hips rose, and he fit the butterfly over her mound and arranged the lace at her hips. With the sensation of the vibe against her core, her fingers tugged on his jacket as she lowered herself back to the seat.

"Wow. I've never had one of these," she said, curling over his back and breathing loud between his shoulders. Her desire sheened through the lace, and he exhaled with pleasure.

"A first. Good," he said, empowered by her excitement. He reached into his coat pocket and felt for the remote. "Honestly, I'm not ready to share the most beautiful view in Paris. You need panties for the ride to the top of the tower. However, you need to be reminded of what will happen when the tour is over." He tapped the on button and the vibrator hummed softly.

Kat's dark lashes dropped to the top of her cheeks, and her teeth scraped over her lower lip. "Oh, my . . . it's . . . you can't do . . ."

"I will," he announced, with a satisfied and teasing smile. He turned the vibe off, and rested his palm on the side of her face. "Rosy pink. I can't get enough of your flush."

"You're really not playing fair, Monsieur Renard."

"I'm not playing at all."

Her breath caught. Marko had no time for games. He wanted her. He needed her. And there was nothing that was going to stop him from having her. His life was moving too fast to wait any longer. He needed to discuss the career choices and life-changing options he was chasing. The possibilities would ease her reluctance. He'd find a way to bridge the miles between them. Little did she know that his international itinerary had been booked the previous Monday. He had a ticket and reservations to spend a week in New York. The moment he'd accepted one of the new positions, he'd intended to make Kat his and bring her back into his life.

"I'll do anything to get you where I want—where you belong—sweetheart."

He touched the remote control and her chocolate-colored eyes went darker. Color crawled back up her neck, and he traced the heat with his hand. Kat fell against the seat as the buzz intensified.

She sighed softly, her beautiful mouth dropped, and her eyes glazed with passion. The woman was absolute heaven. He couldn't deny it, and more than anything, he wanted his name on her lips as pleasure reigned through her body.

Bringing her to the edge and then making her stop wreaked havoc on his control. Every nerve ending in his body was strung so tight, he'd explode into a thousand pieces if he didn't touch her.

The car came to a stop, and Marko briskly spoke to Jean-Luc. She'd begged Marko to let her come, rather loudly, and the partition had been down the whole time. There was no way the driver had missed her whimpers and moans, but Marko wanted her completely to himself. He needed her.

Exiting the vehicle, Jean-Luc engaged the locks and strolled behind the car.

Marko removed the remote control from his pocket, chose a medium setting, and placed it on the seat. With measured effort, he shrugged out of his coat and jacket, then loosened the knot of his tie.

"That's it, *bella*. Ride the ecstasy," he said, folding his body on the floorboard between her legs. He pushed her knees apart and kissed up the length of her thighs, all the while admiring the sensual unraveling of the woman before him.

Kat's unfocused eyes spoke volumes. Her hips bucked off the leather, and he instantly pushed her dress up and cupped her ass.

"You're driving me insane," he said, worshiping the soft skin with his tongue and sliding beneath the lace barrier to taste her. "This has to go." He tugged on the lace. "It all has to go."

He ripped off the panties and tossed the vibrator to the side. His patience was spent. He needed to taste her, feel her unravel, and all as quickly as possible. She tangled her fingers in his hair and held him against her intoxicating center. He licked through her wet folds and suckled the excited nub into his mouth, unable to satiate his hunger for the woman. He wanted all of her. Needed her.

Spreading the moisture between the swollen folds, he pushed a finger through the muscled resistance of her backside and thrust his tongue inside her honey. Her body trembled, and as he feasted on the woman he hungered for, her climax hit.

Her hold tightened in his hair. She called his name.

"Marko. Yes. Marko," she repeated, shattering beneath his mouth. "My Marko."

"Your Marko," he confirmed, kissing the insides of her thighs and resting his head on her leg. His heart pounded so hard in his chest, it was difficult to breathe. He caressed her trembling legs and wrapped his fingers around the beautiful curves. "My Kat, completely and fully and always mine."

She smoothed her hands through his hair, and breathed softer as the waves of pleasure subsided and her body relaxed.

"I want one more," Marko said, leaning against her thigh and fitting a finger inside her. "I want to feel you come again."

"My body can't take more," she insisted. "I won't be able to walk."

"I'll carry you. We have so much time to make up for, so many orgasms to capture." He curved a second finger inside her channel, and found the special spot hidden within. "This one is only for me."

She ground against the heel of his palm. He circled her clit with his thumb and stroked her G-spot between his fingers, coaxing more sighs of submission from her lips.

"Come for me, sweetheart. Come hard."

Chapter Ten

Kat's neck couldn't support the weight of her head, so she leaned against the softness of the seat and watched as he poured a glass of water. She accepted it and slowly sipped the cool liquid, allowing time for her mind to clear and feeling to return to her jellied limbs.

Her strong and powerful man meticulously cleaned and dressed her, sliding her own pair of silk panties up her legs and lowering her dress to cover them. She still wasn't able to move, but she was suddenly aware of their surroundings.

"Where is Jean-Luc?"

Marko lifted his chin and indicated the area behind the car's trunk. She turned to see the driver speaking with an officer. "He's probably sweet-talking his way out of a citation."

She gathered her coat and wrapped it around her knees.

Marko laughed. "No one can see in, sweetheart. The tint provides full privacy." He smoothed the coat over her legs and worked the buttons. "Jean-Luc is probably spinning a beautiful tale on our behalf. He's quite the romantic. I wouldn't be surprised to hear him telling that pretty police officer that we are in need of some time to settle a lovers' quarrel before we tour the Eiffel Tower."

The only thing settled was that Kat was completely and utterly owned. Marko had owned her heart for years, and now he owned her body. She'd never responded to a man like she did to him. She was completely spent and totally consumed by the man. She'd shed all her inhibitions and ignored logical boundaries. She'd never be able to limit future interactions to simple friendship again. She was truly fucked. She couldn't deny needing him any longer.

Whereas she'd been adrift in emotional and sensation bliss, and totally incapable of coherent thoughts, Marko had focused on her needs. He'd seen to her and her alone. It was only right for him to find his pleasure. For her to see to him.

"No thinking," Marko reminded her, dropping a kiss on her lips. "You promised."

"I was thinking," she admitted, feeling her skin prickle at the brazen thoughts flashing through her mind. "I was thinking that you are the most selfless and generous lover. You didn't get off."

She reached for him and pressed an open palm over the impressive bulge at his groin. He was so hard.

"Oh, but I will," he promised. "*After* we get the sightseeing part of our agenda out of the way, and when I have my two hours."

"So our car ride doesn't count toward your two hours?"

"No. I'll take all the time I can get." He reached for the purple vibrator and tossed it in the paper package. "Kat, you have a way of altering everything I plan. The original idea was for you to wear the damn thing on the ride up the tower. I was going to make you wait. You were supposed to climax at the top, but the gorgeous color and delicious scent of your excitement couldn't be put off. I needed to see you come as soon as possible. I need you again."

"I need you, too." Kat reached for him and let her fingers explore his magnificent mouth. She ran her fingers over his lips, and her heart filled with love and admiration as he sucked on them, before claiming her mouth in a slow kiss. His tongue glided over hers, coaxing her to surrender to the chemistry that sizzled between them. The opportunity to enjoy his kind strength wouldn't last, but she was damned if she wouldn't revel in it for the moment.

As if seeing her inner thoughts, he broke the kiss and took her other hand, tenderly easing his thumb over her knuckles. He turned it and placed a kiss in the center of her palm. "Are you ready to experience the Eiffel Tower?"

She nodded. She was ready for anything she could have with him.

Marko rapped on the window, and Jean-Luc swiftly appeared and opened Kat's door. He offered Kat his hand. "*Mademoiselle, c'est bon?*"

"Yes, I'm fine." She looked into telling seafoam-colored eyes, and a tingle ran down her spine. Jean-Luc knew what had happened in the vehicle, but he approved. The comforting green gaze offered pleased assurance.

"Ask Marko to stop at the snack bar before you enter the lift," the driver said in a low tone. "The chocolate croissants are divine."

"*Merci*, Jean-Luc," she replied, making room for Marko to stand beside her as the driver stepped away. She reached for Marko and adjusted his tie, placing her palm on the white dress shirt and smiling. "I'm with a handsome man, in a gorgeous city, and counting my lucky stars. I'm so glad Paul and Justin told you I was coming. I'm even grateful for the feature competition."

"Yes. You came to Paris. You came to me."

True. From the moment she'd decided on the trip, she'd known that rendezvousing with Marko was highly likely. If she were honest, she'd admit it had been her secret motivation. Honesty took guts. She wasn't brave enough for such an admission. "Amongst other things, it really gives us time to catch up. Thank you for making time."

"Making time?" Marko shook his head and sucked air between his teeth. "Not how I'd describe it, *bella*. I've been counting time waiting for you." He fit a finger beneath her chin and angled her face to his. His mouth lingered inches above her lips, and his warm breath tickled her senses. His dark gaze settled on her eyes. "It's also not about catching up, sweetheart. Don't fool yourself or lie to me."

Marko closed the space between them and settled his lips on her mouth. Patient but sure, he waited until her lips parted and her tongue swept out in search of his. The kiss was sweet and quick. He lifted his head and gave her a wicked smile.

"What?" Kat asked.

"Selfish thoughts, my dear. Very selfish." He traced his thumb pad over her trembling lip. "Men like their toys. Your body is my dream toy. I can't wait to explore every inch. To touch every trigger. And to turn you on so hard that you will writhe in my hold and beg me for more."

Heat crawled up her neck. She dropped her gaze to his chest. "I think you've already managed to make me beg."

"Not nearly enough to satisfy my ego," he said, straightening, tucking the wrap around her, and arranging her beret. "The wind will be cold."

She wanted to tell him that if she fed his ego any more, it would swell to an unmanageable size. But she didn't. His ego and arrogance were part of his allure.

He laced her hand through his arm and led them into the crowd of tourists. English, German, Italian, and Chinese words floated in the air. Vendors peddled their souvenirs. Police moved stragglers along. There was so much going on, but all Kat could feel was the way Marko's fingers closed over hers.

"Don't get me wrong, because I'm not complaining. I'm actually very grateful, but I'm also baffled," Marko said. "You are so responsive, *bella*. Absolutely sexy and beautiful. How is it possible that some shrewd New Yorker doesn't have you tied to his bed and at his mercy?"

She released a slow, long breath and shook her head. *It's because no shrewd New Yorker could measure up to my arrogant overseas god.* "It's not that simple."

"Why is that?"

Kat shrugged and stared straight ahead at the iconic steel structure.

"Do you trust me?" He squeezed her hand and urged her to look at him. Concern and something she couldn't recognize filled his dark eyes.

"Of course," she replied. She trusted him completely. She'd always trusted him.

"Then you will let me know everything you want and desire, regardless of circumstances or timing. Everything. Understood?" He tightened his hold. "I will see to everything you need and give you everything you want. The only requirements are your honesty and trust."

Nodding her agreement, Kat continued her deep breathing and focused on walking straight ahead. Images of her hands and feet tied at the corners of *his* bed and of herself at *his* mercy played in her head.

"Would you tie me to your bed?" She mentally kicked herself in the ass the second the words were out.

"In a heartbeat," he replied.

Wanton desire hissed through her body and sizzled between her legs. He meant it. Marko would fulfill her every fantasy. She didn't need to hide her sexual hunger and she didn't need to ignore her longings.

"What are you thinking?"

"I'm thinking we should hurry to the top of the Eiffel Tower, see the beauty of the city, and retreat to a private place." She glanced up at him. "Toys are designed for play. I want you to play with your toy."

"*C'est bon.*" He grinned and hastened his stride.

Marko was pleased, which in turn pleased Kat. She had done the right thing. She'd told him what she wanted. Kat walked on clouds, impatient to reach the lifts and finish the tour. She could see the long lines of tourists, and was tempted to call off the excursion and spend the remainder of her time satiating her carnal cravings.

The reality of the situation kept her silent. She needed the research. She wanted the byline. If she allowed herself to follow her heart, she'd lose herself and all she'd worked for. Being with Marko always carried that risk.

A young boy approached with a bronze replica and offered it at a special price to the "pretty lady." Marko drew her close and raised his brow in a negative response, surprising Kat with the harsh manners.

"Unfortunately, he is not an innocent child," Marko said against her ear. "The athletic shoes he's wearing cost well over two hundred euros." He stopped in front of a table dressed in a tattered gold cloth. "We'll choose something from this woman. It seems like she can use the business and will appreciate the support. She's also not harassing the other tourists."

The woman held out a heavy marble paperweight depiction of the Eiffel Tower. "Dis?"

Kat smiled at the elderly woman, who motioned for her to examine the souvenir. Truth was, she didn't care for a tchotchke. "The apartment is rather small. I don't want to crowd it with dust collectors," she explained in a whisper for only Marko to hear. "Something smaller in size, please."

The older woman pointed to a silver heart keychain, with a small, dangling Eiffel Tower in the middle. "Dis?"

"Um . . ."

"*Bon,*" Marko said, taking the keychain and adding a pair of silver earrings to the mix. "*Merci, madame.*"

The vendor quickly wrapped the jewelry and tchotchke in a floral paper, offering it to Marko. He dropped the package in his coat pocket and handed her a hundred-euro bill, lifting his hand to indicate for her to keep the change.

Kat looked up at him and laughed. "When are you going to wear dangling, rhinestone-encrusted Eiffel Tower earrings?"

"I'm not. But I know a little girl who will love them," he said, turning his back on the souvenir stand. "Plus, I think that lady deserves the money. She doesn't hustle visitors and works hard for a living. You can see it in her eyes."

Saying she was proud of him seemed vain and inadequate. It was more like she admired him and his insight. "Thank you for the keychain. It's perfect."

"*Bon, bella.* Now are you heeding Jean-Luc's advice and stopping for a bite before we enter the lifts?"

"Yes, that sounds wonderful. It seems like the French air makes me famished."

He grinned, smug as ever, and took her hand. "I'm sure it's the air."

Shaking her head, she took a deep breath, and snuggled close to him. She'd missed his self-assured remarks, but damn if the man was ever wrong. "You know you're just a bit cocky."

"So you've said." His dimpled chin lifted a little higher. The man was so incorrigible. He always thought he knew best, and Kat secretly, only secretly, admitted to believing he was right.

Marko's analytical mind and determined will were unstoppable powers in the world of business. On a personal level, he was respectful and caring to all he loved. People, places, and products amongst them all.

Smart, good looking, and loyal, the prominent man was any mother's dream for her daughter. On more than one occasion, Kat's mom had asked what had happened to her best friend. Past . . . that was the past, she reminded herself. He wasn't hers. She had no right. *Keep things simple, Kat.*

"Is being cocky how you went from a growth"—she hooked two fingers of her free hand into quotation marks by her head when she said growth—"position at the World Bank to being one of the greatest assets and the youngest junior partner at the largest financial company in all of Europe?"

"I like that version," he said, squeezing her hand. "Even more, I like that I'm not the only one who has kept tabs on an old schoolmate."

Busted. He'd never discussed his career with her, but she'd confessed to knowing it well. She sucked on her lower lip, but didn't miss a step. "It was hard not to stay in the know where you're concerned. You were splashed on every society or finance page at every newsstand."

"Right. At some point today, I'd like to talk about some business meetings I have tomorrow, *bella*."

She pressed her palm against the dancing butterflies in her stomach. "Is it bad?"

"No. It's all good. Let's table the discussion for later though." He led her through the crowd, and without asking, he ordered a single chocolate croissant. "This should hold my little chocoholic for an hour or so. We'll enjoy the real deal from the *boulangerie* next door to the apartment. Antoine makes the best croissants, obviously his late wife's recipe."

"I'm looking forward to trying your local bakery," she said, eyeing the pastry. In what she knew to be a very non-French move, she opened her mouth wide and sank her teeth into the prettiest and best-smelling croissant she'd ever seen. Once the flaky dough met her tongue, she closed her eyes and savored the taste of every chew. She swallowed and looked up at him. "This one is divine." She took another bite and slowly repeated the delicious experience. When she opened her eyes again, she licked her lips. "It's better than sex."

Marko narrowed his gaze and cocked a brow.

"Present sex-company excluded," she added quickly then gave him a sultry wink.

"I would hope so. You beat down my manhood with a mass-produced-for-tourists croissant," he said, pulling her into his arms. He lowered his mouth and licked at the corner of her lips. "Not bad. But maybe it's the tasting method."

Kat laughed, happy to see his pompous play. He'd been serious and intense after their stroll, and she craved his smile.

"Hurry, *bella*. We have a tower to visit." Marko took a big bite and smacked her ass. "Then, we'll see what you think about present-company sex."

She popped the last piece in her mouth, smacking her gloved hands to shake off the golden flakes. "In that case, *allons-y,*" she said, taking his hand and pulling him toward the line at the lift.

Waiting in line wasn't something Marko generally did or liked, but if it meant he did so with his arms wrapped around Kat, he'd stand as long as possible. Her small frame fit perfectly against his chest, and he couldn't get enough of the sweet scent of her hair. Lavender and vanilla. Same as always. He held her tight, taking deep breaths, and sending up a prayer of gratitude for the second chance that had come his way.

"You made your papa proud. Not many young women could have handled his business the way you did," he said, rubbing his chin on her hair and swaying her in his hold. "You were probably the busiest aluminum-siding company in New York."

"The busiest?"

"With such a beautiful boss at the helm, I'm sure every contractor wanted to work overtime and bring in as many new jobs as possible." He pressed his right leg against the back of hers and stepped forward. Left leg next. "There's no doubt I'd do anything to spend as much time with you as humanly possible."

She turned her head toward the metal staircase. "You know, the faster we see this landmark, the faster we'll be at your place."

"Stairs," he said. "The stairs will be faster." He pulled her through the crowd and directly to the metal staircase. Speaking with an attendant in rapid-fire French she couldn't understand, he motioned for her to start up. "Stay on your toes, sweetheart. Not sure those heels will do well on over seven hundred metal stairs."

"How many?" Kat asked in a high voice.

"Seven hundred and four to be exact," he replied. "Get going, *bella*."

"Maybe we should wait on line," she offered. "Seven hundred and four steps is a long way up."

"No way you're issuing an invitation to get you alone faster and then making me wait." He playfully swatted her bum and growled. "Climb."

She glanced over her shoulder and shrugged. "Okay. You asked for it."

Marko took the first few flights two steps at a time to keep up to her. The woman proved to be a speed demon on heels. Paris rooftops dropped away and other landmarks came into view as they scrambled high above the ground. They had almost reached the first-floor entrance before he leaned an arm across the metal banister and kept her from taking the final four steps.

"Are you still addicted to your stair-climbing routine?" Marko snarled in order to conceal the effort of catching his breath.

"Sort of," she said, showing no strain in her composure. "I've added arms and moved onto an elliptical machine since the last time we worked out together."

"How long?"

"What do you mean?" She darn well knew what he meant, yet she batted her eyelashes like an innocent bystander.

"How long do you spend on the stair machine each day?" He tightened his arm and pulled her against his chest. "Checking for stamina, sweetheart."

"Oh," she puffed, feigning a shocked look. "About seventy-five minutes daily."

"Good. I'll carry your coat. Take it off now." He allowed her just enough room to maneuver the wrap and wool coat off her shoulders and down her back. Cupping her ass, he slid his palm over the tight globes and down her toned thighs. "If I'm marathoning up these stairs, I'm going to maximize the view."

"You are horrible," she said, laughing and draping the coat over his forearm. "How much further?"

"A few more steps," he said, laughing as he drew back his arm and let her pass. "This is the renovated first floor. The restaurant has a line of reservations as long as the line for the lifts. It's a mecca for lovers to connect . . . or reconnect."

He briskly walked her through the level, pausing only for a few seconds so she could take some photos with her phone. While she studied the bustling city, he spoke to Jean-Luc and instructed him to arrange for quick access to the lift to the third floor.

"What an amazing sight," she said, her voice full of admiration. "Seeing Paris above the rooftops is like seeing over a forest's canopy."

"There's a gift shop on this level as well." He pointed to the establishment, but didn't enter. "The transparent glass flooring is a very popular part of the renovation, allowing visitors to appreciate where they stand while looking directly at those beneath them." *Hence the reason for the return of your panties*, he added silently. Being able to see down meant others were able to see up. Marko had never been good at sharing.

Releasing a slow breath, he also silently and unwillingly acknowledged that he would give her anything she needed to be fulfilled. Including sharing her, even if it didn't meet his needs.

"Let's go. The second floor awaits." He directed her to enter the stairwell ahead of him, and marveled at the ease in which she managed the numerous flights.

He reviewed the attractions on the second floor, pointed to the historical landmarks, allowed her a few more minutes for pictures, and headed to the front of the line for the lift.

"Thank you, Gabriel," he said, once the attendant nodded for them to enter.

Nobody seemed to notice their obvious shortcut, but neither did he care if they did. He wanted the tour done and Kat to himself. The elevator doors closed and they rode to the top of the Eiffel Tower with only a recorded female voice for company.

"Do you know Gabriel?"

Her sweet voice pulled him from his thoughts. Shit, he royally sucked. Here was Kat, willing to share one of her life's dreams with him, and he was rushing her through the experience so he could get her in his bed.

"No, not really." Guilt swelled in his gut. "I had Jean-Luc speak to his supervisor on the ground level. He informed them of our time requirements."

"Time requirements?" Her big dark eyes filled with confusion.

"Fine. I lied and finagled my way past the lines." He shifted his weight away from her and looked everywhere but at her eyes. "You're an international dignitary, on a really tight schedule, and you can't afford to be recognized because of security reasons. I'm a pompous ass that is too impatient to wait on line and wants to get you to the top observation deck as soon as possible." Basically, because he wanted to get her down as soon as possible.

She smiled and wrapped her fingers around his forearm. "That's sweet." Leaning closer, she brushed her lips over his jaw. "It's flattering to have you throwing your influence around to make this good for me."

"Sure. That's what I did," he said in a low rumble he hoped she couldn't comprehend. He managed to meet her gaze, clear his throat, and smile. "It's my pleasure, sweetheart."

Marko placed a palm in the small of her back and led her out to the observation deck. Being the man Kat needed meant meeting all her needs, not just the ones that suited him. At the moment, she wanted to bask in the glory of Parisian dreams. He wasn't about to disappoint her.

"The view is absolutely breathtaking," she exclaimed, taking a few steps onto the platform and throwing her arms out at shoulder level, twirling like a dancer.

"It certainly is," he agreed, admiring the spirited woman before him. "Paris has never been so beautiful as it is today." He reached for her and skimmed his fingers over her waist as she turned. "Absolutely gorgeous."

She stopped before him, arched her back over the curve of his hold, and looked up at him. Lush lips curved into the most beautiful smile he'd ever seen. The twinkle in her eyes lit up the skyline, and the swirl of her thick hair, brushing against his cheek as she pressed a kiss on his neck, called for him to proceed with caution.

His heart was on display for all of Paris to see. He loved this woman with every fiber of his being.

He fit her coat over her shoulders, wrapped the cashmere around her throat, and guided her along the metal railing. Marko made a conscious effort to fuel her enthusiasm with tales of the romantic city and its sights, taking care not to rush through her first experience on the tower.

The way she leaned on his shoulder and lifted on her toes for the perfect view between the upper fence grids made him smile. The upset little circle of her mouth, when he explained how vulnerable Paris had been to foreign invasion, made him want to hold her tighter. The wonder and awe of her every comment and observation warmed his soul.

"I'm honored to be joining you on your inaugural tour of the Eiffel Tower," he said, lifting his champagne flute to hers. "To my *bella* and her Paris."

They drank and he studied her questioning gaze over the rim of the plastic glass. Her dark eyes asked so many questions. Bewilderment and concern filled the space between them, but she didn't protest. She was his, whether she admitted it or not.

"I don't have a single picture of the two of us. Can we take a selfie?" she asked, snapping out of the reverie and sliding up against his chest. She settled her head next to his cheek and waved her cell phone before them. "Please."

"Let me." He took the phone from her hand and tucked her tight against his shoulder. "My arm is longer."

He glanced behind them, making sure to have the Seine and the Notre Dame in the background, then pressed the button. Smiling like a doting tourist. He dropped a kiss on her hair. And finally, he rested his cheek against her head.

"Now we have a few," he said, flipping through the photos and forwarding each one to his number. He returned the phone and brushed his lips over her forehead. "I promise we'll take more."

"Do you mind if I post these? I won't tag the staunch businessman. Won't even mention your name." She teasingly waved the phone. "Friends back home will enjoy them, and it proves I'm in Paris with a devastatingly handsome man."

For that alone, he'd definitely break his rule of no personal pictures on social media. He wanted everyone to know she was with him. "Post away, sweetheart."

Chapter Eleven

Kathryn snuggled close to Marko and enjoyed the ride through the city as he continued to point out the attractions. "You're the perfect tour guide, *monsieur.*"

"Thank you," he replied, placing a finger beneath her chin, and tilting her face to his to seal her mouth with a kiss. When he broke away, she kept her eyes closed and her lips pursed. He chuckled and urged her to open her eyes. "Take in the sights, *bella.* We're almost there."

"Your home?"

"Yes," he replied. "Are you up for an afternoon café and one of Antoine's croissants?"

"*Oui.*" Her mouth watered in agreement. She had a definite soft spot for croissants. When Jean-Luc drove onto the quaint island in the middle of the river, it was like stepping into a fairy tale. She didn't speak again until they were seated at the picturesque café, looking directly at the elaborate elegance of the Notre Dame.

"We're so close, I can practically feel the curves of the arches and the details of the sculptures," Kat breathed, holding out her hand and pretending to trace a finger down the stunning Gothic lines of the cathedral. "It's magical."

"I'm glad you like it." Marko stretched out his arm and closed his fingers around hers. He pulled her hand to his lips and kissed inside her palm, his lips warming her heart and making the moment truly magical. "It is pretty."

"Pretty?" She pulled her hand away in protest and pointed to the magnificent church. "It's surreal. Your choice of adjectives is maddening. We're sitting on an island that has been frozen in time, in the middle of the Seine, enjoying *café crème* and yet another chocolate croissant, and the best you come up with is pretty."

He shook his head, and his relaxed laughter filled the air. She liked seeing him relaxed. Being with this man was a comfort and thrill. She didn't want their time together to end. She rubbed the heel of her hand in the center of her chest, massaging the foretelling knot of heartache.

Their time would end. Unfortunately, what made him the powerful and successful Marko Renard didn't mesh with Kathryn's life goals. If their time together didn't end, one of them would be lost. The ache spreading through her chest confirmed it would be Kathryn. After years of living on autopilot and taking care of responsibilities she hadn't asked for, she'd just managed to get her shit together. She couldn't lose herself.

Staring at Marko and all he was to her, she battled with her desire to try and claim her dream of living with real love. Living a life with Marko. Unfortunately, love made you vulnerable. Exposed you to hurt. And fate had a way of taking away joy, and the people one loved, at the most inopportune times.

Kat wasn't sure she was strong enough to take the risk of having everything stolen from her if she chose to reach for happiness. She couldn't leave her predictable and boring life. She didn't dare try to fulfill her every dream with the man of her heart. In the same way, she couldn't ask him to alter his plans or life. He'd offered just that after her father had died. There was no doubt he loved her, no doubt he believed he could make it work, but there was always the possibility he'd end up resenting her if it wasn't all they hoped. She let out a long breath and stared at the rays of sunshine dancing on the river.

"What's wrong, *bella*?" He tenderly swiped the pad of his thumb across her cheekbone and brushed his mouth over her temple. "Why so contemplative?"

She took another deep breath and forced her lips into a smile. "Nothing. I guess the sentimentality of the setting is doing a number on me. Not only is Paris at our feet, but the activity at our backs feels like history come to life. There are bakeries, butchers, cheese shops, and even eccentric craft places woven into these streets. It feels like a village from hundreds of years ago in the middle of a modern city."

"That's exactly what Île Saint-Louis is, sweetheart. It a little slice of peace set in the middle of the Seine, which runs down the middle of a bustling city. There are no large department stores or food giants to alter the flavor of the island. People escape to the island and enjoy the simplest and best things in life."

"Is that why you live here?"

"Partly," he said, trailing a finger down her face and across her jaw. Fingers caressed behind her ear and sank into her hair. "It's the closest thing to home. It may not have the rows of almond trees and the carefully sculpted vineyards, but we do have Antoine's croissants and the soft jazz drifting over the bridge from the Right Bank."

The tender intimacy tugged at her heart and amplified the ache. Pulling away and reducing the physical contact, Kat turned her attention to her plate. In a cowardly gesture, she swept her hair forward and covered her ear. Chewing on the flaky croissant, she considered her next question carefully. For years, she'd wondered why Marko hadn't returned to claim his position in the empire his grandfather had built, but she'd never thought it appropriate to probe into his family life. He'd never seemed willing to offer the information.

"If I'm out of line, please let me know," she said, glancing sideways and meeting his gaze. "If I remember our old conversations, your father should be retired by now."

"He is," Marko confirmed.

"Your uncle only wants to work the land. Château de M is your legacy. It's so obvious that you adore your home and everything about it. Why aren't you back in Provence and at the helm of Château de M?"

He folded his hands on the table and looked downstream. A tiny muscle at his jaw clenched. She feared she'd overstepped and upset him. Reaching for his hand, she rubbed his knuckles and asked him to forget she'd asked. It was none of her business.

"No," he insisted, shifting and covering her hand with his. "It's a legitimate question. The answer is a bit long, though."

She leaned forward and looked into his eyes. She didn't speak.

"When we first met, I had every intention of doing exactly what you describe." He released her hand and combed his fingers through his hair. "The plan was to get a graduate degree and acquire all the skills and knowledge necessary to grow the family business and succeed in a global economy. It didn't matter if the name of the school was famous or not, because I was planning on going home and implementing what I learned with Château de M. Bringing our wines to tables in every corner of the world had always been my father's dream."

"So what made you change your mind?" Kat detected a tone of mourning in his voice. Something terrible must have happened.

"It's not that I changed my mind—I changed the methods necessary to achieve the goal." That was a major difference between them. Marko always had his sights set on the goal and would do anything to achieve it. Kat was more into making the journey worthwhile. He gave her a quick wink. "Remember our discussions on Machiavelli's 'the ends justify the means'?"

She nodded. Of course she remembered. That simple statement had given her opportunities to stay and be with him for many nights. She smiled at the memories.

"Well, to make a long story short, my family isn't the typical Mediterranean family with many children. On my paternal side, there are three siblings. My father, Marcel, is the oldest and married my mother, Angelique. My mother miscarried three times before she gave birth to me. She insisted on stopping at one child."

Kat remembered that Angelique had been born and raised in Italy. Marko had told her his *grand-père* had belittled her peasant upbringing at first. He hadn't believed she would be a suitable mother for his grandchildren. However, Marcel loved Angelique, and he'd threatened to leave Provence and his family if they didn't accept her as his wife. Needless to say, not only had Marko's *grand-père* accepted Angelique, but he had grown to love her as his own daughter.

"Uncle Maynard is the second son. He married my aunt Laurel and had my cousin Martine. She's more like a twin sister than a cousin to me. She was born just weeks after I was, and we spent our childhood playing in the same backyard." At the mention of his cousin, his eyes filled with pride and he smiled tenderly.

"Are you still close?" Kat had wished for a little sister or a baby brother, but her parents had stopped at one child as well.

"Very close. She's always been there for me, listened to every concern, and given me all sorts of honest advice. Unfortunately, she went through a lot these past few years, but Martine is one of the strongest and smartest women I know, and she's come through the turmoil like a champ. The two of you will be good friends."

"Maybe," she said below her breath.

Apprehension spread through her like wildfire at his assumption. She'd known about the family business and about his mother and the difficulties she'd originally had with his grandfather, but Marko had never really opened up about other family dynamics before. He was painting a mental picture for her, and not only did she like what she saw, but she also craved it like a junkie.

She wanted to tell him to stop dangling dreams that were unattainable in front of her, but she couldn't. For Marko, anything was attainable. He wasn't exactly spoiled, but luxuries were part of his daily life. He didn't flaunt his affluence; rather, he lived it with ease, all the while making no secret of how important the simple pleasures of his home and family were to him. She didn't doubt he valued people more than things. That was what made it easy to accept the materialistic stuff he offered—money and wealth weren't his priority. Family and home were. Kathryn had set herself up for a day of bliss to be followed by much longer devastation. She didn't know if she could truly handle being with him and walking away.

"My aunt and uncle were the topic of much town talk. They were the first and only people in the family to ever divorce." He went on with his story, not breaking to acknowledge her hesitation. He shook his head as he spoke about his uncle and aunt, but an approving twinkle lit his eyes. "They remained very close friends after, and they even lived in neighboring homes. Better friends than when they were married."

"I've heard of such relationships. Sometimes, people may truly love and care for each other, but they may not be good together as a couple. Did you say they lived in neighboring homes?"

"They did. They do," he corrected. "They still share a vegetable garden, and Aunt Laurel babysits my uncle's young twins, Michel and Morell, on Thursday nights so he and Cecile can enjoy 'private' couple time. The whole family, including both of my uncle's wives, gathers every Sunday for dinner. It's a unique relationship."

"Wow. That is unique," Kathryn said. It took a lot of courage for people to go for what they really wanted regardless of how it would seem to others. "It's nice to hear that there are divorced couples that remain close and co-parent their children. How did it work out for Martine?" she asked.

"Great. She now has two little brothers to spoil. The boys just turned nine. They are something else. Loud, active, and very identical." He held out his cell phone and scrolled through the pictures. "Here they are with my aunt Michella after a concert last month. Michel is on the right and Morell on the left."

An attractive and regal blond woman, dressed in a black gown, sat behind a grand piano with the two dark-haired boys at her side.

"My auntie Michella never had any children. She is the baby of the family. She's also a renowned pianist and married to her music. Due to her traveling, she's the only one missing from our regular Sunday dinners. She tries to make it when she's in town, but she always finds a way to call when she's not."

"Your family sounds great," she said with admiration, understanding the need for him to be close to home. No wonder he was so proud of his heritage. It wasn't just the family business that grounded him and kept him so close to Provence. It was the people and their connections. "It's much bigger than my family. Since dad died, it's only been me and my mother."

"And Ralph," he added.

"And Ralph," she agreed, shifting her thoughts to the happiness her mother had found. "I'm so glad for her. They both found love again, and they really do look like a young couple in love. I think Mom looks fifteen years younger because of Ralph."

"Do you have a picture of them?"

Surprised at his interest, but happy to share, she swiped through her pictures and showed him one of Ralph and her mother on a sailboat with two other couples. "Ralph's brothers are avid sailors. The *Sea Princess* is their weekend lover, or so their wives claim."

"Do you go out with them on the boat?"

"I do," she said, filling her chest with cool air and straightening her shoulders. "Who do you think took the picture?"

"I see," he replied, drawing a finger down her nose and leaning forward to place a kiss on the tip. "Your family is bigger than you thought."

She hadn't thought of it that way before, but Marko was right. Her family had multiplied when her mom and Ralph had married. They too shared regular dinners, even if they were at the local seafood restaurants.

"What's the story behind that smile?" Marko asked.

"Our dinners are usually at Fisherman's Wharf or a little Italian restaurant in town. No one is willing to take a chance on going hungry with a homemade meal." She chuckled at the charred attempt at barbecuing a specific catch last Labor Day. "They're all horrible cooks. Can't even get the charcoal right to grill."

"I'm good with charcoal," Marko offered, placing the phones on the table between them and folding her hand into his lap. "If you handle the salad, I'll handle the grill."

His suggestion stole her voice and filled her mind with unexpected scenarios. She'd never thought of Marko with a spatula in his hand, but the idea of putting a family meal together really pleased her. So much so that it was scary. She smiled and sucked on her lower lip.

Keep it simple, Kat. Sweet and simple, she thought.

"Your original question, and the start of the story was why I'm not in control of Château de M." He rubbed the hand he held in his lap and settled against his seat. "I haven't turned my back on my family. I oversee and advise on a daily basis. Martine is in charge, though. She holds the title of CEO. Technically, I'm the CFO."

Once again, he'd surprised away her ability to respond. She stared at the man before her, watched his lips move, heard him speak, but wasn't sure she truly comprehended his words. She retrieved her clammy hand and wiped it over her coat.

"After a difficult end to a bad relationship, Martine found solace and happiness in the work. At first, I think it was a way for her to cope with the insecurities that the jerk had planted in her mind. Proving to others, but primarily to herself, that she was strong and capable. That singular incentive kept her going. She needed it. Even more, she was good at it. As success after success rolled in, my beautiful cousin pieced her life back together and her confidence soared."

"She means a lot to you."

"A lot," he confirmed. "Martine and I grew up together. She is the sister I always wanted. I'd do anything to make her happy, and I am sure she would do the same for me."

He'd stepped away from the family legacy to give his cousin room. The aggressive do-anything-to-get-ahead student and cutthroat businessman had a heart. Kathryn's lips curved into a smile, and something peculiar tingled in the center of her chest. She leaned closer to him and returned her hand to his. Fitting it snug inside his hold, she let out a long breath.

"She's actually a very tough leader and an innovative thinker. We work together, but I have no desire to step into her spotlight," Marko said. "I'm very proud of all she's overcome and achieved. Martine is incredibly strong."

"Is that why you're in Paris?" Kat finally found her voice.

"Yes," he admitted. "The week before I came to school was the first week Martine had come out of the house and surfaced from the massive depression that had taken her under. We feared she'd been damaged so bad that she wouldn't be able to climb out of it. When she did, it was like a true miracle. We didn't want to do anything to upset her or risk her slipping away again."

"That must have been difficult for the whole family."

"Devastating. She was always carefree as a child. So damn cheerful and sweet, her optimistic nature hurt my teeth. Her laughter was so loud and happy. Then, silence. Martine had closed herself off from the world." He spread his free hand across his forehead and massaged his temples with his thumb and middle finger.

"We were all shocked when she went to my father and asked him to give her a job. She already knew how the vineyard operated on the soil, so she wanted to learn about the office. She wanted to be the best assistant she could be for me when I returned. But Martine wasn't assistant material. She analyzed and made decisions. She brokered deals. She was a powerhouse in the body of a five-foot-five-inch woman."

His words added layers of respect to her perception of the man. He cared so much for his family. He would do anything for them. Kathryn inhaled and wondered what that level of love from Marko would mean to her. No man, outside her father, had ever cared for her so unconditionally.

"I understand," she said. "Your cousin is as strong as you are. It'll work out."

"No doubt," Marko said, sitting taller and grinning at her. "As for me professionally, I decided to make my way outside the shelter of Château de M. I'm establishing my reputation, gaining invaluable experience, assisting Martine when she asks, and I'm near enough to the whole situation for when circumstances should change. My original goal is still intact."

Kat didn't understand how the circumstances would change, but there was so much information to digest that she didn't ask. She looked at him, smiled at the intense dedication and force of his presence in Paris, and decided that she had to simply accept what he offered for the day. She needed to experience him fully. No reservations, in spite of the long-term consequences.

"I didn't know that you remained in France to stay close to the family and Château de M." Her fingertip traced over his knuckles. "You had always said you wanted to live in a thriving city and keep a finger on the pulse of financial innovation."

"True," he replied, grinning slightly. "It wouldn't make me very marketable to big international firms if I said I wanted to return to my family land and expand our business from within. Most importantly, returning to Provence on my own didn't seem appealing. It's a place for family. I was a bachelor."

"Hence, being in Paris provides the long line of beautiful models and socialites always on your arm," Kat said, not happy with the photos she'd seen over the past few years. "You seem to enjoy the eligible bachelor lifestyle."

"Hence, being in Paris," he mimicked, "allowed me the opportunity to wait and prepare for what I truly want." He skimmed his fingers down her face, and Kat shivered at the sense of possession that filled her body.

"Kat, how would you feel about making us a reality?"

Surprise filled her chest. She couldn't speak.

"As I've mentioned, I'm in the market for a new firm. I have the experience and clout to further my career, but I want nothing more that to have you in my life. I'd take a lesser position if I knew that to be the case. You are more important to me than any job could ever be. The meeting tomorrow gives me the opportunity to come to New York. Would that make you happy?"

Happy? Marko in New York? She nodded, then shook her head. She didn't know what to say. If the distance between them was no longer an issue, how could she justify keeping him at arm's length? How could she make him understand that she wasn't meant for his world?

"Marko, you need to take the position that will further your career. Any firm would be lucky to have you. I trust you'll pick the best one for you." She met his gaze and gave him the sultriest smile she could manage. "As for us, we are who we are. I want to enjoy this time with you more than you could imagine. I am enjoying this time with you."

"Enough to stay in Paris?"

Her heart beat against her ribs. She simply shrugged and held out her arm. "Look at this view. Who wouldn't want to see it on a regular basis?"

Chapter Twelve

"It's time for us to enjoy this view from a higher elevation," Marko announced, fitting a bill beneath the shot glass containing their receipt and motioning to the waiter. She may have avoided his questions, but he knew what she craved.

Ironically, Kat needed simultaneous limits, guidance, and freedom to grow. She needed her emotional and physical needs acknowledged and met. And even if she didn't know it, he was the man to give it all to her.

Impatience and anticipation were getting the best of him. He wanted Kat in his home. In his bed. Marko had not lacked for female company while he'd been apart from Kat. By no means was he a celibate or sexually deprived man, but what he'd always desired had only just arrived. He sensed Kat's hesitation to see the truth, but he was determined to make her understand exactly how much his personal goal had never changed.

He knew who he wanted on his arm, who he'd always wanted, and he was prepared to give her all that she needed.

Marko wanted Kat.

He stood and held Kat's coat. "The apartment is above the café."

"Seriously? That is amazing." She looked out over the river, fitting her arms through the sleeves and shrugging the heavy wool over her small shoulders. "You get to watch the sun set here every night?"

"When I'm home on time," he replied, loving the starry-eyed gaze on her face. "Tonight, we can enjoy it together."

Marko arranged the cashmere wrap to shield her chest from the wind and offered her the beret.

"I thought berets were démodé," she said, pursing her lips in a tease as she angled it on her head. "Would a real Parisian wear a beret these days?"

"I haven't given it much thought," he said. "Probably not. But this one is very soft, keeps you warm, and is adorable on you." He dipped his head and touched the tip of his nose to hers. "You are adorable."

She laughed and reached for him, lacing her hand through his arm.

"The entry is around the corner," he said, stepping from the café's glass enclosure, and shielding her from the bitter chill that had returned while they'd been warm inside. He led her the few meters to the entry.

Entering a security code on the keypad, he unlocked the old wooden door to the townhome and steered her inside. They bypassed the elevator, and climbed the steep staircase to the first level. He was eager to see her reaction once she walked into the comfortable living space. She'd love the tall windows overlooking the river. The view had been his reason for buying the entire building. He had three stories of beautiful views . . . views he wanted her to find irresistible.

Reaching the first-floor landing, he opened the door and stepped back for her to enter. Instead, she looked up at him, placed her hands on her hips, and made a very animated and annoyed face.

"You don't lock the door?" Kat asked.

"No. No need," he said, chuckling as she scrunched her nose. "There is no other resident in the building."

"Oh," she breathed, and turned toward the magnificent view. "Oh, wow." She stepped inside the apartment and walked directly to the seating area by the windows. Clasping her hands to her chest, she stood before the grand windows and slowly shook her head. "This is gorgeous."

Mais, oui, he silently agreed. *Absolutely gorgeous.* His gut clenched and his feet remained glued to the entrance hall, immobilized by the vision and the desire that crashed over him. He'd arranged the furnishings to optimize the view, but he'd done a much better job than he'd originally thought. Kat was stunning in that space.

The grey light filtered through the glass panes and silhouetted Kat's frame to erotic perfection. The long coat draped over her slender shoulders, adding to the dark allure.

"Take off your coat and stay awhile," he said, finally dropping her bags on the side table and managing to walk around the tall-backed white leather couch. She stood catty-corner to a love seat, her body angled so she could see the activity on the Right Bank. Her thighs pressed against the lucky arm of the love seat, and he wanted nothing more than to have her pressed completely against him.

He stepped behind her and lowered the coat off her back, then tossed it on a plush chair in a far corner. Aching to skim his fingers over her arms and brush his lips up the side of her neck, he closed his eyes and inhaled her sweet scent. Contentment swelled within his chest. The image was real. She was finally here . . . with him . . . His.

"*Bella, you* make these sights beautiful," he said.

Kat closed her eyes and savored the warmth of his breath. Her skin heated, and with each glide of his tongue, tingles shot through her body. She pressed against his hard length, reveling in the feel of his erection against the upper swell of her buttocks. He wanted her as much as she needed him.

Weighted by desire, she forced her eyelids to remain open and leaned her head to the right to grant him complete access against her neck. His lips closed on the soft flesh of her earlobe, and his hands splayed across her rib cage. She couldn't get enough of him. Every inch of her body craved his touch.

"Only one thing could improve the view," he said and stepped away.

"No," she breathed. Every cell in her body protested the distance, displeasure coursing over her at the loss of physical contact. She turned and found him looking down at her with a smile on his lips. Kat wanted that mouth on hers. Her chest rose and fell with anticipation, and her breasts grew heavy with need.

"Patience, *bella*," he said, cupping her face in his large hands and feathering his fingers across her cheeks. "I've waited a very long time for you to come back to me. Indulge me. Let me satisfy my curiosity on how the light from outside the window shadows the lines of your naked form."

He lowered his mouth and took her lips, slowly coaxing her body to wait for his command and settle against him. Her palm pressed over his muscled chest, and she found the quick beat of his heart matched her own. Needing to feel his bare skin beneath her fingertips, she moved up to his neck and tangled her fingers in the dark hair at his collar. Somehow, between the passionate possessions of his tongue, she managed to break free to take a slight breath and taste the dark, shadowed temptation at his jaw.

She pushed his jacket off his broad shoulders, and as if on autopilot, she loosened his tie and unbuttoned his shirt. It was her turn to step back. She met his dark gaze, and the passion embedded in those telling eyes inhibited her logic and captured her heart.

"This is perfect," he said, his accent strong and defined. His fingers gripped her hips and he returned her body against his. "No more distance. No more denial," he insisted. *"Finalement."* He touched his lips to her mouth. *"Ici."* His tongue swept over her lips and she opened to him. *"Avec moi . . . finalement."*

"Yes. Finally," she breathed and released her uncertainties. No matter the outcome of spending time with him, she loved this man. Being with him was not about the sexual gratification or physical need; he was everything she'd ever desired. She'd allow for the heartache, if necessary, to experience one day of that everything. Her fingertips moved over sculpted muscle and through the tempting dark trail to his belt buckle. In spite of his sharp inhale of breath, he kissed her, slow and tender, and additional pieces of her heart melted with each caress.

"You are mine," he said, closing one hand on her fingers and stilling her actions. With the other hand, he cupped her cheek and his eyes held her gaze.

Waves of need rolled over her as she read the promise of determination in his eyes. He rested a thumb on her trembling chin and caressed down the side of her neck with sure fingers. She nodded her head in agreement.

"I need to hear you say it." His mouth remained a mere inch from hers, teasing her lips, but not satisfying them with a touch.

"I'm yours," she whispered, tears welling in her eyes from the verbal acknowledgement. She'd always been his, but she'd never dared ask for him to be hers. "I am yours, Marko."

One hand curved on her nape, he claimed her mouth with a guttural groan that thrilled and empowered her. Her lips instantly yielded to his strength and demand to open. She swept her tongue over his, tasting the hunger in his kiss and feeling the burn of his possession.

"Mine." He grasped the hem of her dress and pulled it over her head.

Eager nipples peaked, rubbing against abrasive lace. The once dainty bra was laid to rest with the dress. Indoor heating in Paris was not like it was in New York. Her skin prickled from the cold, but it was a race for skin to feel skin, and Kat sucked in a breath as she pressed against him and the chill in the air disappeared.

Marko wrapped his fingers on the thin straps at her hip and snapped the panties from her form. He stepped back and let his appreciative gaze travel down her body.

"Now this is a beautiful sight," he said, motioning for her to spin on her heels.

She did, but playfully jutted her chin forward and noted the inequality in their situation as she turned. Still wearing her boots, and dressed in only her stockings and garter, all the pertinent parts of Kat's body were exposed to his view. Her nipples grew harder under his visual exploration, and the moisture pooling between her legs heated her thighs, in direct contrast to the cool air.

Marko stood before her, barefoot but clothed. His straining erection was sheltered inside his dark slacks and tucked secure beneath the buckle of an expensive leather belt.

Shoes were scattered across the floor. Clothing draped on every surface. But he was not available to her. Pouting, she cocked her head and she made an obvious show of reviewing his disappointing state of dress.

Grinning, he crooked his finger for her to return, and she stepped into his embrace. Beneath the urgent exploration of his hands, her pulse raced, pressure built between her thighs, and she ached with the need to give all of herself. As if she'd never known a man's touch, each caress awakened new sensations and she silently begged to feel him more.

His kiss simmered from her lips to her very core, blazing a trail over her nerves and stealing the oxygen from her lungs. With impatience, she broke the kiss, and falling to her knees, she unbuckled his belt and pushed the last pertinent barrier between them down his thighs. Exquisitely tailored slacks fell to his ankles, and his large erection sprang free. Her mouth watered at the sight and she leaned forward, grasping the rigid shaft and kissing the smooth tip. Her fingers wrapped around his base and stroked. She curved her lips around the head, taking him deep into her mouth.

"*Arrêter*," he rasped, pulling away and urging her up on her feet. "*J'ai envie de toi. Maintenant.*"

He gathered her in his arms, lifted her off the ground, and fit her to his chest. Once she was snug against him, the strong beat of his heart soothed her spirit, the familiar fresh scent of his skin enticed her senses, and the possessive splay of his hands grounded her soul.

An electric charge passed between them. She didn't know what had happened, or why he'd stopped her. But in saying that he needed her, he'd fulfilled an aching need deep inside her soul. She welcomed the sense of belonging and settled against him as he wordlessly carried her up the staircase.

He pushed open the door with his shoulder and crossed the large space to stand her on her booted feet by the bed. Touching her cheek, he tilted her face and met her gaze, once again stealing her breath with a branding kiss.

With one muscled arm secured around her waist, he tipped her back onto the mattress, and, following her down, owned her will. She was in his bed, in his arms, and she embraced Marko into her heart and soul.

His long, hard body covered hers, as she arched to take all of him, and bask in the spell he wove around her. Large hands smoothed down her neck, over her shoulders, and to her ribs. Dipping his head, his mouth followed wicked fingers as they teased her taut nipples, beaded tight not from the cold, but from the anticipation of his touch.

With his thumb and forefinger, he rolled one hard bud, while his mouth claimed the other breast, sucking and nibbling the tender flesh until she bucked beneath him, unable to stand the teasing pleasure. "Please, Marko. I need you."

His mouth trailed down her stomach until strong hands grasped her hips. He rose and fit her legs around him, entering her in one, smooth glide. She nearly came at the first touch of his cock. He filled her so completely that she fought to keep her orgasm from consuming her immediately and ending the heavenly action too fast. Her vaginal muscles quivered in excitement and clenched tight around him, taking him deeper with each delectable thrust.

Kat's stockings snagged on the heel of a boot, as she linked her ankles around his waist and angled her hips for total contact. He rounded and ground against her moist heat, stroking every bit of her and building the frenzy for release. When he caressed the bundle of nerves nestled at the tip of her heat, her passion liquefied to a hedonistic longing for submission. She quivered beneath him. Bit her lower lip. Inhaled with all her might.

"Maintenant, mon cœur. Ensemble."

A prism of pleasure splintered over her and the buildup of pressure devastated her control. With a low groan, Marko pushed through her clenched muscles to the top of her womb, rubbing hard against her clit. She cried out and shattered in his hands. Marko threw back his head and released deep inside her shuddering body. The haven of his strength blanketed her restless tremors. Her vision spotted and, secure in his hold, Kat surrendered to blissful darkness.

With reluctance, Marko lowered beside the woman in his bed. He ran his fingers over her face in concern. Sultry eyes peeked from beneath her long lashes, and she reassured him with a smile before wrapping her leg over his thigh. Kat burrowed against him and slept.

He took her hand in his, kissed the center of her small palm, and then tucked her closer. Cuddling her body beneath the white down comforter, he relished the sound of her soft breathing and the manner in which it swept over his bare skin. Male satisfaction turned up the corners of his mouth in a heartfelt smile. He was truly happy.

He released a content breath and rested his chin atop her head.

Marko breathed in lavender and vanilla, nuzzling closer to the source of the sweet scent. Kat also burrowed closer to Marko, moaning sensually and fitting the plush white comforter to just below her nose. In contrast to the warmth of her naked body, leather smoothed over his thighs.

Dark clouds rolled through the sky, promising the arrival of torrential rain within minutes. He needed to make a fire and adjust the temperature controls before all the heat in the room was gone.

Careful not to wake her, Marko untangled himself from the shapely limbs, and rose from the comfort of Kat's warmth. With a glance under the covers at her booted feet, he smiled down at the gorgeous, almost-naked woman and made a mental note to properly undress her once the fire was going.

He dropped a kiss atop her head, then quietly moved to the limestone mantel. When she woke and saw how it stretched to the ceiling, she'd love it. He squatted, quickly built the fire, placed an additional blanket over Kat's shoulders, and collected his cellular off the side table. If she was going to adjust to the time change without much of a problem, she needed to eat properly and remain hydrated.

Marko scrolled through his contacts, hitting the number for the *boulangerie*. He spoke with Antoine, ordered a fresh baguette, and asked his friend to do him the favor of delivering a picnic of sorts to the apartment.

"Was that the beautiful Katerina I saw you with at the café?" Antoine asked.

"Kathryn," Marko corrected. "And yes, she is beautiful."

"It's about time, my friend. I've heard so much about her since the day you moved in. Now, I see why you are so taken with her." Antoine's booming voice was full of understanding and held no judgment. "When will I have the pleasure to meet your lovely woman?"

When she realizes she's my lovely woman, Marko thought. "She is here only for the day," he replied a little hesitantly.

"Well, then. You must convince her to stay longer. I will prepare a nice snack for the two of you, but a nicer dinner in our city is in order. Make those plans, *mon ami*."

"I'm on it," Marko said, gathering the discarded clothing off the furniture. "See you in a little while."

"*D'accord.*"

Nourishment would arrive in thirty minutes. He grinned like a cat that had discovered a bowl of cream. There were so many seconds in those thirty minutes, and he wanted to spend each of them with Kat.

Marko hung their coats in the foyer, collected the packages that had been delivered before they'd arrived home, then placed them beside the remainder of the clothes he'd folded on the staircase. He'd carry them to the bedroom when he returned.

He started a fire at the hearth in the living area before heading to the kitchen. The opulent space finally felt like home, and he knew it was because Kat was there. He'd purchased the property because it was exactly what would make her happy.

With more satisfaction than he'd thought possible, he poured a mix of fresh squeezed juices in a tall glass. He carried the red concoction back through the living room, hooked the packages in his fingers, and secured the folded clothing beneath his arm, then started up the stairs and back to Kat.

Curled on her side, Kat slept soundly.

Placing the glass on the nightstand, he sat on the edge of the bed and smoothed back the damp hair at her forehead. He remained as quiet as he could manage and admired the treasure in his bed. Kat's soft breathing made him smile, and he lowered his head to taste her lips. Sweet. Addictive.

He dipped lower and suckled her nipple, allowing it to harden between his lips and circling his tongue on the tight bud. Even in her sleep, she was so beautiful and responsive. She moaned and writhed beneath his touch.

Her eyelids lifted and she smiled, a bright twinkle in her dark eyes.

"*Ciao, bella,*" he whispered.

She stretched her arms and pressed an open palm to his heart. "Hello to you, sir."

He wanted her to rest comfortably, so he needed to remove her boots.

"You can wear these to bed again," he whispered, caressing the sides of her thighs. "And the boots. I want the leather over my shoulders."

At his words, her eyes opened and her seductive gaze swept over him. He unzipped the boots, slid them from her feet, and dropped them to the floor with an unintended thud. Her eyes closed, but an appreciative sigh escaped her lips as she extended her other leg. She smiled, placing her small foot in his hand.

"My feet ache bad. How about a massage, handsome?"

More than willing to oblige, he rubbed each of her dainty toes, smoothed the arch of her foot, then trailed up her calf, and settled on the heat at the apex of her thighs. He moved over her naked skin and to her garters. She squirmed as he touched the sensitive area and hooked his fingers on the material. He rolled the decadent garment down her legs, and released the silk stockings, brushing his lips over the tip of her hips.

"You were made for me," he said, clasping her wrists with long fingers and pulling her hands over her head. Her back arched and her chest lifted to him. He kissed the underside of her breast and licked the creamy flesh. He slid his fingers between her swollen folds and slipped inside her, leisurely coaxing her body back to surrender. Claiming a pretty nipple between his lips, he tasted her desire.

Another sigh escaped her lips as a second finger joined the first, and he caressed her tight moisture and watched the need for release spread over her flushed skin.

"I want to reach for you. Want to give you the pleasure you're giving me." Her breath grew ragged as she spoke. "The heady sensations in my mind and your hold on my wrists imprison my abilities," she confessed, twisting beneath his touch. "You're driving me wild with longing, Marko. I can't find the energy to move."

"Then accept the pleasure," he said, kissing down the flat length of her belly and plunging his fingers deeper inside her heat.

"Good. Accepting. Offer," she rasped.

A sense of accomplishment surged in his chest, as he realized it was the first time Kat had accepted freely. His tongue dipped into her belly button, and his thumb circled the raw desire pulsing between her legs. She curved off the bed and against his hand. Stroke after stroke, her sweet moans pleased him, and when her heat squeezed his fingers so tight and her thighs trembled with need, he called for her climax.

She cried out his name.

Marko loosened his fingers from her wrists and lowered her hands from over her head. He held her close, feeling the pleasure roll through her body and straight to his heart. Everything she felt, everything she did, everything that was Kat was what really mattered to him.

The doorbell chimed. Kat sighed and looked at him.

"Wait in bed," he said, rising and tucking the comforter around her shoulders. "Keep the sheets warm. I'll be back in a minute."

"Just the sheets?" Kat teased, cupping his groin and spreading teasing fingers over his already erect shaft.

"Wait. In. Bed." Marko forced himself to step away. She'd passed out after the previous orgasm, and he wasn't about to let her deplete her energy. She needed her strength. "Wait."

Chapter Thirteen

Antoine had the code for the front door, and he'd never send a regular delivery boy. He was a true gentleman and rather discreet, so Marko knew he'd come himself. After all, Antoine was doing him a favor by bringing much more than fresh bread.

The bell chimed . . . again.

"*Attendre!* I'm coming," Marko hollered, buttoning his jeans as he rounded the stairs. He opened the door and could barely see the big man behind the numerous paper bags and packages. He took the first bag, and patted his friend's back in appreciation. "Looks like you brought a lot of food. Don't even think about joining us."

"*Hé là,*" Antoine said in greeting, laughing and moving past Marko to the dining table. "*Tout est fin prêt. Une baguette.*" He unwrapped paper from a crisp loaf and the scent of fresh bread wafted in the air. "*Le Beurre Bordier, fromage, jambon, brandade de morue, croque monsieur, et croque madame. Bon?*"

"*Oui,*" Marko said, clasping Antoine's hand and shaking it gratefully. Typically, Marko limited his friends, but the local baker had proven to be a loyal and good choice. He knew that such friendships were rare. "It's perfect. You've thought of everything. Thank you."

"So, do I get to meet your Katerina?"

Marko shook his head. Negative. He wanted to return to bed and keep her to himself. Food, sex, shower, sex, more sex, and by then the rain should have subsided—

"Of course," a female voice sounded. Kat stepped off the last stair and extended her arm in greeting. "Hello. I'm Kathryn."

"What happened to waiting where you were?" Marko grumbled, pretending annoyance. He liked how she made herself at home. Kat parading through the house in his underwear did great things for his ego.

"*Faire la bise*." Antoine ignored her hand and pulled the tousled woman close, placing the traditional set of kisses on her pink cheeks. "I would be an insult to men in all of France if I pass the opportunity to kiss a beautiful woman—even if it is Marko's woman. *Je m'appelle Antoine*. I am Marko's friend."

"Ah, Antoine." Her bright smile lit up the room. "You're the man responsible for the most delicious croissants in the world."

"*C'est moi*." Antoine puffed out his chest and pounded his fist in the center. "I am happy you enjoy them. Now, you must try my baguette."

"Thank you so much," she said, giving him a quick peck on the cheek, conscious of the fact that the French rarely hugged when just meeting.

Back at university, it had taken Marko more than a few attempts to grow accustomed to skipping the kisses and giving her a hug in greeting. He grinned at the memory and at the way she'd insisted on wrapping her arms around his shoulders and counting to ten before releasing him. She'd claimed that was the only way he'd grow used to being hugged.

Truth was, he may have stretched the need for training a bit longer than necessary. No one could blame a man for wanting a woman like Kat wrapped around him.

"Please join us for some lunch," Kat said, walking around the room and looking between the warm hearth and the darkening sky. "Looks like it's pretty nasty out there. Please stay for a bit."

"He can't. Antoine needs to get back to the *boulangerie* for the afternoon rush. Parisians need fresh bread for their dinner." Marko squeezed the other man's shoulder. "Thank you for bringing this by."

"*Non, non*," Antoine insisted, giving Marko a mocking look. "Thanks for the concern, my friend. It is my pleasure to join you for a glass of wine. I'd like to get know Kathryn a little before I go."

The damn man was doing it on purpose. The gleam in his eyes and the smirk on his face were more than telling, but Marko couldn't blame him. He, too, would want to spend more time with Kathryn.

"Just great," Marko muttered, turning his back and pretending to read over the labels of the wine selection on the granite counter. There was no need for any real study, because each of the bottles was from his vineyard. But, he wasn't going to give his friend the satisfaction of witnessing his possessiveness over a woman. He'd even make a trip to the wine room to prove how easygoing he was. Maybe.

What was the big deal about having company for a glass of wine? Other than the fact that Kat had dressed in one of his white undershirts and a pair of his boxer shorts, and the woman looked too good to be looked at by another man, there was no problem. Right? Plus, she had finished off the outfit with a pair of black Merino socks.

Marko kept reading the labels. He couldn't suppress a grin at the pretty vision Kat created. He wanted to see that image every day.

"I have been looking forward to meeting you, Kathryn. Marko has told me a lot about you and the times you shared in New York." Antoine pulled out the chair nearest to the fireplace and gestured for Kat to have a seat. He sat beside her.

"He has?"

"Oh, yes. *Many* stories." Antoine stretched the pronunciation of many.

Marko closed his fingers around the neck of a favorite vintage and brought it to the table, along with three glasses. He'd spent too many late hours refurbishing details of the apartment with the other man, who had a talent for woodworking, to let him speak alone with Kat about their conversations. He'd definitely changed his mind about heading to the wine room for a different bottle.

"My Aimee especially likes the one about how you saved the kitten from beneath a car's tire. You used your weekly spending money to buy cat food and supplies for the animal to *weewee*, only to find out you are very allergic to cats."

Kathryn giggled. "I had to move out of my room until I found a home for her. I couldn't breathe, let alone sleep, with a cat living under my bed."

"Those hideous welts on your body didn't do much for your coed image, either." Marko took the seat across from Kat, uncorking the bottle and placing it in the middle of the table so the wine could breathe.

"Ha, ha." She feigned annoyance, waved a hand across her face, and turned to address Antoine directly. "Do you know that your friend made it practically impossible for me to soak in his tub? It wasn't like the dorms I lived in had bathtubs, and Marko was the only one I knew who had a 'private' bathroom. He had the nerve to try and persuade me not to use his 'private' bathtub." She had used air quotes with each mention of private.

"My *private* bathtub was shared with two soccer players. You wanted to sit where they placed their grimy feet." She'd come to his apartment at three o'clock in the morning and begged for a soak. Of course, he'd spent an hour scrubbing and sanitizing the communal tub before he'd let her step foot in the thing.

"They were nice guys," she said.

"What was nice was sitting with a naked woman for two hours and pretending to help her study for her midterm, while her skin got all wrinkly in an oatmeal bath that kept draining and exposing more blotches than she realized." He cocked his head and winked. "Rather fun Saturday night."

"Yeah, but thankfully those soccer players had more than a few boxes of oatmeal." She tapped a finger on the back of Antoine's hand for emphasis. "Marko was the perfect gentleman. I think he was more embarrassed by our situation than I was. He added oatmeal each time we added water."

"At least that's what I made you believe," Marko said.

Laughter filled the comfortable space, and Marko leaned back in his chair. Life was good when Kat was in it. With her brilliant smile and teasing laughter, her spirit and beauty were palpable in the atmosphere. Even his sullen friend had fallen to her charm. Usually, Antoine only smiled for Aimee. Today, the corners of his mouth were in a perpetual upturn and his eyes held a mischievous vividness. Kat chased away the melancholy.

"So what else have you and Marko spoken about?"

"A lot." Antoine put down his glass and reached for the baguette. "Honestly?" He paused and broke off a piece of bread.

"Always," Kat replied.

"Meeting Marko has helped me more than it has helped him. He is a late-in-life friend. A true friend."

"The feeling is mutual," Marko said. "You and Aimee have been a big part of transforming this apartment into a home. Maybe Kathryn can meet your princess soon?"

"*Absolument,*" Antoine agreed. He closed large fingers over Kat's small hand. "My daughter would enjoy meeting you very much. She lacks feminine influence, and it would be good for her to know a strong and attractive woman."

Clearly in tune with the sadness in Antoine's tone, Kat looked to Marko in question. He nodded.

"If I may be so bold to ask such a personal question, what about your wife?"

"My wife passed a few months after she gave birth to Aimee." The burly man gazed at the fire, tears shining in his eyes. "My daughter doesn't remember her mama."

Kat leaned over and wrapped her slender arms around his shoulders. She pulled Antoine into a hug, regardless of French etiquette. "I'm so sorry."

Inhaling loudly, Antoine dropped his head. "We went to the doctor because Talia was having problems sleeping through the night. Her breasts hurt too much. We were trying to have a baby, so we were hopeful that was the reason. The day we learned that my wife was pregnant, we also discovered that she had a very aggressive form of invasive carcinoma. The surgery was done immediately. We fell from clouds when we learned it was a cancer too aggressive for hope."

"I'm truly sorry," Kat repeated, rubbing his back. "It must be very difficult."

"Before I met Marko, when I was left alone and Aimee visited her grandparents for a few days, I would spend the nights with a bottle of wine . . . or two . . . or three. The dark became very ugly when vodka replaced the wine. Since Marko came, I have been preoccupied and more productive with those nights. Manual labor helps men."

Marko nodded and agreed with his friend. "Yes. It does. However, you helped me as much as I helped you."

"The place is to your liking, no?" Antoine asked Kat.

"Very much. It's exactly what I've always thought Paris would be like."

"*Bon*," Antoine said. "Marko was very specific in all the renovations."

She glanced at Marko, who simply shrugged. "I bought the place last February. I had professionals in for the major work, but as Antoine said, manual labor helps a man. I did what I could, and Antoine did even more with the woodwork."

"Unbelievable. This place is perfect." Kat splayed her arms in a grand gesture and spun on her heels. "The views are surreal. The flooring exquisite. And even if the kitchen is loaded with every amenity, it looks like royalty has lived here forever. Very authentic. Right down to the two fireplaces—

"Three," Marko corrected. "You haven't seen the third level."

Kat had always had a thing for cozy fireplaces. He remembered how she used to tell him that if he was going off campus to live, he had to find an apartment with a fireplace. She'd warned she'd move in with him if he did. He hadn't been able to land an apartment with a fireplace—and it wasn't for lack of trying. But on more than a few occasions, he'd pick her up in her room and walk across the quad just to sit by a fireplace and study.

"First, we drink to the love of my life. My beautiful Talia." Antoine poured the wine and handed them each a glass. They raised them high in the air and clinked them together. "To Talia."

"Second, we drink to friendship."

"To friendship."

They drank and ate, laughing over memories and speaking about the must-see Paris attractions. It was too bad the rain had ruined the afternoon picnic at the Pont Marie quay, but a house picnic worked. Contentment and joy filled the room, and Marko was actually glad to show Kat a little of his local life. He also wanted to show Kat off to every person in his life. He wanted to share everything with the woman he loved.

"Marko said you are here for work. How long can you extend your stay?"

Taken aback, Kat shook her head. "I can't. I need to present my article in a few days. I'm heading home tomorrow."

"When will you return?" Antoine asked.

"I'm not sure."

"She's not leaving," Marko said, stretching his legs beneath the table and nudging her with his foot. "Not if I have anything to say about it. You can fly out Monday and be back in plenty of time."

"And Aimee won't be home until Sunday night," Antoine added.

"You have to give Aimee her present, sweetheart." Marko grinned and turned to the other man. "While we were visiting the Eiffel Tower, we picked up a pair of earrings for your little one."

"I wish it was possible. Unfortunately, this is an important deadline."

"I remember. You are a writer." Antoine trailed a finger through the air, as if signing his name. "Marko says a great writer. What about your novel? Did you finish?"

Her gaze flitted to Marko. Her novel was a secret. She hadn't told anyone other than Marko about her publishing dreams.

She didn't answer. She sucked on her lower lip and looked down at her empty plate. Marko cut a piece of cheese and placed it there. Antoine offered her the crisp corner of the baguette. Her hand shook as she raised her glass and sipped on her wine. Antoine didn't ask more questions, and neither man spoke. They waited, like people who really cared, and allowed for courage to build, for her to speak.

"I did," she breathed into the glass. "I finished."

Marko exhaled, apparently out of relief. Dropping his napkin, he pushed back his chair, and rounded the table. He pulled her from her seat and crushed her mouth with a celebratory kiss.

"Congratulations, *bella*. I'm so happy for you. So very happy."

"Now you finish, now you stay," Antoine concluded.

"I can't wait to read it," Marko said. He beamed with pride. They'd fleshed out the characters together, each covertly putting pieces of themselves in the romantic duo, but she'd never shared the ending. "Do you have a copy on your laptop?"

Kat's insecurity surfaced, and she pulled out of his arms and turned toward the hearth. She gazed at the fire. She may have finished the story, but the ending wasn't what she'd wanted to write or what he'd want to hear.

"It wasn't a big deal. The book needed an ending," she said, hunching her shoulders toward her chest. "That's all."

"How does it end?" Marko asked.

Kat didn't need to see Marko's face to feel his eyes on her. It was a silent dream they'd shared, something they'd never admitted to, but a dream nonetheless.

"She becomes a successful attorney, making partner by thirty-five."

"And?" His voice, lower than usual, coaxed her to answer differently. She knew he knew. He didn't really want to hear the ending she'd written.

"Having it all, she still wants a child. She makes it happen via a reputable sperm bank." It wasn't perfect, but nothing in life was ideal. "She lives happily ever after with her beautiful babies. Twins."

"Where is he?" Marko asked.

Kat swallowed hard and closed her eyes. "He's also very successful. An esteemed researcher that lectures all over the world, he's the most intellectual eligible bachelor. Other than the pictures she sees in the papers, she doesn't know much about him. They drifted apart. Live separate lives."

"I see." Marko stepped away, and the loss of his heat on her back chilled her heart.

Awkward silence descended.

It was fiction—they knew it was fiction. But something about the writing was so real. Small quirks and big personality issues had found their way to the page, identifying the author's true thoughts. Unable to admit to the desires in the book, she'd keep the finished manuscript hidden away and never let another person read it. It was fan fiction of the life she led and the life that was out of her reach.

She'd put more of herself into the story than intended. Hurt and loneliness were common characteristics of the heroine. At least she'd found joy in the babies.

The arrival of a text message sounded. She turned back and looked from Marko to Antoine, but neither moved. Glancing around the open space, she saw her bag by the door. A second alert dinged.

"It's yours," Marko said, crossing his arms over his chest. She read the agitation in the posture, saw the anger in the color of his face, but she accepted the momentary reprieve from their situation and went in search of her phone.

While she rummaged through the tote, Marko and Antoine resumed their conversation in French. They spoke quickly and at a low volume, so she wasn't able to process what they said. She didn't mind. Actually, she didn't want to know. Kat needed space to save her sanity. Getting wrapped up in a day's fantasy wasn't the way to succeed.

It's about time, KittyKat. I see you're enjoying Paris and Marko. Just do it!

She couldn't help but smile at Paul's innuendo. She wasn't shy and bashful any longer. She could give as hard as she got.

Just do him?

Hitting send, she strolled back to the table and dropped into her chair. She held the phone in one hand, reached for her wine with the other. Her thumb hovered over the keypad, waiting for Paul's inevitable smartass response.

Now you got it. Don't worry about the piece. Charlie has it covered. Just enjoy your man and remember to come—

An immediate second ding had her collapsing the keyboard to continue reading.

Get your mind out of the gutter!

He'd added a picture of an old-fashioned metal garbage can.

What I meant was - come back to us. Maybe bring the foreigner?

Right ☺ Like I have any control over the foreigner. Wait, what do you mean, forget about the piece?

He couldn't be serious? She'd traveled to Paris for research. She wanted—no, *deserved*—her byline. Downing the last of the wine in her glass, she folded her forearms on the table and dropped her head into them. She wanted to scream. "No fucking way," she lamented in a whisper.

"What's wrong?" Marko rubbed the tight knot between her shoulders, and sat in the chair previously occupied by Antoine. "Who is it?"

"Work," she said, peeking over her arms and looking at the empty wineglass with longing. "Paul is being an ass."

"Typical," Marko said. He reached for the bottle and refilled her glass.

Paul's reply dinged. She sipped on the wine, then looked at the screen.

Fucking enjoy yourself and fucking fuck Marko in every position known to man. Do NOT waste your time on research and do NOT write the article. Charlie has more than enough material to do a 'bang up' job. The ship is crawling with handsome specimens. You should see the pics she sent me.

The next ding was for a picture of a man's snug ass, covered by a pair of Levi's jeans worn low on his hips. The next was of three men in exaggerated flex positions by the pool.

Best In Suit Contest. I like the one on the right, KittyKat. You?

F-off. I'm writing the damn feature. Don't think of cutting me out!

She placed the phone face down on the table and drank more wine. A flush crept up her neck and settled on her cheeks. "He can't do this. He's such a dick."

"Do not let work ruin your time in Paris," Antoine said. "Work is work. It is not worth disappointment."

"It's just Paul," Marko added. He reached across her and moved the wine just out of her reach. Cutting a small piece of the smoked ham, he paired the meat with some bread and held it by her lips. "Eat."

She opened her mouth, but didn't taste what she was sure was a delicious bite as she chewed and swallowed. "I'm not listening to him. I'm not."

"Okay," Marko agreed. "You always find a way to get what you want, sweetheart. Dealing with Paul is not an exception."

"Third, you must be true to yourself," Antoine boomed, rising from his seat and coming around the table to place a hand on her shoulder in a show of his support.

"Thank you," she said in a small voice. It was as if the wind had stilled and her sails had dropped, but she wasn't giving up. She was getting the byline.

"I want to give my friends a little advice. A few words an old man once said to me, but I was too young to understand and follow. Today, now that it is too late, I appreciate them," Antoine said, meeting both of their gazes in turn.

Kat reached and picked up her glass, but Antoine indicated for her to return it to the table.

"I do not need a drink to say this," Antoine said. "I may want to shake some sense into Marko for not acting faster, but I do not need wine."

The imposing man stood between them, first touching his fingers to his heart, then dropping a heavy hand on each of their shoulders.

She glanced at Marko, who was unsuccessfully trying to hide his annoyance at the turn of events. The little muscle in his cheek pulsed, and lines of restraint marked his forehead. He met her gaze, warning her to stay the course. She looked down and squared her shoulders in the opposite direction.

Antoine's fingers squeezed tighter. "Do not waste a second more when you can live with love every minute. Make every hour count. Live every day. Do not push away what is in your heart."

A lump the size of France settled in Kat's throat. She blinked back her own tears and forced a smile. If only it were that easy to embrace what was in her heart.

Marko didn't budge. Thankfully, Antoine did.

"*Et maintenant*, I must return to the *boulangerie*," he said, and gave her a reassuring smile. "*Faire la bise, ma douce chérie.*"

She performed the ritual air kisses and said good-bye to her new friend. Kat turned her back just in time to hide a solitary tear. She walked toward the sitting area, listening as Marko thanked Antoine for the meal and bade him farewell.

They were alone.

Chapter Fourteen

K at wrapped her arms across her middle, stared at the rain stream-ing down the tall panes, and dug her fingernails into her palms. The fairy tale had come to an end prematurely. She had to get out without falling apart.

Silently, Marko returned to the hearth and tended to the fire. Ten-sion rolled off his broad shoulders as he added wood. She'd made Marko feel like shit over the ending of her story, and the feature was being pulled from under her feet. Things were on a quick downward spiral.

She wanted to go to him, to run her fingers over the muscled arms and tell him that the novel was just fiction. But she wouldn't lie. They each had their lives, and the reality was that their paths may have crossed, but they weren't meant to merge. She turned back to the icy chill drizzling on the beautiful church and waited for him to speak.

"Don't worry about Paul. You'll get him to come around." Big, warm palms closed on her upper arms. He leaned into her and settled his cheek against the side of her head. "I'm more sorry about the weather. Our picnic at Pont Marie is postponed, but we'll take a walk along the quay once the rain stops."

"It's okay. We've had a great day. Thank you," she said, casually lifting a shoulder and trying to hide her nervousness. "I really should get going anyway. I need to check in at the hotel and start working on the piece while everything I've seen today is fresh in—"

"No."

"What?"

"No," he repeated, his fingers holding her steady.

The intensity in that single word froze her in place. No amount of wood on the fire could chase away the chills that raced down her spine.

He trailed a single finger across her arm, immobilizing Kat as he circled to stand in front of her. He cradled her face in his palms. Stroking his thumbs over her cheekbones, he lowered his head and brushed his mouth over her lips, licking slowly between them and urging them to open.

Her lips parted and closed around his tongue. She sucked on him deep and long, wanting to commit his taste to memory forever. She closed her eyes and held back most of the tears that had threatened numerous times in the past hour. She couldn't help it.

Sinking against him, she let his strength carry her. His hands moved down her back and cupped her ass, pulling her closer and pressing his arousal against her tummy. Need spread over her, but her mind fought the sensation. The hurt in her chest from the realization that she couldn't have what she most wanted intensified.

Breaking the kiss, he smoothed away the moisture from her cheeks. Fitting a finger beneath her chin, he lifted her face and looked into her eyes. "Are you ready to tell me what happened?"

Marko recognized the look. Hated the look. He wasn't going to let it stand.

"Paul said to forget the article. He said Charlie could take care of it. I should have a fucking fun time." Her voice trembled. "I guess I'm not good enough for a byline in his mind. I'm just pretty and flighty. . . ."

"You know that's not true," Marko said. "You know you're more than good enough, and you know Paul knows it, too." Her apprehension had nothing to do with her writing, and they both knew it. "You'll write the feature. You'll give *City Wings* a real choice on which article to publish, and I bet you'll get your byline. I'm not saying that your friend isn't a good writer; I'm just saying you're a great one. You always accomplish what you set your mind to. Set your mind to it and write the article."

Kat worried her lower lip so hard that Marko feared she'd make it bleed. He pressed his thumb to her swollen mouth and forced her to stop.

"You're right," she said, nodding her head and stepping back.

He saw the emotional shield drop, and he clenched his jaw, grinding his teeth until they squeaked. He dreaded her next words. He knew what she'd say.

"I'm going to do it. I'm writing the article." Her gaze darted around the room, as if searching for something to grab on to. She wanted support. "I just need to get to the hotel and regroup—

"No." He reached for her hand and closed his fingers around her wrist. "You're not leaving. You're not going anywhere."

Concern crossed her face. She looked into his eyes, seeking an explanation.

"Seriously, I should act like a true professional, get to the hotel, and start writing."

"We settled that. You're a professional regardless of where you are," he replied, refusing to allow her to justify any time apart from him.

"The hotel is prepaid and I'll lose the money if I don't show. It's a waste."

"You know the money doesn't matter. Not to me. Not to Paul," he insisted. "So if it makes you feel any better, give me the confirmation and I'll take care of it. You're not leaving. You relinquished yourself to me for the day. I say what happens. I decide."

Relief replaced her concern. From the soft flow of her breath to the moisture in her eyes, to the return of her color, she told him everything her mouth wouldn't. She didn't want to go. Marko released her wrist, and she didn't step away. She remained by his side. Relief flooded through him, as well.

"I warned you that I would not allow you to run."

She needed this. He needed this.

Kat held his gaze, her breathing loud and her curiosity piqued.

"You will find a way to write the damn thing, regardless of where you are. You're not leaving." He added the *me* silently. "I won't let you go. However, I will discipline you for considering the ridiculous idea."

Her mouth dropped into a pretty circle and her pupils dilated wide. The black practically covered all the beautiful color of her eyes. A pink flush marked her cheeks, and her chest rose and fell rapidly. The cotton T-shirt did nothing to conceal her hard nipples, while his cock jerked against the harsh denim.

He sat in the center of the couch, spreading his legs to accommodate the painful swelling in his jeans. She still hadn't moved. She watched him with a hunger in those dark eyes that begged for him to continue. His Kat craved limits. She needed restraints.

"Come here," he said, pointing down at the plush carpet.

She shuffled and stood between his feet.

"Good." He rewarded her with a tap on her ass. "Take off your shirt." He held his hand out, palm up, and watched as her fingers fumbled and lifted the white cotton over her creamy, tempting skin. The full smoothness of her heavy breasts bounced free as she tugged the shirt over her head, and his damn cock burned for her.

Still wordless, she laid the shirt in his palm and stood with arrogant pride. Her breasts pushed forward, curving slightly upward as her nipples grew even harder.

"Very nice," he said. Rewarding her obedience, he circled a fingertip around one nipple until she moaned. He pinched it between his thumb and forefinger, then gently tugged on the excited peak to make her shift her stance and face him.

Her breasts were inches from his mouth, offered seductively as she looked through her long lashes at him. He could suck and lick her to orgasm if he chose, but . . .

"I promised to mark your ass so you couldn't sit comfortably for a flight, but now you require punishment for errant thoughts as well." He rolled the tender flesh, and she gasped. He pinched it hard enough to let her know this wasn't a gentle act.

Taking the other delicious bud between his lips, he kept her in his mouth, nipping at her softness with his teeth, then soothing the ache with his tongue, only to suck harder and deeper the next time around. Teeth grazed a little bit closer to the taut tip each time he repeated the actions, until he felt her knees release and come to rest against his thighs.

Moaning, she arched her back. Her legs strained to hold her.

Greatly responsive, she would submit quickly.

He licked and nibbled, first one, then the other nipple, until her control broke and she straddled his thigh. He allowed her to work herself up, grinding against him, sliding a hand inside the boxers, and rubbing herself toward a much-needed climax. Her face flushed, her chest heaved, and the honeyed scent of her sex filled the air.

He wanted to watch her like that for a very long time, riding the edge for hours, and pining for a release only he would grant her. The power she gave him in knowing that he could either keep her from what she yearned for or grant her what she desired was so addictive. He shook his head. He had to focus.

"This is a punishment. Stand," he instructed, lifting her effortlessly off his thigh.

Somehow, she managed to steady her shaking legs and find the energy to stand. Her hand, still shoved in the boxers, moved beneath the cotton with sinful intent. The guilty look on her face confirmed she continued to work her clit, even as she dropped her gaze to his feet.

He had to fight to keep from smiling. Greedy little wench. She'd learn to wait.

"Clasp your hands together behind your back," he reprimanded.

She did. He pressed his face between her breasts, then leaned around her and secured her wrists with the T-shirt. The sound of the material tearing as he pulled it tight startled her and she jumped. He nipped at her breast and she stilled. "You're very responsive, *bella*, but you need to learn patience and how to release control."

"Okay," she whispered, a plea in her tone. "I'll do that."

With a small tug, he lowered the oversized boxers off her hips. "I don't believe you know the meaning of letting go, but if you don't learn fast, your ass will be so sore that you won't be able to sit for weeks."

He guided her over his knee, smoothing a hand up her spine and draping her silky hair over her shoulder. "*Tu est très jolie comme ça.*"

The first smack landed on the underside of her right ass cheek, but before she'd finished crying out, the second followed in the middle of her receptive flesh. Her skin promptly displayed two pink impressions that were so maddeningly pretty.

She groaned in pain and he was almost tempted to stop. Almost. The way her shoulders relaxed and her body went spineless urged him on. She needed this.

The soft sigh escaping her lips had him raising his hand above her ass and deciding on the next landing.

"The first two were to keep you uncomfortable on the plane. The next five are for disappointing me with your thoughts," he explained. "They will sting more than the first."

"More?" Kat's question was a whisper.

"More," he confirmed. "Next time, I won't be as gentle as I was on the initial ones, nor will I be as lenient on the amount. Count." He snapped his wrist and met her soft flesh.

"One!" she cried, her nails digging into her fisted hands.

"Two!" Her legs tensed and kicked back.

"Fall into the burn."

"Three."

"*Très jolie.* Let the darkness relieve you."

Sweat beaded on the small of her back, but her arms had relaxed and her hands were held together only from the bound material.

"Four . . ." Kat said, when his hand slipped between her legs and found her soaked with desire.

"Not quite, sweetheart." He rubbed through her swollen folds and circled her nub. "This is a caress. And it's not your ass that I'm caressing yet."

Her head fell freely. He released her hands from the binds. One arm remained atop her back and against his torso, the other dropped to her side. She'd let go. She'd sunk in to the pleasure of the sting. His Kat had truly placed herself in his hands.

Four and five were light snaps, but she was too far gone and he could barely hear her count. So damn responsive. "Why did I wait so long?"

Securing her in his arms, he rose from the couch and carried her toward the stairs. There was only so much control left in his own body, and he needed to be inside her with an urgency he'd never known. There was no time to take her upstairs and be gentle.

He needed her.

"Hold on to me," he said, slightly shifting her body and placing her arms over his shoulders. "Don't let go, sweetheart."

"I won't," she breathed, linking her hands behind his neck and nuzzling into him. "I won't."

He pinned her back against the wall, holding her feet off the floor and brushing his mouth over hers. She responded, and they kissed and kissed and kissed, sharing a passion that had been denied for too long.

"I want you," he said, supporting her with one arm, while the other hand unbuttoned his fly. "Tell me you can take me now."

"I can take you," she rasped, wriggling beneath him, searching for footing.

"Wrap your legs around my waist," he said, freeing his erection and pushing up against her sweet heat.

Thankfully she'd retained the ability to wrap her legs around his waist. He stroked up his length, positioning himself at her opening, and in one sure movement, drove into her welcoming body. He thrust long and hard, setting a grueling rhythm that had her tightening around him in seconds. He sank into her warm and moist haven, rougher than he logically knew was right, but he was unable to satiate the need to stake his claim until he felt her building climax push her over the edge.

First to surrender to the ecstasy, her muscles convulsing around his driving cock, she called his name. He freed his control and joined her in a blinding orgasm that kept rolling through them.

Marko gathered her close, holding her in his arms and turning to sit on the steps. Her breath was ragged and her body spent, but he soothed the shivers from her back and somehow he had managed not to collapse into a heap on the floor. He held her on his lap, dropping kisses on her hair and inhaling her sweet scent.

"Je t'aime, bella. Je t'aime."

Chapter Fifteen

"Bella, you need to sit in the tub. It's a soothing oatmeal bath. Your favorite."

She knew the voice. Had heard the words before. She tried to turn over, but hit a wall of muscle. More resistance.

"Wake up, Kat. You need to soak or you'll be very sore later."

Awareness dawned, and she didn't appreciate the light invading her sleep. Marko was holding her in a candlelit room, over a steaming fragrant bath. It wasn't just oatmeal. A sweet field of lavender called to her. But, no matter how lovely it smelled, she didn't want to wake up.

"I can't," she said, burrowing into his chest. "Please let me sleep."

"It's okay, sweetheart. We'll do this together." He took a step forward. His thigh brushed her sore backside as he lifted his leg, and she groaned her discomfort. Hearing the water splash and feeling his lips on her forehead soothed away any anxiety. She returned to the tranquil euphoria of his strong arms.

"I'm going to sit in the bath now. Don't be shocked when you feel the water." Marko lowered them into the aromatic indulgence and fit her snugly between his outstretched legs. He wrapped an arm beneath her breasts, and reclined her head against his shoulder. "Sleep. I've got you. *Je t'aime.*"

He'd said it earlier. He had. Kat had heard his husky proclamation, but her voice wouldn't work and her eyes wouldn't open. She stayed in the security of his hold, warm and happy in his embrace. Her body and soul complete in that specific moment in time. And again, she slept.

* * *

When Kat opened her eyes, the image of the handsome man sitting on a cream-colored lounger, his bare feet resting on the edge of the bed, filled her chest with warmth and belonging. She watched him, appreciating the stretch of the grey sweater across his shoulders and the long lines of his legs in slacks down to his bare feet. But so much more about Marko held her heart. He was the total package of a dream man. In her book, nobody else compared.

She didn't speak, and her heart thundered in her chest as she recalled just how much of the total package he was. He was loyal, caring, and more than she'd imagined in the past. He truly valued the people he let into his life. Maybe a little arrogant on his abilities, but he'd certainly earned, even deserved, that personality trait with his track record of success.

The concentration in his eyes as he scanned the tablet in his capable hands gave her a small glimpse of his business prowess. Oh, the hands . . . those wonderful hands, the mere thought of the security and safety coupled with mind-blowing sensuality had her squirming beneath the comforter. She groaned as the soft cotton scraped over her tender backside.

"*Ciao, bella,*" he said, as he caught her staring. He smiled and blew her a kiss.

"*Ciao, bello,*" she replied, returning his kiss and snuggling against the down pillow at her side in order to reduce the pressure on her butt. Damp hair fell over her shoulder, and she was grateful for the added warmth of the fireplace.

"Did you wash my hair?"

"Had to." He dropped his feet to the floor and placed the tablet on the side table. "It was full of oatmeal . . . like the rest of you."

He lowered the screen on the laptop, which was perched on an ottoman, and placed the computer beside the tablet. Like a jaguar leaning for his prey, he reached and tucked a strand of hair behind her ear. "How do you feel?"

"I feel great." And she did. Stretching her arms over her head and sticking her toes past the edge of the mattress, she twisted and turned, feeling more energetic than she had in ages. She rearranged the covers, folded her hands under her cheek, and gave him her best come-hither look.

"Great?" Marko asked, raising a sexy brow and pointing to where she'd moved the comforter off her bum.

"Okay. A little sore," she admitted.

"That's better." He grinned, then joined her on the bed. Spreading out that wicked body next to hers, he ran a large hand over the curve of her waist to the swell of her hip. "Otherwise, we'd need to press rewind and repeat."

Cozying up against his solid warmth, she lazily kissed the side of his neck. The yearning to strip off his clothes and paste her naked body up against his bare skin gained in popularity with each yummy taste of the man. "I don't know. Maybe it's not as sore as I originally thought."

"It's always an option, baby." Holding her chin between his thumb and forefinger, he lowered his mouth and swept his tongue across her lips. "Or I can put some more lotion on that pink little ass of yours."

"You really marked my ass?"

He leaned over her shoulder and nodded. "Absolutely. I promised I would."

Excited by the image his words created in her mind, she pushed off his chest and tried to get up so she could catch a glimpse in the mirror. But he snaked an arm around her waist and pulled her back to the bed. She kicked her feet, but playing too hard made the soreness burn.

"I want to see. Let me up."

"Lotion," he growled, turning her on her stomach and clasping her wrists in one hand. He softly leaned over her legs and secured them between his thighs, keeping his weight on his knees. Marko kissed between her shoulders and held her still. "I'll take any excuse to keep you in bed and to myself."

"I like that idea."

"Which one?" When he dipped his head beside hers and looked at her, a daring twinkle played in his eyes. He traced down her nose and settled on her lips.

"Both of them," she said, sucking on his finger and swirling her tongue over the tip. "First, let's get done with the lotion. Then we'll think of what else we can do."

He straightened and set to his original task. Cool, gentle fingers soothed over the burn and silenced her. She closed her eyes and allowed herself to feel the message those fingers relayed. No words needed. He was taking care of her. Kathryn sighed and buried her face against her arm.

Minutes of pure bliss passed, he released her legs, then kissed the spot between her shoulders. Once satisfied she was relaxed and comfortable, he settled on the pillow next to her. "That's better."

"It is," she said, turning on her side and touching his jaw. "It wasn't that bad before, but whatever you did was heavenly. Thank you."

"Anytime, *bella*. Anytime."

Curling around him, she pressed against the man of her dreams and slipped her hand down the clichéd washboard abs women expected on the hottest men. Her heart skipped at the knowledge that there was nothing cliché about Marko, and she was privileged to have firsthand experience on that front. Those muscles supported a body and mind that surpassed any woman's stereotype of a hot man.

"So not typical," she said, lifting his hand to her lips and circling a fingertip. Licking down one finger and up the next one, then taking it into her mouth and enjoying the anticipation that lit his features. Question lines formed at the corners of his eyes and across his forehead, but she continued over all his fingers with no explanation. At last, she suckled on his pinky as if it was the tastiest treat in the world. Which, for the record, it almost was.

She splayed her hand over his stomach, skimming beneath his sweater and loving the way the soft hair, just below his belly button, trailed to the world's true tastiest treat.

"I don't think it's fair that I'm totally naked under here and you're totally clothed," she said, raising her brow and giving him a taste of his medicine. She pushed the sweater up. "This needs to go."

"Never let it be said I'm less than accommodating," he said, pulling it over his head and tossing it on the lounger.

She skimmed slowly down his chest, loving the feel of taut muscles and the soft sprinkling of dark hair.

The buttons at his waist were easy enough to undo and the zipper slid down with little effort. Quality was quality. With his help, she managed to rid him of the urban dreamboat pants, and was pleased to find he hadn't bothered with underwear.

She cupped her hand around his heaviness and moaned with pleasure as his cock jerked from her touch. Rubbing his thick erection in long, hard stokes, she pressed a slow line of wet kisses from his belly button, over his goody line, then nuzzled and tasted beneath and around the treat she ached to enjoy. His breath caught and his delicious skin prickled each time her tongue licked over it.

Consumed with the desire to please him, she couldn't get enough of him in her hands and mouth. She worked to grip him tight, stroke up his length, and keep him in between her lips, as he swelled in her hold. Her tongue lavished the broad smoothness of the round head, and her mouth watered at the first taste of his excitement.

A groan sounded his erotic appreciation. Strong fingers tangled in her hair, cupping her head and massaging her nape. Kat licked up and down his length, and when his intoxicating flavor was too much to deny, she tried to relax her jaw muscles and take as much of him as she could in her mouth. Marko slid over her tongue, stroked the back of her throat, but as the heaviness between his legs tightened, he pulled away and hauled her up his body.

His hand found her wet heat. His thumb circled her throbbing bundle of need. Muscle control disintegrated, and her body liquefied. Her head lolled back on her shoulders and her hair brushed her lower back.

"This way," Marko said, firm hands guiding her to straddle his body in a full contact position. "Kiss me, Kat. Take me and give me everything."

She did, moaning with pleasure when he sucked her lower lip into his mouth and rubbed her clit with the same measure. Heavy sensations built in her lower belly. Her hips circled his groin, and the feel of his hard length gliding between her swollen folds grew to an unmanageable hedonistic indulgence she craved.

Pushing upward, Marko filled her body and met her desire, impaling her on him and driving them closer to the edge of reason with each thrust.

"Come with me, *bella*," he said, breathing freedom into her heart and tumbling them off the cliff. He caught her in his arms and held her as they fell. Together.

Knowing he may regret reminding her she had a job to do, Marko had to do it anyway. Kat had to know she could work when she was with him. She could do anything she set her mind to. "We're going out. Research for the article, sweetheart. Your dress is on the bed," he said.

"You bought me a dress?" She lowered the makeup brush to the vanity and turned to look at him.

Merde, she was beautiful. Standing in the bathroom in only a bra, dark nipples peeking through the lace and a neat little patch of curls set between her legs, he didn't want to take her out. Didn't want her to dress.

"Yes. What you brought isn't appropriate for the weather. Guaranteed pneumonia if you step outside in either of those dresses tonight."

"They aren't that bad," she said, waving her hand in dismissal. "My coat is long, and that lovely wrap you gave me is perfect protection against the wind."

He had to stop fantasizing about bending her over the Italian marble and fucking her gorgeous ass. He'd make her watch in the mirror. More importantly, he'd watch. His cock swelled and throbbed painfully with the image.

The thought of her staring back at him with the smoky look in her melted chocolate-colored eyes . . . He'd push through the muscled rosette and stroke into her tight hole . . . So fucking tempting . . . The bounce of her full breasts . . . The tightening of her nipples . . . The flush on her face as she worked to take him . . . His cream dripping over the lattice of pink that he'd left—

"*Merde!*" He wiped his palm down his face and stepped back. He wanted much more than mind-blowing sex with the woman. He had to focus on the big picture.

Only an hour earlier, Kat had been content to stay in Marko's bed for the remainder of their time together. Then, his sappy conscience and realistic side insisted on them seeing more of Paris . . . supposedly for research.

He needed more than sex from Kat. He needed everything she had to give, and in order to get that he had to have some control of the carnal urges that had dominated his day. Being with her after all the time apart made minimizing the physical need practically impossible.

"Fine. Don't get so worked up." She threw her hands up. "I'll wear your dress."

"Good," he clipped, turning and walking away. He needed distance to maintain his composure. "Wear the boots. Your garter and stockings are beside the dress. No panties."

"No panties equals pneumonia," she called, giggling to his back.

The problem was he hadn't thought of buying panties. He'd have some delivered.

Accompanying his cousin during a few of her shopping expeditions, he'd grown comfortable with spotting clothing he wanted to see Kat wear. In spite of Martine's teasing about his newfound interest for woman's couture, he'd purchased a few outfits in anticipation of her visits.

In all the time he'd known her, Kat had gushed over only one designer, so he'd visited the Emilio Pucci boutique on Avenue Montaigne more than a few times during the summer. As a result, silky and bold patterns hung beside exquisite monochrome gowns and dresses in what he had intended would be her closet. Not once had he considered buying appropriate lingerie for her to wear beneath any of them.

He shrugged and stepped into the closet, choosing a shirt off a hanger and putting his hands through the sleeves. She was still 'fixing' her makeup as he went downstairs, not appreciating the greater distance between them.

Walking through the sitting area and past the kitchen, he went directly to the wine room and selected his favorite vintage. He finished a first glass of the potent drink, cleared the remains of their lunch from the table, and set to the task of making sure the hearth would be secure in their absence.

He was placing two glasses of red wine on the counter, when the sexy clicking of stilettos sounded on the marble stairs. He turned and his breath caught in his chest. Wine spilled on his hand and he wiped at it with a towel he promptly tossed across the counter. The bohemian princess strolling toward him, the most beautiful woman in the world, was all he wanted to see.

Her hips swayed with each step she took toward him, mesmerizing him and keeping him in place with the melodic movements. He was her prisoner.

"*This* is a Chloe," Kat exclaimed, her smile growing brighter with each swoosh of the fabric around her legs. She pulled the skirt to the sides of her thighs and twirled on her toes. "How does it look?"

"Beautiful." Marko walked to where she stood and took her face in his hands. Stroking his thumb over her cheeks, his gaze traveled from her big eyes to her full lips. Her free spirit on full display made her absolutely irresistible. "Damn, Kathryn. You're so damn beautiful."

"The intricate jacquard and the soft fringe are like ornate feathers on a—"

"Fuck the dress," he interjected. "It's you that is one hundred percent beautiful." Taking a step back, he kept a hand on the soft skin of her exposed upper arm and allowed his gaze to sweep up and down the rest of her body. "How is it was possible for anyone to look so good?"

"Thank you," she said, wrapping her arms around his neck and squeezing tight. "I love it. It makes me feel wonderful. No matter what you say, this dress is gorgeous, but I don't think my boots do the gown justice."

"The dress is black. The boots are black. They match," he assured, switching from whipped to man mode again. "Give me a few minutes to check on the fire in the bedroom, and I'll be right back. There's wine on the table."

He took the stairs two at a time. Turning into the bedroom, he was greeted by her lingering scent. He smiled. At last, her scent filled his room. He planned on keeping it there. It was their time.

The faint glow of embers in the hearth was almost out. He repeated what he'd done in the living room, secured the screen, and made sure there was nothing flammable within a meter.

He hurried back to the woman, who for once, had done as instructed. She'd dressed in what he'd given her, even chosen to go wonderfully braless. Nothing to restrict the movements of her lush breasts for him and no lace outlines under the dress for her. No panties—well, in truth, he'd never considered them necessary, so he'd never considered them. Then there were those cock-teasing boots on her feet, which added character to the free spirited dress she wore so well. A true bohemian princess, she stood by the window.

"The city sparkles," she said, leaning into his chest as he rubbed his hands down her arms. "I can see why it's one of the most romantic destinations in the world."

"Anywhere with your other half is the most romantic place in the world," Marko said, fitting his lips against her neck and kissing up to the sweet spot behind her ear. "Personally, I'd stay right here if it meant holding you in my arms all the time."

He felt her shiver, and smiled before suckling on her soft skin and feeling her body heat against him.

"Thank you. I have you all to myself tonight and I couldn't be happier." Marko described the quaint café nightlife of the Isle to her. "Many cafés have braziers or propane heaters on the terraces. It's rare for Parisians to give into the cold weather." They watched the boats glide past the historic buildings, and spoke of all things Paris, not moving away from the window view.

When the Eiffel Tower started twinkling, she gasped and danced on her toes. She turned and handed him her wine glass.

"Wait here. I need my phone." Kat looked around the room, trying to remember where she'd put it last.

"I'll get it. It's on the table," Marko offered.

"No," she insisted, pushing on his shoulder for him to turn and look out over the city. "Stay there. I want to take a picture."

Picking up the phone, she immediately pressed on the camera button. The tower twinkled behind Marko. She clicked at least a dozen pictures of his silhouette before he looked over his shoulder and nodded for her to hurry.

"Get over here. The show only lasts a few minutes." Marko reached for her hand and took the phone. He pulled her against his chest and rested his head on hers. "Selfie?"

"Yes, please," she replied, turning and placing a loud kiss on his cheek.

He captured the kiss and a few more pictures, before he lifted her off her feet and into his arms. "Kiss me properly."

The ricocheting contentment in her chest pinged off her heart and hit every happy nerve in her body. Kat was happier than she'd been in years, and she knew that Marko had everything to do with those feelings. She traced his jaw and lowered her head, licking slowly over his lips, and slipping her tongue through them. Passionate tingles flowed into her soul as he gently glided through her mouth and sucked her into his until the tower stopped twinkling.

"If we don't go now, I'll keep you here forever," Marko said, lowering her feet to the floor.

Forever with Marko was very tempting. Was it too much to want everything? "Okay, let's go. We have a city to see, research to do, and a feature to write."

She longed for everything. Marko, career, happiness.

"*Allons-y,*" he said, and arranged the wrap snug around her body, leading her to the foyer. "Do you want me to carry your phone?"

It was such a couple thing to do. She could be quickly lulled into thinking this little break from reality could be a forever situation, and she couldn't help the warmth that filled her at his suggestion. At least they had the night. "Sure. Thanks."

The business card tucked into the side pocket of her tote came to mind. She'd certainly found what she'd initially been looking for. She rummaged through the receipts and pulled out the invitation from the romantic Cyril. Asking for her phone, she took it back from him, lifted the rubber casing, and fit the card inside. She handed the cellular back to Marko, who promptly slid it into his pants pocket.

"What's that?" Marko asked, holding open her coat and waiting for her to slide her arms through the sleeves.

"A hidden gem," she replied, shrugging into the coat. "I'll explain later."

She didn't argue when he handed her the gloves and fit the beret on her head.

Chapter Sixteen

Happy with her hand once again tucked neatly into Marko's coat pocket, Kat bumped against his shoulder and puffed out little clouds of breath. The chill in the night air stung her cheeks, but the stroll along the quaint streets warmed her soul.

"I can see why artists have flocked to Paris over the years," she said, holding out her arms and twirling like a child. Happy and carefree, Kat walked beside Marko in the city of her dreams.

The picturesque character of the storefronts was distinguished, yet inviting. Time-worn stones whispered romantic tales down the long lanes. Bright red doorframes had her making mental notes of where to return, while retracted awnings identified the proprietors' intents and marked their passage through the cobblestone paradise.

She stopped before a chocolatier's window and regarded the creative display with amazement. A chocolate park sprawled through the shop, covering all shelving and featured table rounds. Dark chocolate trees with gold leaves at their roots, creamy little pavilions with colorful candy roofs, and even a magical playground, with a tall old-fashioned slide and an intricately carved carousel, called for the child in her to wander through the gourmet wonderland.

"Such an enchanting masterpiece," she breathed.

"Not only is his work art, but it's also delicious," Marko explained, squeezing her hand in agreement. "Don't tell Antoine, but this is one of my favorite places for a sweet indulgence on the island. I sneak a Grand Marnier truffle at least once a week." He looked down at her and nuzzled a kiss behind her ear. "When the weather warms and the season is right, I'll bring you dark-chocolate-covered *fraises des bois* every night. I promise."

He promised. He always kept his promise. Forest strawberries were best in the summer. The season started in mid June. Sadness filtered through her. She wouldn't be here in June. He'd have to break his promise. The first she knew he couldn't keep.

Wiping a gloved finger over the corner of her eye, she shook her head. She must have read too much into a simple comment. He hadn't meant it literally. He was being nice and adding to her research. There was no real promise.

"You need to stop thinking so hard," he reprimanded. "It's only chocolate."

"I was thinking about your neighbor," she said. Somehow, she recovered and skimmed over the truth, perplexed as to why he'd never spoken of Antoine before. "Is he your best friend?"

"Antoine?"

She nodded, relieved that she'd managed to shift the topic of conversation back to Marko's life and away from her dark considerations of a lonely future.

"I never really thought about it, but I guess you can say he is." Marko wrapped his arm around her waist and commenced walking. "From the first day I saw the apartment, even before I bought it, we became friends. He offered me a coffee and welcomed me to the neighborhood."

"So, he's a new friend. You bonded as neighbors at that beautiful home."

"Yes. And I'm so happy you think the apartment is beautiful. It needed a lot of renovations when I first saw it. However, the location was excellent."

"It is. I can't get over the views," she added. "And it's very spacious for a city place. Very spacious."

"The three levels were being used as three different units, for three different families," Marko explained. "It took some time, but when they were combined, space was not an issue."

Kat had never seen the third floor—or, in U.S. terms, the fourth floor. She loved the first level with the sitting and dining areas. Impressive, yet cozy, it welcomed long conversations and gatherings. The comfortable seating, gorgeous view, and openness of the space called to her family nature. The kitchen was very modern, and come to think of it, that level also had the wine room.

The next floor had the master bedroom, which was a suite much grander than any apartment she'd ever lived in. He'd suggested his study as a place to set up her laptop and keep any notes she wanted to collect; then he had also shown her two more impressive bedrooms. She'd never realized there was more to the home.

"When the majority of the demolition was done and the foundation had been restored, Antoine asked to see the place. Since he also lives on the isle, he was familiar with the architecture. He agreed with the idea of preserving the historic integrity on the property, and he understood our need for modern amenities. Antoine offered to help me when Aimee was visiting her grandparents. He did a lot of the trim and woodwork in the formal areas."

"What is on the third level?" Kat asked, referring to the fourth floor as a true Parisian would.

"There is a formal living room, dining room, and what you could call a large kitchenette or a small kitchen. It's more for entertaining and those type of events. I prefer the first level. Not too high from the street, but it still affords stellar views."

"It really does," she agreed. "You could see everything, including the expressions of the people walking on the street."

"Exactly."

They fell silent and walked toward the river. Sultry jazz floated past a wooden door, issuing an invitation of warmth out of the wind. Passing an old-world bistro, she reached out and ran her hand over the regal blue iron bars on the window and along the blue walls as they rounded the corner.

"This restaurant has been through some recent changes, everything from the menu to new owners, but it's a classic landmark on the island." Marko explained.

"Lots of clientele for such a small place," Kat said, sidestepping a couple exiting the club and two others heading inside.

"It's not so small," Marko said against her ear. The music drifting out the door made it difficult to hear. He squeezed her hand and spoke near her ear. "Long and narrow, they manage to serve a lot of people. There's a lower level, too. How would your book have ended if the lawyer and her academic frequented this place?"

Very differently, she thought. Kat lowered her gaze and stared at the tips of her boots. She shuffled over the cobblestone in silence.

"Step down," Marko said, supporting her elbow as she moved on autopilot.

The wind whipped around her ankles, and she shivered. Walking along and trusting Marko to keep her safe, she flipped through the final fictional scenes in her mind. "I sort of gave up on them. They couldn't get their act together, and I needed to end the book. Though they're not together, they each have a happy ending."

He didn't say anything and she didn't elaborate. They walked in silence for a few minutes. Marko steering. Kat staring at her toes.

"Look up, *bella*."

The Pont Marie stretched across the river. Lights, framing the impressive structure, glittered on the water. The pretty bridge resembled a fairy's crossing, sprinkled with pixie dust. "Just wow," she said, a smile crossing her face. "Cyril was right. I can see the appeal."

"So can I," Marko said, looking down at her and positioning his back to the wind, sheltering her from the cold. "If you look carefully, you'll notice how each of the five arches differs in design. I'm not sure why it was made that way. Regardless, the bridge is as unique as any of the bridges spanning the Seine. Each bridge has distinctive architecture. The real mystery with the Pont Marie is why there has never been any statues built into the niches of the arches."

"Maybe it was done intentionally." She snuggled against him and fit her head on his shoulder. "Fill-in-the-blanks architecture."

She studied the illuminated curves and the steady traffic over the bridge, wondering what it would look like if different statues filled the niches. The possibilities were endless. While considering the empty slots, she reflected on what could have been different in her life had she made different choices.

Rather than feeling like something was missing on a daily basis, she could feel content and complete. Speaking with someone who understood her on every level definitely added to a sense of satisfaction. Not to mention having the most amazing and nourishing sex on a regular basis.

With its missing statues and the options the blank spaces offered, the Pont Marie inspired all sorts of promises. Pressure swelled inside her chest. Hope enveloped her heart and pushed against her ribs. Kat looked up at Marko and simply considered her options.

He cupped her face, leaned in, and kissed her. A soft and gentle kiss, as reassuring as it was strong, confirming that he was a very real possibility. No words. No preamble. Gently, he licked over her lips, his tongue soothing the chill and softening her resolve to protect her heart.

Kat's lips parted and she kissed him back, breathing him in and growing suddenly very aware of how vulnerable she was to his every attention. She wanted him. Needed him. The heaviness in the center of her chest increased with each glide of his tongue, as he stoked the yearnings she'd kept buried for years.

"I should have ordered out for dinner and kept you in bed." Rubbing a thumb over her cheekbone, he took her mouth again, deepened the kiss, and stroked every bit of reason from her head. Consumed by the taste of him and the intensity of his mouth, she closed her eyes and let the kiss take control. She didn't want to think any further.

Dinner was at a quintessential bistro, hidden inside a pedestrian lane midway between the Pont Marie and the apartment. Decorated with black and white photo portraits, of subjects she guessed to be locals on burnt-orange-painted walls, and steel lanterns hanging from the ceiling, the bistro had an ambiance that was casual and humble. The aromas tickling her nose were not. Rich flavors floated in the air and spurred her appetite. Her stomach actually growled in response.

Flattening her palm on her belly, Kat giggled and scraped her teeth over her lower lip. She was famished.

"The daily fish is always delicious," Marko suggested, looking toward the chalkboard. "Grilled turbot tonight."

"With Béarnaise sauce," she added enthusiastically, and dropped the menu on the table. "That settles it. I'm ready."

Marko chuckled and raised a hand to call for the waiter. "We'll start with the escargots in Provençale butter," he said in French, glancing her way for corroboration.

Mouth watering with anticipation, she nodded. He knew her well. Had paid attention from the first day they'd met, so he had never needed to guess what made her happy. He knew. He selected a bottle of wine and ordered their meals, then placed an arm around the back of her chair.

"I'm loving my research," Kat admitted, a wave of happiness flooding through her as she leaned into Marko. "The city is so much more than I expected. I'm totally falling in love with Paris."

"You're going to fall doubly in love with the chateaux. Provence in general," Marko said, dipping a crusty corner of the baguette into the buttery sauce and feeding it to her. "The scenery and atmosphere are just what you like. Not the hustle and bustle of the city, but there is so much to enjoy. Plus, I think you'll like the family. I know my family will fall in love with you."

Inhaling through her nose, her chest rising visibly, she chewed, licked a tasty drop off her lip, and then swallowed hard. More than a little nervous about meeting his parents, she didn't think they'd appreciate her crashing their family dinner.

The Renards were a bit out of her league. Actually, a bit was putting it mildly. His family wouldn't like her at all. She didn't have an elegant French bone in her body, nor was there a colorful Italian gene in her makeup. She was an outsider. She had nothing to bring to the table.

"They're my parents," he said. "Salt-of-the-earth people, who will adore you."

"Do they adore all the other women you bring home?"

Stormy darkness clouded his face. The tiny muscle in his jaw ticked.

"I think that statement may require another session over my knee, *bella*." With a single finger, he turned her to look at him. His words had a devastating effect on her resolve to distance herself. Her cheeks flushed, and she couldn't look away from his displeased eyes. "For the record, I have never taken a woman home. I've never wanted another woman in my home. *Comprendre?*"

"Okay," she whispered.

"Do *not* compare yourself to anyone else," he continued, in a low and steely tone. "You are you, special, and exactly the woman I want to bring home." The space between them dissolved and a heated kiss sent messages of encouragement and strength into her body and mind. "You need to trust me for more than just a few hours. I have no doubt in what is right."

She touched his mouth and trailed over his strong jawline. Spellbound by his words, she brought her lips close to his. He kept his gaze steady, leaving her no room to deny what he'd said. Somehow, his knowing what was right comforted her. It made everything all right. She could keep her heart exposed. A sense of belonging overcame her and outweighed any risk she envisioned. The last thing Kat wanted was to walk away from the security his knowing instilled.

"Okay," she repeated, realizing she'd been looking for a way to goad him into an argument so she could avoid being vulnerable. "I'm sorry. I do trust you. I do."

"*Bien.*" He motioned for the server to refresh their wineglasses.

Chapter Seventeen

"I didn't mean to sabotage our night by being negative. I agreed to let you make decisions for the day." Kat intertwined her fingers and placed her hands in her lap. Her thumbs twirled quickly as she spoke in a very soft voice. "You've been wonderful, Marko. You're wonderful with anything you do."

Kat, a competent and extremely headstrong woman on the surface, dropped her shoulders each time a future with Marko was mentioned. Beneath that surface, and only on personal relationship issues, she lacked confidence. Doubt had crossed her face more than once during their walk. She hid her reluctance to believe in herself well, but not well enough. He'd seen it.

Fuck. Marko swept a hand down his face and rubbed his jaw. He should have kept her at home and cultivated her submission until she was totally secure in her feelings. Casual physical contact didn't suffice to keep her grounded and comfortable. He'd misjudged the depth of the situation.

She'd repressed the truth for too long. He'd allowed it. There was no way he'd let wrongful assumptions, supposedly based on logic, come between them again. He owned up to his shortfalls and steeled his determination. She'd only decide when she was honest with herself and with him. And only after he'd exhausted every avenue to prove to her that they belonged together.

"Thank you for your trust," Marko said, raising his glass. "I do know best."

A twinkle lit her eyes and she smiled. Her body visually relaxed. "I guess you haven't outgrown the bigheaded attitude."

"Why should I?"

"Why, indeed?" She clinked her glass with his. "To you knowing best."

The glow of acceptance accentuated her loveliness, and he knew that by night's end she'd agree to stay through the weekend. The rest . . . he would work out.

"Have I told you how beautiful you are?"

"Not nearly enough," she said, her fingers playing for more.

"You are so damn beautiful, *bella*."

Her back straightened, and she sat up tall. He settled a long wisp of silky hair behind her ear, and caressed the soft skin of her pretty ear between his fingers, unable to sate the need to touch her. Truly lovely, she graced him with a bright smile, and just like that, Kat returned to the moment.

She sipped her wine, chatted with glee between courses, and ravished the grilled turbot. "Is everything in Paris so flavorful?"

"It's what we make of it, and flavorful is a perfect way to describe being with you," he replied, taking her hand and lifting it to his lips. He turned it gently and placed a kiss on the underside of her wrist. "So, so far, what is your most romantic landmark?"

"It's difficult to choose. The whole city dazzles my mind. The Eiffel Tower is more breathtaking than I expected. The café mentality is extremely romantic. The Pont Marie is as Cyril described—"

"Cyril?"

"Cyril is the man from the plane. He was the one that said when you stand by the Pont Marie, you're supposed to kiss the person beside you." Kat offered. "He kissed, or was kissed by, his first love beneath the bridge."

"I can relate," Marko said.

She fidgeted a little in her seat, and then held her hand out on the table and asked for her phone. Removing the case, she produced the card she'd placed in it earlier. "Cyril also invited me to this place. He called it a hidden gem. Said when I found what I was looking for in Paris to head on over."

Marko knew this *gem* well. He knew Cyril. When he'd learned that his friend would be on the same flight as Kat, he had requested Cyril look out for her and make sure Kat would be comfortable. His friend had done exactly that and obviously more. *He* wasn't comfortable with the other man being on a first-name basis with *his* Kat and personally inviting *his* Kat to the club, but giving her a peek into reality did suit his long-term goals with the woman.

"Would you like to go?" He took the card and flipped it through his fingers, studying her face.

Kat shrugged. "Why not? He was correct about the bridge. His suggestions were very romantic. Even sexy."

With no intention of convincing her otherwise, Marko nodded and placed the card in his pocket and retrieved his cellular. "Then we'll go. I'll arrange for a car."

"Marko?" Slender fingers closed around his wrist and prevented him from lifting the phone to his ear.

"What is it, sweetheart?"

"I was hoping we could walk over the bridge together?" She raised her left shoulder and tilted her head. "I know it sounds corny, but it's like crossing into the future. If you don't mind, I'd enjoy the walk. The weather is cooperating."

"It does not sound corny," Marko insisted. "The club is off the Champs-Élysées, so we will need the car to get there." He placed the call and arranged for a car to meet them on the Right Bank later in the evening. Motioning for the server to approach, he requested a thermos of *vin chaud*. "However, we will have a little outdoor picnic and a quick walk along the Seine."

"Thank you." Her eyes sparkled with excitement. She leaned across her seat and kissed him sweetly on the cheek. "I've always dreamed of strolling by the river. You're making this the most memorable night of my life."

Merde! Kat could hardly anticipate how memorable the night was about to get.

"This evening is so dreamy . . . so perfectly romantic," she said, curling her fingers around the thermos of hot wine. Kat practically bounced in her chair. Her big eyes, brighter than usual, seared him with a sensual invitation. The blush coloring her cheeks displayed her sexual desire. Marko's body couldn't help its innate response. He was a man, a man who wanted his woman. He tapped a fingertip over the rosy center of her left cheek, and her delicious lips parted. Immediately, he envisioned doing things to her mouth that were not very appropriate considering their location.

"It's more than romantic. It's sexy to the point of being painful," he said. Taking her hand, he placed it over his groin to show her how sexy he thought it was.

"It is sexy," she agreed, splaying her fingers. "A little discomfort serves as a nice aphrodisiac. No?"

His cock agreed. "More than you know, *bella*." The red marks on her curvy ass had certainly served as an aphrodisiac. "I think we should hurry to our picnic. We have a few things to discuss before we visit the club."

"Or maybe detour to the apartment?" Kat offered in a whisper. "We could enjoy a different sort of picnic there."

"Yes. We can," he agreed, deciding on the perfect spot to enjoy their *vin chaud*.

His cock swelled painfully in his pants, and he was the one in need. He needed the cold air to stall his libido, or he wouldn't wait for privacy. He'd take her on the very table on which they'd dined.

"*Allons-y*." He grabbed the thermos, pushed back his chair, and reached for their coats.

Marko kept a hand on Kat's hip, holding her close as they walked through the lanes. He explained the basic premise of the private club, elaborating on its open mindedness and inclusive nature. He didn't outline specific activities or events, but he allowed her enough insight to change her mind if she wasn't comfortable.

They walked past the café from the afternoon and rounded the corner to the street entrance of the apartment. She tugged on his arm as they stopped at the door. "Is it a real sex club?"

"It is," he stated. He entered the combination on the keypad, opened the door, and showed her to the elevator. "You will be with me. I will not allow for anyone else. Remember, you have given me the night. As for the membership at the club, it is exclusive and by invitation. Consensual play only."

The elevator was larger than most private lifts, but she squeezed in close to him and tightened her grasp on his arm. "It's a bit intimidating, but my curiosity is greater than my fear. I think it'll be interesting to see," she said. "Am I dressed right?"

"You will be." Marko dropped a kiss on her head and closed his eyes. She was finally embracing what she wanted. "However, once we walk into the club, you become my responsibility. There will be no doubts or questions."

"Seriously?"

"Seriously," he repeated, no smile on his face.

"Okay," she said. "I understand."

At that, Marko smiled. Kat was taking a big step and trusting him.

The elevator stopped on the third level of the home. He led her through the foyer and into the formal living room, which from its mere location was meant to impress. Stark white walls rose to an intricate crown molding, which was dusted with gold roses. The wooden beams on the high ceiling added a distinct warmth and complemented the polished floors. Wanting her input on the décor, he'd chosen to wait on the majority of furnishings. Only a white leather seating group, as on the first level, sat before the tall windows and beside the fireplace.

Kat gazed around the vast space, once again a look of awe on her face. When she reached to undo her coat, he stopped her. "There's more."

Their footsteps echoed as they crossed the room. The staccato rhythm of her heels coaxed his cock back to full attention. No matter how he tried, he couldn't stop envisioning Kat in the club. Physical submission and the acceptance of pure pleasure would add a definite link to their bond. A link she hadn't openly admitted she needed, he cautioned his eager body.

Strong and capable, she'd managed well on her own and put away a good nest egg for her mother to retire on. Her success did not negate the need for support. He was the man for her support. He *had* supported at the expense of delaying the inevitable. Requiring assurance, loyalty, and commitment didn't make Kat a submissive in every part of her life, but he knew she craved to be just that in certain points. It was his duty to identify those times and to fulfill her desires.

Stepping out onto the balcony, he indicated the spiral staircase. "Our picnic awaits, *mademoiselle*."

Taking care to stay off her heels, Kat climbed the iron staircase on the balls of her feet. When she reached the upper turn, and the rooftop came into view, her mouth dropped.

Strings of lights trailed over the low wrought-iron fence and framed a canvas awning against the back wall, casting a radiant glow over the terrace. Set in an alcove between two of the building's stone sidewalls, plush couches with big red pillows were arranged beneath the retractable canopy and offered an unobstructed view of the city sprawling below them. The comfortable seating area featured a low cocktail-style table with a rustic fire pit as the centerpiece.

"Marko, this is heavenly," she said. She held his arm while turning in blatant appreciation. He placed the thermos on the table, then reached for the remote.

Fire flamed in the pit and the awning retracted. "Why didn't you show this to me earlier?"

"Sometimes we need to be patient. Plus, it was raining, Kat," he said, laughing as he pulled her into a hug. He linked his hands at the small of her back and swayed to the soft jazz drifting up from the street level. "Did you say something about corny?"

"Not corny. Absolutely not," she whispered, her sweet breath teasing his lips. "We should've started with the terrace. It's the most beautiful and the most romantic place I've ever seen."

He closed the distance between them and kissed her. Savoring her taste, he reveled in every caress of her tongue and the softness of her lips.

Enfolding her in his arms, he devoured her mouth with each step he took toward the couch and was still unable to get enough of her. He didn't want to let her go, but they had a picnic to get on with and an interesting night ahead of them. He lowered her onto the over-stuffed cushions and sat beside her.

Breathless, she sidled onto his lap. "Do you mind?"

"Never."

She looked into his eyes and tangled her fingers in his hair. Her mouth, swollen from his kiss, curved into a radiant smile. "Marko?"

"Yes, baby." His body objected to the lazy lingering, but his heart wanted to remain in the gentle moment. He wound his arm around her waist and settled his hand on the curve of her hip.

"I . . ." She sucked on her lower lip and exhaled. She tried again. "I . . ." Her lip trembled.

"Sh," he breathed, cupping the back of her head and brushing his lips over her forehead. "I know, *bella*. I know."

Kat released a low breath, then pressed a kiss against the side of his neck and relaxed on his shoulder. "You do know."

Chapter Eighteen

Warm from the spiced wine and the euphoric effects of the time she'd shared with Marko on the terrace, Kat skipped into the bedroom and tossed her coat on the lounger.

"I can't believe you really picked out clothes that are appropriate for a sex club," she said, sitting on the edge of the mattress and pulling off her right boot.

"Truthfully, you don't need clothes for the club. Your birthday suit would be nicely welcomed, but I'm not about to share that exquisite vision with anyone else."

She dropped the left boot to the floor and turned to find Marko, who stood in the doorframe with his arms folded menacingly across his chest. Her body heated beneath his dark gaze, and she was compelled to go to him, to feel his touch.

The Chloe design swept across her calves, reminding her to sashay rather than walk, but in all honesty, she wanted to run across the room. She had to make an effort to move slowly, but when she reached him she had to feel him. He radiated pure masculine sexual prowess. As her eyes followed the defined lines of his forearms, strength and resolve traveled from her fingertips to her core. She shifted on her feet, trying to minimize the tingle spreading between her legs.

"Has my gentleman turned into a he-man?" Kat asked, looking up through her lashes and trying her best to portray a shy maiden.

"I'm invoking my two hours once we arrive at the club. Strip, Kathryn."

Kathryn! Strip! "Just because I was issued an invitation to a sex club?"

"No." He glanced at the time, then walked to the closet. "Because you belong to me, and I'm taking you to a sex club. Have you had a change of heart? Or are you procrastinating?"

"I'm sorry," she replied, not exactly sure why she was apologizing. She just didn't want to disappoint him and ruin their perfect evening. Lifting the lovely dress over her shoulders, she placed it on the bed, and shook out her beret hair. She wanted to look perfect for him.

"Come here," he said, stepping from the closet and holding out a black leather mini-skirt. He knelt and waited for her to approach. When she did, he lifted each of her feet in turn, caressing under the arches and over her instep, and then raised the softest of leather to her hips. He reached around her and zipped the skirt into place. "Pretty."

His approval drew a smile. Kat couldn't look away as he rose to his full height and ran a finger over her lips. Of its own accord, her tongue flitted out and tasted.

Marko retracted his finger and returned to the closet. "In the club, you will touch when I allow you to. You must listen to instructions. You need to trust that I will take care of you."

"Okay," she said.

He opened the top drawer of a built-in dresser, and brought out a skimpy black bra hanging from his fingers. Slowly, he fit her hands through the straps and settled the sheer material over her breasts, hooking the front closure with meticulous tenderness.

"I haven't worn a front-closing bra since high school," she admitted, not voicing her concern about how much support it could possibly offer.

"We can reserve that fantasy for a different night. Tonight, I own you."

With no material to contain the moisture, her thighs were coated with her excitement. Thankfully he'd allowed for the stockings and had thought ahead to leather.

He slipped her feet into the boots, then stood back and looked at her. He raised an appraising brow and shook his head. "*Merde, tu es belle.*"

Smoothing the back of two fingers down her cheek, he dipped lower, over her shoulder and outlined the swells exposed above the bra. Her breasts grew achingly heavy. She arched her back for control, but her nipples had hardened and were straining against the transparent covering for his attention.

"Beautiful and ready," he said, trailing his knuckles over her right breast and capturing its crested peak between his fingers. "No boundaries. No reservations. Completely mine."

She was his. She placed her faith in him. Having only read about the famous sex clubs in Paris, she wasn't sure what to expect. Would there be orgies on the dance floor? Were sadists breaking the physical limits of their slaves? Did couples interchange partners and loan out sexual desires? The carnal possibilities were too many to consider, and the excitement for the experience mingled with fear.

Curling tense fingers around his wrist, Kat brushed her thumb across the heel of his palm and looked into his eyes. He lowered his head and his breath warmed her lips.

"I've got you, Kathryn," he said in a low voice. He slanted his mouth over hers and a sense of safety seeped into her. Secure in his capable hands, she was his.

Flames licked over her skin. The heat between her legs burned. *His.*

He pulled a leather jacket from the closet and fit it on her shoulders. Taking the red wrap off the bed, he settled it around her neck and nodded. *"Allons-y."*

Marko cursed the cold. The small leather jacket did little to keep her warm, but walking into the club with a coat or warmer clothing wasn't an option. Additional coverage would make her stand out in the wrong way. Kat needed total immersion in the night's experience. There was no room for any discomfort.

"Walk fast, sweetheart," he said, squeezing her hand as they stepped onto the bridge. "There'll be plenty of other opportunities for a casual stroll."

The red cashmere, tucked into the lapels of the jacket, covered her chest. The unprotected legs and pussy were a different story. The boots and skimpy leather left too much exposed. Angling to her left, he hoped the length of his coat cut the effect of the wind.

The convenient location of the Pont Louis-Philippe was the greatest benefit to using that specific crossing. Only meters from their door, it was rarely crowded with pedestrian traffic at night. It didn't have the romantic allure of promised kisses from strangers like the Pont Marie, nor was it weighted down with street performers like the Pont Saint Louis. They walked quickly, and in silence, into what Kat had identified as their future. A car, with impeccable heating, waited on the Right Bank.

Seeing the driver's door open, Marko waved her off and steered Kat to the waiting vehicle. He opened the rear door and a blast of warm air surrounded them. "Hurry out of the cold, *bella*."

She scooted inside, and once she'd folded her legs close to her body, she rubbed her soft gloves over the sheer stockings. Marko settled beside her and hastily removed the red shawl from her chest to wrap it around her legs. He rubbed one hand up the side of her right thigh, while he pressed the left against his coat.

"*Bonsoir, monsieur et Mademoiselle Kathryn,*" a sweet feminine voice called from the front. "*Heureux que vous êtes hors du froid. Et merci de me garder hors de lui.*"

Kat turned to look at him.

"*Merci, Stella. Nous allons au club par les Champs Elysées.*"

"*Oui, monsieur,*" Stella replied.

"Stella said she's glad we're out of the cold. She's grateful she was able to stay in the car and keep warm," he explained. The privacy glass promptly lifted into place. Done with the formalities and greetings, Marko smiled down at her. "Better now?"

"Much. That wind was vicious," she said, snuggling closer to him and fitting her legs beneath his knees. "Where's Jean-Luc?"

"He's off on Friday nights." Marko cupped her cheeks and circled his thumb over the bright red in the center. "*Bella*, it's important you decide on an easy safe word before we arrive at the club."

"I don't need a safe word. I'm with you."

Elated by her reasoning, he pressed his lips to her mouth and kissed her until the oxygen in his lungs was spent. The woman, who had insisted on taking care of everything on her own, felt safe with him. *Merde*, he wanted to break out the champagne and celebrate her gift.

"The scenes are not always exclusive. There may be things that make you uncomfortable, and admittedly, some of those things will be rewarding if you choose to explore them, but you do have limits. I'm not a sadist, Kat, but we may reach a limit that you do not wish to explore. The safe word is for your comfort."

"I trust your judgment."

Damn if his cock didn't stand and salute.

"You need a safe word, *bella*," he insisted.

She didn't reply; rather, she placed her cheek against his chest and rubbed her hand over his heart. Nothing had ever felt so right. He would fulfill her fantasies, just as she had just fulfilled his greatest aspiration. They stopped at a traffic light, and the perfect word pulled up beside them. He dropped a kiss atop her beret.

"Your word is Porsche," he said. "When you feel that you want to stop any activity or you want the evening to end, you will say Porsche."

Worrying her lower lip, she looked up at him.

"You will make me proud, not disappoint me, by using your safe word if you feel you've reached your limit," he explained. "I'm very happy to own your trust, Kathryn. It means everything to me. But my job is to show you pleasure like you've never experienced. I will push your body, and I will push your mind. There will be times when you may question my actions, but I will not hear those questions from your lips because you will not dare voice them. Your safe word is Porsche."

"Okay," she said, her eyes darker than usual. The chill had left her skin, and her cheeks burned pink. "Porsche. I got it. Okay."

With a gentle nudge on her chin, he angled her face up and brought his mouth to hers. "Okay is officially my favorite word."

Chapter Nineteen

The car stopped before a brownstone structure. No neon lights. No flashing billboard. The only indication that they were at the correct address was the scrolled sign beside the door. It read CLUB PRIVÉ.

Assuming the burly man in the dark coat was Jacques, she practiced silently mouthing his name in the privacy of the car.

Stella came around to open the door. Marko stepped out and offered Kat his hand. She accepted it and, careful not to flash Jacques, she exited the vehicle.

"*Je vais attendre de votre appel, monsieur,*" Stella said, lowering her gaze in obvious respect with her offer to await his call and instructions.

"*Merci, Stella.*" Marko smiled down at the petite young woman.

And in a very unexpected move, the pretty driver did the *bise* thing and peppered kisses on either side of Kat's face. "*S'amuser, Mademoiselle Kathryn.*"

Stunned by the intimate gesture and suggestion to enjoy, Kat barely remembered to smile back at the other woman. "Thank you, Stella."

"Welcome, Marko." Jacques opened the door and motioned for them to proceed.

"Jacques," Marko replied with a nod and confirmed Kat's assumption. He placed a hand at the small of her back, and led her inside the club.

"Has Stella been driving for you long?" Kat asked, confusion over what had just happened spurring the curiosity.

"No," he replied flatly. "She's been with me for two weeks."

He pushed past her and took her hand. "She is a friend who needed help. I gave her a job and an escape. Now, enough with the questions or there will be consequences to pay. We'll check our coats to the right."

Her gaze darted to his face and then down to her almost bare chest. She didn't voice the question.

"Clarification," he said, sliding a finger down her nose and circling her open mouth. He pushed between her lips, then stroked gently over her tongue. "We'll check my coat and my good girl's wrap."

Handing over the red cashmere, she released an audible breath. Her poor jacket must have gotten confused as well. Between the hard pounding of her heart and the sudden whooshing of air, it had dropped open and exposed her left breast. She shrieked and quickly yanked it into place, gripping it so tight that her fingers hurt.

Marko laughed, removing his coat and placing her hat and gloves in one of the inside pockets. He then threaded the wrap through the sleeve and passed the articles jointly to the attendant. Still chuckling, he leaned down to kiss behind her ear. Slipping a warm palm inside the jacket, he cupped her breast and feathered his thumb over the peak. "Thank you. That's a very pretty nipple, sweetheart. Tell me your safe word, Kathryn."

"Give me a sec," she said. Her hands worked on securing one more of the buttons.

"No," he insisted and stilled her hand. "We are inside the club, and in order to continue, I need to know that you remember it."

At that moment, a very good-looking man, dressed in faded jeans and a tight fitting T-shirt, and a tall naked woman crossed their path. A fine, thin chain hung from gold nipple hooks and was linked to a second thin chain the man held between his fingers. He led her down a slate-colored hallway with sure steps. She followed quietly, her gaze lowered to his heels. He didn't look back to check where she was, but he held out a hand and she took it. He turned and kissed her until soft moans filled the hall.

Clearly, the tall woman was a submissive, but she had a serene and happy look on her face. Her perfect body was flushed with heat and her gait was more than willing. Having her body adorned with gold chains, kissed until her legs buckled, led by a handsome man to a pleasure chamber, had its appeal.

Kat couldn't stop looking at them.

"Porsche," she said, against Marko's ear. "But I don't want to leave."

"I know that, sweetheart." He nipped up the curve of her ear, and played with her nipple between his thumb and finger. "When will you use your safe word?"

"When I'm uncomfortable and have reached my limit. If it gets to be too much, and I want to stop or go home."

"Very good," Marko said, removing his hand from her breast and rearranging the jacket. "We'll start at the source of that lively rhythm. Feeling the beat helps welcome most newcomers to the scene. It's a public space."

"It's just a different kind of dance club. A little more explicit than others, but a club with lots of people," she whispered to herself, her shoulders lifting in a tiny shrug. "Same music as the Marquee and Space."

"Whatever gets you through the night, sweetheart." He took her hand and started down an electric-blue hallway. "We'll sit at the bar."

Controlled by motion sensors, the automatic doors swept open. The room glowed and music roared. There were the neon lights to indicate the club scene and black lights to accentuate the white furnishings. A long bar curved around the dance floor for optimum access. There were more candy dishes full of condoms—condoms of all sizes and flavors, she noted on closer inspection—than drink glasses on the bar and end tables. Tall, backless bar stools, spaced in no apparent pattern, allowed for a lot of standing room.

Most impressive was the ballet-style chrome barre that rimmed beneath the long surface. Patrons gripped it for support while they engaged in a variety of sexual acts.

"I may be overdressed," Kat said, glancing around the room. Women in corsets were most common. Some wore only lingerie. Others were completely nude.

"You're perfect," Marko said, straddling a stool and pulling her up against him. He fit her between his thighs, with her back to his chest, and dropped a protective hand on her abdomen.

Kat couldn't look long enough to take in all the action. People in all states of dress, or undress, jammed the dance floor and lounge areas. Nearest to them was a couple squeezed onto an armchair. The woman, in only a demi bra and heels, bent over the arm and arched backward as her partner pounded into her. A second woman kneeled before them, alternating between lapping on the first woman's breasts and sucking a man's cock.

Then there was the young man with a collar secured around his muscular neck. A leather pouch squeezed his scrotum and cock into a confined package. He was doubled over the back of a couch, a man's cock in his mouth, a woman fucking his ass with a dildo, while a different man ate at her pussy.

"She's punishing him with the straitjacket," Marko said. "The pressure doesn't allow for an erection, yet he must perform."

A few feet further down, a groom held his bride on the bar, her gown around her waist, and her legs spread wide to accommodate the blond head of a bridesmaid. With every couple of bobs of the neatly coiffed head, the bridesmaid would pull back, finger the bride, then offer the groom a taste. A groomsman fell in line behind the bent-over bridesmaid. He lifted her skirt, and exposed a naked ass. Without warning, he drove into her and thrust her face up against the bride's pussy.

A man wearing a mask that concealed his identity brought himself to release on the bride's face, and a second masked man came on her heaving chest. The groom snapped the strap holding the plunging A-line bodice in place and exposed the bride's breasts, kneading the flesh with force. He rubbed the other men's release on the pebbled nipples, then motioned for two more men to shoot their loads on her face. Cum, mixed with makeup, smeared over her face and dripped down her chin.

Shuddering, Kat turned and glanced at the mirror over Marko's shoulder. The romantic euphoria slipped away. There was sex everywhere. Women with men. Women with women. Men with men. Couples, threesomes, foursomes, and more.

"She wants it. The bride is what is known as a cum slut. There is no judgment and there are fewer limits in the club," Marko said, smoothing his palm down the side of her face. He looked into her eyes and trailed his thumb over her lips.

Kat wanted to ask how often he partied here, and she wanted to know if he enjoyed participating in the orgies, but he'd said no questions. Did that mean no objections or argumentative questions? Or did it mean no questions of any sort?

"What do you want to ask?" Marko said, resting his thumb on her chin.

Nervously, she sucked on her lower lip and took a deep breath. "Do you come here often?"

"Rarely," he replied, smiling when she exhaled. "Only if there's a prearranged rendezvous. I take it it's not what you were expecting?"

She shook her head.

"I know, *bella*." He curled his hand at her nape and pulled her to him for a soft kiss. "It's not the sex that bothers you, but the nature of it."

She nodded, feeling her throat constrict with apprehension. She'd wanted the night to be perfect.

"The partners are dispensable," Marko continued. "There is no emotional connection between the partners—well, other than the bridal party over there. But you consider masked strangers participating in such a manner as using her. The truth is, she's using them. Regardless, the hollow pit in the bottom of your stomach is hurting you."

Amazed, she looked up at him. Relief flowed through her. He'd described exactly what she felt. He knew.

"Drink this." He placed a cool glass to her lips.

Kat sipped at the amber liquid, and was surprised to find it wasn't alcoholic. "Fresh apple juice?"

"To soothe your throat and boost your energy level." He caressed her cheek and tasted the juice on her lips. "Don't forget the vitamin C benefits. We took a risk walking the bridge in the cold. I don't want you getting sick."

Marko spoke as if they were sitting at the kitchen table. The caress of his hand up and down her spine and the gentle tone of his voice relaxed her. She took the glass in her hands and ran her fingers up the frosty side. Sipping on the juice, she relaxed and tuned out the hammering beat of the music. She was with Marko, and no matter where they were, she was good.

"There is nothing wrong with wanting more out of sex, sweetheart. It's what you want. However, some people crave only the carnal pleasure. That is what they want." He brushed his lips on her forehead, and calming warmth spread back into her body "Neither is wrong. You take what is right for you."

She nodded, trying hard not to judge. A dispensable fuck buddy wasn't right for her. She did want more. She wanted it all in a nice little package, with a pretty bow on top. Maybe that was why she'd never been satisfied with any man other than Marko. "I'm so fucking doomed."

"What was that?" Marko leaned forward, and placed his ear near her lips.

"This is what's right for me," she said, sucking gently on his earlobe and kissing down his neck. When she reached the collar of his shirt, she licked a slow and lazy pattern inside it, tasting the essence of the man that defined what she considered as right.

"Enough. Or we'll be the next exhibit on the bar." He pushed on her hips and pulled his shoulders back. Taking her hand, he placed it on his hard erection, and then stood. "Feel what you do to me, *bella*. I'm the one in charge. I thought I was supposed to be seducing you, not the other way around."

She laughed, which gained her an approving smile.

"Leave the juice. We'll head to the next room."

"Okay," she replied.

"Again with my new favorite word," Marko said, hugging her close.

She dropped her forehead against his shoulder, closed her eyes, and inhaled his scent. Everything was good again.

"Come on, *bella*. Let's go." He took her hand and folded it tight against his lower back, shouldering past anyone who didn't see him coming and move in time.

When a door slid open and they stepped out, she sighed her relief at the fading thump of the music. The furious techno beat, the building heat from all those bodies, and the intimate exposure to the orgy had been a lot. Too much.

"I'm such a chicken," she admitted. "If it hadn't been for you, I would've used the safe word in that room."

He stopped walking and turned to look at her. "That's what I'm here for, Kathryn. It's my responsibility to keep you safe and allow you to feel secure enough to experience what you truly need."

Perhaps his body was larger and his physical strength greater, but it was his acceptance of responsibility that she treasured. She couldn't resist him, and she'd do anything to please him.

"There are five communal rooms in the club. We already saw the dance club, and established that I don't visit it often, so now, let's see one I do frequent," he said.

"Which one is that?" Her pulse raced and her skin heated. She'd get to see what Marko wanted. One more layer to the man. Then the eagerness to learn crashed. What if, just like in the dance club, she didn't like what she saw?

"Patience, Kathryn. You'll be okay."

The room looked like any other indoor café. The walls were burnt amber, with art subjects ranging from pictures of simple flowers to erotic acts at eye level. Big suede couches and small mosaic bistro sets served as seating areas. The strong smell of freshly brewed coffee lingered in the air. Members milled around, some keeping to themselves, others interacting like old friends.

She blinked in confusion and surveyed the guests. Not what she'd expected of a sex club, either. Two professional-looking men, both in business suits and ties, pants on, sat at a table speaking intently. Two men, clearly lovers, cozied up on the couch and reviewed a photo album. There was a woman, who was naked, sitting on a bare-chested man's lap, laughing at something a fully clothed man across the table was saying. That same fully clothed man was petting a man on a leash, kneeling beside his chair. A gorgeous woman sat alone, enjoying a glass of wine. It was all so intimate and different.

Marko chose a table in a far corner and instructed the waiter to bring over an espresso and an apple juice. He moved his seat close to hers and clasped her hands in his.

"When we first arrived, we witnessed a lovely moment in the lobby. A submissive following her master with such utter longing is very beautiful," he said, placing the juice in front of her.

"He didn't need to look back to see where she was," Kat added.

"That is a very good observation. She trusted he would lead her where she needed to go. He trusted she would follow." Marko placed a hand on her wrist and stroked his thumb over the back of her hand. "Trust is a valuable commodity, Kathryn."

"I understand," she said, recalling the harmony that the couple had emanated as they'd walked by. "They appeared to be a couple that belonged together. Choosing to be bound. Even the way he handled her chain was caring."

"Master Jean is very caring. He's owned the sub for years. They come out and play in the private rooms at least once a month." His gaze narrowed and his fingers splayed beneath her sleeve. "Your body liked what they portrayed. Your body likes it now. There's a soft blush spreading over your chest, and I could see your nipple straining against your bra. Does the idea of being led by your master, your nipples pained by the tug on the clamps, excite you?"

Was it right to be excited at the thought of a master owning her? She lowered her gaze, but he placed a finger under her chin and turned her face up. "Look at me when you think. I want to see what's inside your lovely mind."

"Yes," she breathed, feeling her cheeks burn with the admission.

"Good girl. Thank you for sharing." He moved his finger to her lips and pressed to part them, slanting his mouth gently over hers and kissing her. His hand moved inside her jacket, under the sheer material of her bra, and he caressed her breast with aching tenderness. He pinched her nipple hard and rolled it in his fingers. "Do you enjoy the sensation of clamps?"

"I don't know," she said, a moan escaping her lips. "I've never had any."

He smiled and kissed her again. "Another first to enjoy together. It pleases me."

"Yes," she said, arching her back and pushing into his hand. Pleasing him pleased her. He released her nipple and it throbbed from the rush of blood. She wanted his hand back. Longed for the pain of the delicious squeeze.

"Kathryn, we came here so I could give you a short reprieve from the faith standards we established earlier. You have the opportunity to ask me anything you want. This is the time to do that. You are allowed ten questions, *bella*."

She had so many questions, more than ten, but all she could think about was how she needed his hands on her again. "Can I sit on your lap?"

"Yes," he replied, shifting in his seat and making room for her between his hard body and the edge of the table. He snaked an arm around her waist and pulled her close. "That's one."

She blinked and looked at him. She'd wasted the first question. She could have just slipped onto his lap—or maybe she couldn't. She didn't know. His hand smoothed up her thigh and her disappointment fled. She had nine more to go.

"Here's number two," she announced, and looked him in the eyes. "Will you please continue pleasuring my nipples?"

A wicked glimmer flamed in his eyes and he inclined his head. "Absolutely. I could never refuse when you ask so nicely."

With his fingers teasing the sensitive peaks, she couldn't think of number three. She just wanted him to continue. Heat spread through her body, and a needy sensation built between her legs.

"I can't seem to concentrate," Kat rasped. She struggled to speak, let alone think. She gasped as he rewarded her with a quick and searing tug. His laughter cleared her mind long enough to ask number three. "Do I need to call you master?"

"Only if you choose. Marko works for me, sweetheart."

The leather grew tight on her skin, and she squirmed on his lap. Bringing her mouth to his ear, she wet her lips. "Question ten. Do they sell nipple clamps in this place?"

"Stand," he commanded.

Chapter Twenty

K at dropped her feet to the floor and stood. Marko wasn't wasting another minute on the grand tour. He was taking her to a suite and giving what she'd requested.

"In addition to the five communal rooms, there are numerous private rooms in the club," he repeated, as they walked out of the café and down a dark corridor. "We are going to pass through one more communal hall, the training room, on our way to our private playroom. Do not leave my side for any reason."

As if she could break contact. His fingers closed tight around her hand as he guided her into the room. Masked spectators lined the perimeter of the large space, while half a dozen subs knelt before a bench. At the center of the floor, a man examined a display on a table. He was tall and very well built, radiating power and utter control. He wore tight leather pants, which outlined his muscular physique, and a leather hood on his head. When he turned from the display, she realized the pants were cut out at his groin. While not erect, the size of the man was very intimidating.

The master approached the line of kneeling submissives. Marko halted and wrapped his arm around her. "You may watch."

Broad shoulders glistened with sweat as the dom bent and spoke privately to the first submissive. The young woman bowed and stepped away. Next, he cupped the jaw of a handsome young man. He whispered something to him as well, then messed his hair and dismissed him. Two more gentle dismissals and the master lifted the bound hands of a woman wearing a silk mask. He untied her hands and massaged her wrists, bringing them to his mouth and kissing them. Then, he slowly walked her around the edge of the room, presenting the chosen one to the observers.

Captivated by the elegance and ceremony of the scene, Kat sighed. The attention the dom showed the woman filled her with an unfamiliar yearning. She squeezed Marko's hand and leaned her head on his shoulder.

"I didn't know it's customary to parade her around the room like a prize. Never read anything about that," Kat said.

"It's not," Marko said. "The sub requested the procession in celebration of being chosen. He must oblige her wish. Every Friday night, the club offers members the opportunity to participate in new experiences. She's been here for over a month, making herself available to him at every chance. I fear she's already in love with him."

Kat didn't see a problem with that. Love was a good thing. Even the master deserved love.

"This woman wants to achieve subspace. It is the master's job to see to her needs," Marko explained, moving behind Kat and wrapping her in his embrace. "If you want to stay, we will. However, there is no way of predicting what will be required for her to fall. I have concerns here."

For a moment, she considered asking him to stay and watch. She wanted to see the master at work, but there was a warning in Marko's voice she couldn't ignore. The agreement was no more questions. She didn't have the knowledge to decide, and she didn't need to. She had Marko. He would make the right choice for her. The burden of making a decision lifted off her chest.

Leaning back against his strength, she curled her fingers around his forearm. "I trust your judgment."

"Thank you." Warm breath brushed over her hair. He relaxed his chin on her head and held her in his embrace. "Bow your head as they pass. Then we will go."

As the couple in the center of attention approached, Kat marveled at the poise the other woman portrayed. Her steps were dainty and measured. She followed directly beside the master, perfectly keeping pace. He held her to the inside of the floor and away from the others.

Kat lowered her gaze, staring at the shiny grey floor. She watched bare feet approach, and Marko said something too muted for her to understand, but beginning with the proverbial French *bon*.

"Welcome," a recognizable male voice said above her head. "Look up, our little chocolate lover."

Kat's heart skipped a beat. The master had stopped before them, had spoken with Marko, and now he was speaking to her.

"It's okay, sweetheart. Say hello," Marko said.

She looked up and into a familiar green gaze. Recognition registered. Her breath caught. Jean-Luc was the master. "Hello—"

"Sh." He placed a finger across her lips and smiled. Suddenly aware of their audience, she complied. "I want to wish you a wonderful evening, *mademoiselle.*" He bent at the waist and stepped away.

Marko took Kat's elbow and led her from the room. He glanced over his back to see Jean-Luc securing the sub to the bench. He shook his head and chuckled. The hard-ass master was a goner. The little miss had his balls in her tiny hand.

"Considering I just saw your driver's impressive package, you're in a good mood," Kat said, surprising him with the lilt in her tone.

"Considering you just saw my driver's impressive package, *you* are in a good mood," he growled back, reaching beneath her skirt and pinching her thigh. "I'd contain that enthusiasm if I were you."

Teasing, he pinched her thigh a second time. The noise she made was a cross between a yelp and a laugh, and one of the nicest sounds he'd heard all night. He lifted her in his arms and started for their reserved quarters.

"*Bella*, how are you feeling?"

Her body relaxed and she nuzzled into him. Testing his restraint, her fingers twined in his shirt and rubbed over his chest, while she pressed her lips to his neck. Slow, small kisses tempted him to skip the niceties and get her to comply with his desires. She was responsive enough, and he knew what buttons to push. Kat wouldn't change her mind and she wouldn't need the safe word.

"I don't exactly know how to describe it, but it's almost like being in a dream. You know you're safe and nothing bad will happen to you, but you can't help but hold your breath until the next scene unravels. Your pulse races with anticipation. The exhilaration and thrill won't allow you to wake up. But the outcome is uncertain."

"You described it perfectly," Marko said. Most importantly, she'd described it willingly. There was a small window of opportunity for Kat to embrace all she'd run from for years, and he wasn't about to miss it. He wanted her completely.

Unable to get enough of the woman, he held her tight and rubbed his cheek over her head. He needed her.

Bringing Kat to the club had been a given, and he'd known that Jean-Luc would be center in the training room. Marko had given a lot of thought about whether or not to let her recognize Jean-Luc, coming to the conclusion that it would be best. Strong and even-tempered, Jean-Luc presented as a perfect and capable gentleman. There was more to the man than his driver persona.

As a master, Jean-Luc ruled every scene and met each responsibility. He chose not to get involved with his subs outside the club. And like Marko had, he chose not to engage in intercourse with his submissives in order to keep from giving them false hopes for a potential relationship.

Kat knew none of this, but she was accepting of the fact that his driver was the strong dom in control of the scene they'd witnessed. He'd chosen right. Accepting others would allow her to accept her needs, which in turn would allow her to accept Marko.

"Did you consider using your safe word while we were in the training room?"

"No," she answered, shaking her head and wrapping her arms around his back. "It was different, but surreal. Everything about this place is surreal. The exchange between Jean-Luc and his sub was very intense. Everyone else faded into the background. The energy between them sizzled. I think they're a great couple."

"They're not a couple. As far as I know, it's the first time he's touched her."

"Not a couple, yet," she cooed. Big brown eyes stared up at him, and pride for her keen observation flared in his gut. "You'll see. She totally responded to him. And he was so caring and gentle."

"Gentle may not be the correct word, *bella*." He lowered his head and brushed his lips over her mouth. The optimistic Kat was so adorable. "We left before things changed. You're right about him caring, but it won't be gentle."

"I know what the bench is for, and I saw the whips and the other things on the table. They may not be methods of gentle persuasion, but I think Jean-Luc will be. I saw how he closed his eyes when he kissed her wrists," Kat said. Not only was she smart and beautiful, but she was also hopeful. "For him, it's not about inflicting pain."

She was right.

Marko had his own plans for the night. They were almost to their door, and he wanted to announce the conversation was over, but he wouldn't. Not yet. He could read the need for more clarification in the soft lines that marked her forehead.

"I don't understand why all those people were there, or why the sub wanted to be on display, but if that was me, I don't know if I'd even be aware of their presence. Her focus was on Jean-Luc."

More pride pushed impatience to the side, and smug contentment swelled in his chest. Kat was more intuitive than she knew. She understood so much. "The sub was only aware of her master. As for the others, their reasons vary."

"Is he going to fuck her in front of all those people?"

"Penetration is not allowed in the training room." He stopped outside their suite. "While a hard fuck is good, sex isn't the goal. Achieving subspace is. Jean-Luc will read her body and mind, to take her there. That is what he does."

"Do the observers get off on watching?"

"Questions five and six," he noted. The conversation needed to end. He had one focus, and one focus only. "And yes, some do. I'm not sure if you noticed that a few were masturbating and having oral sex in the room."

"I noticed." Her pupils went dark and her breath hitched. "It was different than in the dance area though. They seemed more connected somehow."

"Most were there because it's the training room. They wanted to learn about or embrace the lifestyle. Others were there to honor her submission—many consider it an act of ultimate beauty. Still others simply enjoy watching, while some enjoy pain, but regardless of why and how, the sub will get what she needs."

"Subspace," she breathed, a look of longing in those expressive eyes.

"Yes," he said, lowering her feet to the floor, while keeping a hand on her lower back. He lifted her face and captured her gaze. "We have under an hour left in my special time. Tell me what you want."

"I want to please you, Marko."

Perfect.

Chapter Twenty-One

As he instructed, Kat closed her eyes and let Marko lead her into the suite. Unaware of his intentions, she clung to his arm with both of her hands, trusting the next hour would expose her to sexual pleasure she'd only dreamt of. In a futile attempt to silence the anticipation playing in her ears, she scraped her teeth on her lower lip and steadied its trembling.

She pressed her torso on the length of his arm and felt her way into the room. With her sight not in use, her other senses went into overdrive. Her skin simmered with the heat radiating in the space. The familiar and comforting scent of sweet lavender wrapped around her body, and she breathed in deep, immediately transported to an open field of the beautiful flowers. The soft music reminded her of waves rolling on a shore and filled her mind of simpler days.

"Keep them closed for a few more minutes, sweetheart." Strong hands gripped her shoulders and positioned her to wait. Lips brushed over her forehead and disappeared.

She immediately felt the loss of his presence when he retreated, and grabbed at empty air. "Where did you go?"

"Silly girl, that's question number seven," he said. "You only have eight and nine left. Choose wisely." His footsteps faded and she guessed that the room was larger than she'd thought.

Folding her arms over her chest, she tapped her toe. "It's not fair. That was a rhetorical question and you know it."

"It was a question nonetheless."

He was back. Steady breaths heated the side of her neck as he pulled back her hair and brought his lips to it. Every tiny hair on her body bristled with expectation and air escaped her lungs. Slow, torturous licks crept up her side to just below her ear, and then he prolonged the agony with tiny, wet circles, spreading erotic heat through her sensory highway.

A soft, silky material stretched across her eyes, and she instinctively reacted by raising her hands.

"Unless you plan on using your safe word, keep your hands low at your side." His amusement registered in her mind, but she didn't argue. She fisted her hands and pressed them to the sides of her thighs.

"Better?" Kat raised her chin and squared her shoulders.

"That's number eight, sweetheart," he answered, tying off the blindfold. He smoothed out her hair, then caressed down her arms and captured her hands, squeezing her fingers in a stern warning. "Think before using the last one."

Fuck! She'd wasted another question.

A mixture of annoyance and excitement raced through her body, but she embraced the marathon of emotions flooding her sensory pathways. Kat's pulse pounded in the darkness of her mind, and her nails dug into her palms.

"No use in lamenting the past, sweetheart. Let's move forward," he said, tracing a finger over the swell of her ass as he walked around her. He stood before her, his touch ever so lightly skimming from her throat to her chest, and coming to rest between her breasts. "You have the prettiest blush. Soft, warm, and absolutely consuming."

"Thank you," she said, feeling her heart thunder against his palm.

Unbuttoning her jacket, he used both hands to lower it off her shoulders. His hands returned, cupping her breasts and unhooking her bra. Cool air swept over her, and her nipples grew harder. He suckled on one and rubbed the other, and her hips moved against him in an effort to ease the pressure building between her thighs.

"Accept. Don't control, " he commanded.

The silky caress of his hair soothed her anxiety, while the rough stubble on his jaw scraped her skin, and had her yearning for more. She arched her back, moaning in pleasure as he held her breasts together and suckled both nipples at once.

"I can spend hours on your breasts." He alternated between sucking the sensitive peaks into the blazing heat of his mouth and then blowing a cooling breath over the heavy ache. "You had a special request, *bella*."

He sucked a nipple back into his mouth, then pinched it between his fingers. Cool metal slid on either side of the sensitive nub, and she sighed in pleasure.

"Nipple clamps," she said with a whimper. "Thank you." The contraption slowly squeezed tight until she gasped.

"Beautiful," Marko said, licking the flesh around the intense pinch. His thumb feathered over the free nipple. "Does this beauty want some attention?"

"Please," she whispered.

He suckled the stiff peak, nipping gently with his teeth, until she was ready. He applied and adjusted the second clamp, caressing softly over the pulsing strain.

"How do you feel, Kathryn? I need to know," he said, tugging gently on the chain linking her nipples and causing pleasure to shoot through her.

"Good. I feel good," she said breathlessly. "The pinch is good."

"In that case, I've heard enough." He placed the chain between her lips, pulling her breasts high and intensifying the sting. "Keep the chain in your mouth. It pleases me very much to see how pretty your nipples look stretched high."

Quivering, she forced out a breath through her nose. Her shoulders dropped and her head eased back, tugging harder on her nipples.

"Slowly, sweetheart. Be gentle." Marko fit his hand at the small of her back, and she gladly accepted the support. "That's it, Kathryn. Breathe for me. Find your balance, and stand for me."

Shivers raked her body, and she fought to catch her breath and stand. Once the mammoth feat had been accomplished, and the shivering had subsided, he splayed his hand across her back and unzipped the skirt.

"Since this is our first time with nipple clamps, you may enjoy them until I've removed the rest of your clothing. Your nipples are so pretty, all dark and distended. So swollen and tempting like tiny little cherries begging to be devoured."

She nodded, and pain zinged from her breasts to her core. She lowered her chin and allowed for less pressure. But the throbbing between her legs grew.

"Go ahead. Feel," he said, lifting her hand to her breast. "One hand. Take turns."

Pulsing like mad, the burning peaks jutted between the metallic clamps, which had the shape of bobby pins, and she skimmed over the tight nubs. She hooked a thumb through the chain and tugged until pressure flashed like white light in her mind.

His tongue trailed behind her finger, soothing the sting in slow swirls. He licked down the underside of her breast, while returning her hand to the side of her thigh.

Placing wet kisses on her hips and her belly, he lowered the leather down her legs. His lips brushed the insides of her thighs; then he slowly urged her legs apart and pressed his open mouth against her heat. "Pure heaven."

Kat wanted to tangle her fingers in the soft waves of his hair, and drop to her knees to kiss him. She burned to touch him, to see him, and to show him how much she needed him. Relaxing her fist, she gave in to the insistent longing and raised her hand.

Large fingers shackled her wrists. He folded her arms behind her back, which caused the chain to yank on the clamps and squeeze her nipples harder. "Intertwine your fingers and keep your hands there. Concentrate on your balance."

"I can't. The burn is too great," she breathed, managing to keep the chain in her mouth, but feeling the massive sting on her tender nipples.

"You can," he said, stroking softly down her hip. "You're my determined and beautiful Kathryn. You can do anything you set your mind to. You please me so much. Every beautiful way you respond makes me ache to bury my cock inside you and stay there forever."

She moaned her delight. She pleased him. She made him happy. Sucking on her parched lip, she nodded and linked her fingers at her back. He would give her what she needed. He knew.

"That's it, sweetheart. You will wait."

But he moved torturously slow, and she doubted her endurance. She needed him inside her, sating the desire that burned and consumed her abilities.

He unhooked the silk stockings from the garter and they slid down her thighs. With tenderness that hurt, he supported her weight and lifted her feet off the floor to remove the boots. Next, he rolled the stockings off her feet and pressed his mouth to the backs of her knees.

He kissed every inch of her body, reverently whispering his admiration and love. With each brush of his lips and stroke of his tongue, the tight ball of protection she'd wrapped around her heart unraveled, one string at a time.

The concept of time ceased. He took the chain from between her lips. She cried out as pain pulsed through her right nipple when he freed it from the clamp and blood returned. His tongue soothed over the throbbing swell, and she floated in a cloud of ecstasy created by Marko's sensual worship.

When she was able to breathe again, he did the same to the left nipple. The torment was so much greater upon the removal of the clamps, but she arched toward him and offered the sore nubs for more play. Her breath sputtered from her lips and she mewed with an impatient urgency she didn't recognize.

"Next time," he assured, blowing pacifying breaths across her chest and slipping his hand between her legs. He pinched the tight bundle at the top and moistness oozed from within her. "Next time," he repeated.

Completely exposed and vulnerable, she groaned her frustration and pleaded for the use of her hands. The ache to feel him was so great, it burned like a wildfire.

"Let me kiss you," she begged, the silk blindfold catching the moisture on her forehead. "Please, Marko."

The sweet words and heated kisses continued, but he didn't allow her to move.

"What are you feeling, sweetheart?" Marko whispered against her ear, nibbling on the soft flesh of her lobe and sending more tingles from her head to her toes.

"I'm shaking, Marko. My legs won't hold me much longer." She swallowed a sob, determined to make him understand. "It's not fair. I need you. I want you. You're here, giving me excruciating pleasure, but you won't let me touch you. It hurts."

"I don't want you to hurt," he said. "I want you to know what it feels to want something so bad, and to be kept at arm's length."

Tears drenched the silk at her eyes, and her heart swelled with a familiar ache. She knew what it felt like to want something so bad and not have it. She'd denied herself for a long time.

"You have the power to change that, Kat. Make it happen." His tongue traced down the side of her neck and her composure drained.

"I don't know how," she cried, sinking into the dark and quiet hopelessness.

Marko caught her as her knees gave. He lifted her in his arms, and kissed over the tiny beads of perspiration on her forehead. She was almost there. She'd discover the way.

He placed her relaxed body in the center of the large bed, then reached for the silk tie on the nightstand. Arranging her arms above her head, he secured her hands to the headboard. He studied the relaxed lines of her body, the smoothness of her lips, and he craved the opportunity to see into the depths of her eyes and soothe her confusion.

Denying his need, he left the blindfold in place and walked away. He retrieved some juice from the bar, and stripped off his clothes while he waited for Kat to emerge from the respite her mind required. The minutes seemed like hours, testing his patience and tenacity to allow time for her realization to dawn. But the reward of having Kat steeled his resolve, and he set to awakening her with gentle persuasion.

Kat's mind may have needed to rest, but her body responded to each kiss. Her breasts weighed heavy in his hands and her nipples pebbled in his mouth. The exquisite flush returned on the heated canvas of her torso, and the musky perfume of her excitement scented the air. When he tasted the sweetness between her legs, her hips lifted and pushed her core to his mouth. He closed his lips around the swollen bundle of nerves, and thrust a finger in her tight heat.

A glorious gasp escaped her lips, and his heart soared.

"Welcome back, *bella*," he said, pushing a second finger deep inside her body and stroking her back to awareness.

She writhed and moaned, tugging on the restraints at her hands, and clenching his fingers with need. He straddled her thighs, careful not to place his weight on her, and gently controlled the thrashing of her legs as her climax built and she struggled for her release. He coaxed her higher and higher, smoothing her cream over her clit and bringing her to the edge and holding her there, but not letting her fall.

"Tell me, what do you want?" Marko demanded against her lips, sealing her mouth in a kiss and delaying her answer. He withdrew his fingers, and slid them through her swollen folds. Her tongue keenly searched his mouth, and she eagerly sucked him into hers. Breaking the kiss, he was instantly rewarded with a sigh.

"I want to come," she rasped.

He plunged a finger into her wet heat and found the special spot deep inside her, returning her to the edge. "Like this?"

"No," she protested, shaking her head. "With you. I want to come with you."

"And what will you give me in return?"

"Anything," she cried.

He crushed her lips in a branding kiss, and covered every inch of her softness with his hard body. Holding himself at her entrance, he removed her blindfold and waited for her sight to adjust.

"I love you, Kat," he said, thrusting into the sweet refuge of her body and claiming her as his own. Taking her higher, and stoking the fire that burned between them, his body shook with need. He cupped her face and took her mouth, breathing his love into her soul.

"I love you," she breathed.

Elated to hear the words on her lips, he threw back his head and buried himself inside her silky acceptance. Relinquishing his heart to her, he claimed her body in deep and urgent thrusts, plunging them off the edge in an earth-shattering and joint release.

He collapsed over her, holding her close and reveling in the heat of her breath on his neck. When the strength returned to his arms, he lifted his weight off her chest and looked at the perfect woman beneath him. His woman.

He stretched up and released her hands. Quickly unwinding the material from her wrists, he rubbed them gently and brought each to his lips. "Thank you."

Long lashes rested over her cheeks, and she burrowed against him with a content moan. He slid to her side and pulled her against him, holding his most precious possession against his heart.

As their breathing settled and his senses returned, he reached for the glass of juice and took a sip. Lifting her mouth to his, he gave her a drink.

With a beautiful smile curving her swollen lips, she looked at him and stroked her fingers over his jaw. "Tell me what you want, Marko."

"More time," he said. "Come with me to Provence. There is so much more I want to show you. Let me introduce my home and family to you. Plus, there is my mama's bouillabaisse on Sunday. I'll get you back to New York with time to spare for the deadline."

"Okay."

His heart soared. "My absolute favorite word."

Sending up a silent prayer of gratitude, he dropped his chin to her shoulder and simply held her.

Chapter Twenty-Two

Marko brushed his lips over her temple and held Kat tight. "Thank you."

"For what?" Kat asked in a soft whisper.

"You've given us more time. You've allowed an opportunity to see and experience my world. Nothing could make me happier than introducing you to my family." Combing his fingers through her hair, he inhaled the sweet floral scent and smiled. "They will be glad to know that I'm not delusional over an imagined lover. You're real."

"I can never imagine anyone thinking of you as delusional. You've got all your shit together—all of the time. You're smart, capable, successful, super handsome, deliciously sexy, and everything a woman dreams of."

He fit a finger beneath her chin and lifted her face to meet her gaze. "But I wasn't enough for you."

"Not true. You're intimidating to most people. To me." She looked away and sucked her trembling lower lip into her mouth. "When your family meets me, you'll realize *I'm* not enough for you."

Confusion punched him in the gut. He hadn't expected those words. Was at a loss for a reply. Not once had he ever imagined she'd felt that way. And not once had she alluded to that in the past. He touched his thumb to her mouth and released her lip. "*Bella*, please tell me why you feel like that."

"Marko, we come from two different worlds," Kat said, glancing up at him.

Easily solved. He would relocate.

"Your family is a respected powerhouse of French aristocracy. Cultured and elegant, they would never welcome the daughter of an ordinary blue-collar worker. We simply run in different socio-economic circles. They won't approve."

Sucker-punched for a second time, he wiped his palm down his face and rubbed his jaw. His beautiful and smart woman harbored archaic insecurities. He searched his mind for a proper argument, realizing his primary responsibility was to her well-being and not to his comfort. It was the first time she'd trusted him enough to reveal an honest objection to their relationship, even if it was wrong.

"Perhaps such reasoning would work with obnoxious and self-righteous families that value people's bank accounts more than people's hearts. You have my word that my family is not one of those families. They haven't met you, and they already love you." In spite of wanting to shake the nonsense from her mind, Marko kept his voice soft and reassuring.

"They already love me?" Kat asked, her pupils wide.

"They do," he assured. "They love you because I love you. *Bella,* you are perfect for me. You are all I've ever wanted. Never doubt how you complete me."

He watched her features change, could see the thoughts churn in her mind, and he recognized the moment she let go.

"Okay," Kat said, slowly nodding. "I trust you, Marko. I do."

The woman he loved had finally trusted him with her thoughts. Thoughts he knew were wrong, but her thoughts nonetheless.

"I love you, *bella*," Marko said, empowered to love her as she should be loved. Taking her mouth, he kissed her with tender appreciation and assurance as he sank into the warmth of her body.

Amidst the soft snores leaving her lips, a loud rumble sounded from her stomach. Marko grinned and reached for the phone, but she stretched over him and stilled his hand. "What is it, Kat? I was just going to order some food."

"If you don't mind, I'm ready to go home," she said. "I'd like to sleep in our bed."

Home. Their bed. No, he didn't mind.

"Maybe we could stop in the club's café for a quick snack?" Kat added, circling a finger in the middle of his abdomen. "I'm sure you need to replenish your energy."

"I think it's you that needs to replenish your energy." He traced a finger up her spine and massaged her nape. "The café it is."

She uncurled from his body and reached for a bottle of water. "I like the cafe. It's peaceful and welcoming . . . and sexy. There is something freeing about being in a place where anything is accepted and we can just unwind."

Fifteen minutes later, she was *unwinding* on his lap and waiting for her bisque to arrive. He liked the feel of her head resting on his shoulder and loved the way her body draped so sweetly over his. He considered keeping her at the club a little longer just to allow her more time to relax. After years of dancing around their relationship, she'd finally relaxed enough to confide in him. She'd trusted him.

"I like you like this," he said against her hair.

"How's that?"

"Carefree and open." He brushed his lips over her forehead. "Willing to accept."

"I'm always open," she said in a rather petulant manner. He tapped her butt. She scraped her teeth over her lower lip and shrugged. "It's this place. Or maybe it's our agreement. Probably it's you. You're a little different. A bit more demanding. You won't let me get away with things any longer."

Fuck. If only he'd read her right from the beginning. "No. I won't."

"It's a relief," she admitted, straightening as the server placed the soup before them. "If you're willing to assume the consequences, it's possible to take a chance."

"This is happening. It's not about taking a chance." He adjusted her in his lap and handed her the spoon. "You and I are a we. In every sense of the word. I'm not letting you go again."

She placed a soft kiss on the underside of his jaw, and his body tightened. Relief and anticipation mixed in his mind. She was his.

"*Bonjour, mes amis*. I am happy to see you have found your way," Cyril said, appearing from behind them.

"Hello, my friend," Marco said, extending his hand. "Please join us."

"It would be my pleasure," Cyril said. He pulled out a chair and sat. "We finally have an abundance of beauty between us."

"We do," Marko agreed and shook Cyril's hand.

"I'm guessing you two are more than casual acquaintances," Kat said, her back going rigid. "Does that mean Cyril being on my flight was a setup?"

"No," Marko snapped. "We discovered the coincidence an hour before you boarded at JFK." He wasn't about to stand for her questioning him any further. He placed his lips close to her ear. "You've exceeded your questions. Eat your soup quietly."

She sucked in a breath and looked down at the creamy concoction. "Okay."

Her spine relaxed. He dropped a kiss on the side of her temple and turned his attention back to his friend and a typical conversation. "Was the trip successful?"

They returned home a little after three in the morning. Considering the repeated lovemaking and the fact Kat had dozed in his arms while he'd spoken with Cyril in the café, she was very chatty in their bed.

"So what did Cyril mean by 'finally'?" Kat asked.

Chuckling, Marko let out a long breath and shook his head. "I think you've exhausted question number nine twenty times over."

"Please. Tell me about it," she purred, pushing against his chest and rising on an elbow. She gave him a sweet look and tapped a manicured finger on his chest. "Pretty please."

"Rather convincing," he said, rolling her on her back. He pinned her hands over her head and lowered his mouth to hers. Ending the kiss, he looked into her dark eyes. "But if you don't want to sleep, I can think of other things to do."

"I want to talk," she insisted. "How do you know him, and what did he mean?"

Marko shifted to her side, and folded his arm beneath his head. "I've known Cyril for years. We move in the same business circles. It was by Cyril's invitation that I came to be a member at the club."

She propped her head on her hand and smiled. "Peculiar how Cyril invited us both to the club. Happenstance, I guess." She smiled dreamily, the fatigue returning to her features, yet she didn't relax. "What did he mean by 'finally'?"

"I've been helping subs find themselves for a while now. Over a year to be exact. I'd orchestrate scenes in the training room, sometimes play in the dungeon, but I never took one to the private rooms."

"You only had sex in public?"

"No." His knuckles strayed down her cheek, and he caressed along her jaw. "I have a rule against having sex in the club. I guided the subs, but I never kept one. When someone achieves subspace, they may lose rational thought, may not even be able to voice their safe word, so it is imperative that the masters act responsibly and on behalf of their subs. A good dom recognizes when his sub has had enough even before the submissive does. I personally believe a person within the grips of subspace may misconstrue sex for lovemaking. I didn't want that to happen."

"We had sex," she pointed out.

"First, you had not achieved true subspace and were in control of your faculties. Second, and most important, we made love," he corrected, clasping her chin between his thumb and finger, and brushing his mouth down on hers. "Because I do love you, Kat. I love you with every fiber of my being."

He treasured the gift of her acceptance above anything else he'd received. At last, he was empowered to look forward, both personally and professionally.

"Now, if we get some sleep, I'll be much sharper during my meeting, and I'll be able to come home to you earlier," he said. "Then we can discuss our options on our own before we join the family and before your return to New York. Please."

"Yes, sir," she teased, snuggling against him, and running a small finger over his chest. "Marko, I love being with you. I love how this feels."

Watching Kat sleeping in his bed had kept him awake all night, but when a man's dream came true, it was impossible to sleep. He didn't like the idea of her waking without him near, but maybe she'd sleep until his return.

Marko showered and shaved, dressed in a lucky suit, then dropped a soft kiss on her head before leaving the bedroom. Fearing the smell would wake her, he opted not to brew any coffee, and placed the burlap bag of beans next to the machine. He searched for her phone, typed out a quick message, then left for his meeting with a smile on his face.

* * *

At the bright hour of ten o'clock, way too bright for Kat's taste, she stumbled into the kitchen and found her phone propped on the coffee maker.

Disappointed that Marko wasn't home for a late breakfast, she was still excited for the day's outcome. If the meeting went well, which she was confident it would, there'd be three viable options for him to choose from. Four, if she counted the step down into the New York office of his current firm. But as she'd told him the previous day, she didn't want him to settle. He needed to choose the position that would be best for his career.

She reached for the phone, expecting a text about the progress, and in its place found a text from two hours earlier instructing her to read the note he'd entered. He hadn't wanted to chance waking her with a text alert at six-thirty in the morning.

Good morning, Bella.

I hate that I'm not with you, but perhaps a café crème and a pain au chocolat from Antoine's will make the morning go by quicker. I've programmed his number into your contacts. He'll bring it up. He has the access code for the door, so do not worry about meeting him downstairs. However, if you prefer a boring American-style brew, the beans are on the counter.

I should be back by noon.

Wish me luck.

M

ps: If you're reading this, get to work on that damn article as soon as the caffeine hits your brain. I want you all to myself later.

pps: If you find you need more research, make plans for whatever you'd like for us to do. Shoot me a text—just in case. I've made arrangements to fly out at six.

Love you!

Holding the phone to her chest, she did a little happy dance in the kitchen. For the first time in years, she saw herself as happily-ever-after material. So what if she had to make changes in her daily life? Her mother was doing well, her career was just starting to take shape, and she could stand to make adjustments for someone worthy. He was worthy. Unlike her, he'd actually shown in November. If Marko was willing to deal with her, she was thrilled to deal with him.

Deciding on good ol' boring home-brewed coffee, she got the coffee maker going and went to set up her laptop in the living room. After all, she was writing about Paris, and the view was the perfect inspiration.

Her fingers flew over the keyboard, and not only did she manage to categorize her notes, but she wrote a pretty great outline of the article. It wasn't difficult finding romantic things to say about Paris. What proved to be challenging was making it generic enough for readers to see themselves in it and not recognize Kat's personal story.

It was almost noon when her phone chimed an incoming text.

If you're up, give me a call. Can talk for the next fifteen minutes. M

She immediately hit the voice call button, and he answered on the second ring.

"*Ciao, bella.*"

"*Ciao, bello,*" she responded. "How did it go?"

"It's still going," he said in a low voice, sounding apologetic. "But, it's going very well, and it's not an opportune time to walk away. We're ironing out a few details, plus they want to examine a new direction they're considering for the company. I estimate a few more hours of discussions."

"That's okay," she said, glancing at the boats on the river. She wished he didn't need to work so they could enjoy a romantic ride down the Seine. But that was selfish of her. She'd do it on her own and add the perspective the article lacked. "I was thinking about heading to the Latin Quarter for a gyro sandwich. According to my research, the Quarter is known for them."

"You are so adorable. You're in Paris and in the mood for a Greek sandwich?" He chuckled, and she could practically see him shaking his handsome head and finger-combing his hair. "I must be easy to forget. Don't you miss me?"

"A lot," she admitted, trying to keep the disappointment from her voice. "I do miss you. I've been working on the article, and I think I need to layer it a bit. Put some non-Marko things in it."

"Why would you want non-Marko things? What's wrong with Marko things?"

She laughed at his disgruntled yet teasing questions. "Nothing at all. I just don't want all the single girls that read my article to flock to Paris looking for him. He's mine."

"He's definitely yours." There was a long pause and a serious vibe thrummed through the phone.

Kat worried her lower lip, and smiled. "I thought subs belonged to the master?"

"Yes, they do, but I belong to mine. I want a real partner, *bella*. I want you."

"You've got me," she said, breathing a cloudy circle on the window and writing their initials on it. She drew a heart around them, then added a whimsical *4 ever* across the bottom.

"I miss you, too, and I'm sorry I won't be able to share your first Parisian gyro," he said. "I'll try to be quick. At the latest, I'll be done by three. Jean-Luc will be by in twenty minutes to drive you."

"No. Please don't send him." She wanted to see Paris on her own, like any girl coming to find true love for the first time. She had to place herself in the reader's shoes.

"Kat, don't tell me you're embarrassed because you've seen his impressive package. Your words, not mine. You can't go off into a strange city on your own."

Giggling, she snapped a quick picture of her window art, and assured him Jean-Luc's package wasn't the issue. She elaborated on what the article needed to be a success. "I'll simply alter the order of events, lose my heart, rather than my panties, to a handsome stranger at Les Deux Magots, and the story will be totally relatable."

"*Merde.* Wear panties, Kat," he said. "And don't go meeting any handsome strangers. There's only room for you and me in this reality." In good spirits and confident he'd join her for an afternoon snack, he went on to suggest the Batobus instead of a tourist river cruise, outlined the stops he thought she'd enjoy, and told her to be ready for Provence by packing a suitcase and leaving it for Jean-Luc to collect before he picked them up for their flight. "Look around the closet in our room. You'll find lots of outfits for a few days with the family. Suitcases are in the closet in the second bedroom."

Tingles of happiness danced through her, from the tips of her fingers to her sock-clad toes. Hey, January in Paris wasn't warm. She smiled and perched on the edge of the couch, looking out at the cityscape and listening to the man she loved.

"Okay. I'll see you at Café de Flore at three-thirty," Marko said, after he'd explained every detail thoroughly. "Be careful, Kat. Call me if you need anything at all."

"Do you know how much these roaming charges are going to suck?" Of course he didn't. Marko wasn't the kind to count pennies. She shook her head, dismissing the thoughts that had plagued her insecurities in the past.

"Kat, I'm serious. Call me with *anything*. I'll answer."

"Knock them dead, Marko. I'll be waiting at the corner of Saint-Germain and Rue St. Benoit." She repeated the address for his benefit. She didn't need him thinking about her when he went back to his discussions. Kat really wanted him to have the best professional choices.

She rinsed out the coffee maker, showered, and dressed, leaving her packed tote and the designer case at the foot of the bed. Thankfully, Marko had thought ahead, and had left a pair of Le Chameau rain boots for her in the foyer. Made of kid leather, and with no heel to speak of, they were comfortable as fuck. She left the apartment with her phone, wallet, and passport in a small cross-body bag. Kat was finally free to explore and accomplish anything and everything.

Dropping by Antoine's for a quick hello, she nibbled on an almond cookie as he gave her directions to the best gyro place in the Quarter. He added his surprise that Marko was willing to let her venture out alone, but he guaranteed her it would be fun and told her to call if she was lost or feeling alone. As long as she was near the river, he could always get to her within minutes.

"You're exactly what he needs. You give him true purpose, *ma chère*. I'm glad you stayed," he said, pulling her into a huge bear hug and forgetting the air kisses. "Marko is a good man. He'll do right by you."

For once in her life, she had no doubts about the future. Kat kissed the big man and started for the bridge. She was off to stroll the streets of Paris as a tourist.

Opting to wait for the gyro sandwich, she hesitantly passed on a Berthillon ice cream cone, but made a note on her phone and added the name to the list of things she would do in the near future. She lingered near the Pont Saint-Louis, enjoying the slue of street performers. Her favorite, a mime, followed her onto the bridge, offering his heart in his hand if only she'd sit with him by the river. She held her hands over her own heart and blew him a parting kiss. The mime was a keeper for her research.

Carrying the secrets of the city and its people, the Notre Dame lured visitors into her Gothic folds, while standing protectively in the center of it all. It was impossible to hurry past the cathedral. Tourists gathered everywhere, taking pictures and waiting for tours, but Kat strolled past, noting the time for Sunday mass in her phone.

The little green bookstalls on the Left Bank slowed her progress even more. Amongst the latest novels and coffee table books, there were old editions of classics that belonged in elegant libraries. Flipping through one of the picture books, she was mesmerized by an image of a large castle in Carcassonne, France, a city near the Spanish border. Her to-do note kept getting longer.

She made a left and a quick right, finding herself walking along the center of the Latin Quarter and all its tempting food windows. The place Antoine had suggested proved delicious, and she added its takeout number to her notes.

Sailing down the Seine in the water service most locals used, she catalogued the new information she'd gathered and realized she had more than enough to write the piece the way she wanted. Maybe she was short on time for the Louvre, but she figured she could lose herself for an hour inside the Musée d'Orsay and still be early for her rendezvous with Marko.

She typed out a quick text, telling him of her plans, then turned off her cell and escaped into a world of enchanted artistic expression.

The time was ten minutes to four. Afternoon clouds loomed dark and heavy over the corner of Saint-Germain and Rue St. Benoit. Kat was about to head into the café when a black sedan pulled to the curb and Jean-Luc stepped out.

"*Mademoiselle, s'il vous plait,*" he said, extending his arm for her to take.

"Seriously, Jean-Luc? I think we can drop the formalities at this point." She stretched up on her toes and did the *bise* thingie, then looked toward the car for Marko.

"Kathryn." His voice low and stern, Jean-Luc took hold of her elbow and steered her toward the sedan. "Please. We need to go. Get in the car. It's about to rain."

"Where's Marko? He was supposed to meet me here almost half an hour ago."

Jean-Luc looked down at her, his eyes shuttered from any emotion, and squeezed her elbow in what was meant to be a reassuring gesture. "Monsieur Renard is fine. He has been called to attend an immediate family situation. I will see you to your flight."

"My stuff is still at the house," she said, growing very uncomfortable. "Are you sure he's okay?"

"I promise, your Marko is fine," he repeated, holding open the door for her. "And I have already collected your bags."

She believed Jean-Luc, so her worry dissipated. "I don't want to sit by myself. May I ride up front with you?"

His features softened. He nodded. "*C'est bon.*" He shut the door and, curving a protective arm around her, he led her around the car and to the front passenger side.

Kat untied the red cashmere from around her neck and pulled off her hat and gloves. Folding them neatly in her lap, she waited for Jean-Luc to explain. He drove them into the busy afternoon traffic, but offered no more information.

"I'm sort of lost, Jean-Luc. What happened?"

"There is an emergency with the family and he will not be joining you. Monsieur Renard tried to call you numerous times, but he said it went directly to voicemail."

Shit. She'd turned off her phone before entering the museum and hadn't bothered to check voicemail when she'd turned it back on. Retrieving the cell from her bag, she found a new and unread text from Marko.

Jean-Luc will collect you.

Jean-Luc handed her a new smartphone. "This is for you. He said there are no roaming costs, so keep it on at all times."

"I turned it off while I was in the museum," Kat explained.

"*Ça va, mademoi—Kathryn.*" He cleared his throat. "It would not have made a difference. I will see that you make the flight."

"Is he meeting us at the airport?" Kat's voice cracked a bit. She wasn't feeling very optimistic about the family visit in the midst of an emergency.

Stopping at a red light, Jean-Luc turned a compassionate green gaze on her. "*Non.*"

"I can't go to his family's home without him," she pointed out, swallowing the panic that formed in her throat.

"You are going home to New York."

Chapter Twenty-Three

K at hadn't known there was an evening flight from CDG to JFK. "It's a direct flight," Jean-Luc explained, as he helped her from the car. "With the time difference, you'll be in New York a little after nine o'clock."

"I have to call my mom. This is such a mess. I have to ask her to meet me at the airport." Kat reached into her bag, but he stilled her hand.

"Don't worry, *ma petite*," he said in a soft and soothing voice. "Marko has made arrangements. He's seen to everything."

That was one dom speaking for another. But it worked, for his words calmed her nerves and her optimism returned. If the circumstances were different, she'd wonder if the words were scripted. They weren't and she knew it. Jean-Luc's assurance was what she needed, and exactly in the tone he'd delivered it.

She sighed softly. Marko had seen to it, he'd seen to everything. He just didn't want her feeling uncomfortable with the family situation. He'd call.

Jean-Luc said something to an officer and left the vehicle in a no-parking zone. He took her hand and led her through the security doors. Skipping the long line for coach passengers at the Air France counter, he walked her directly to the front of first-class check-in. Relieved of the burden, she handed him her passport and waited for him to finish with the agent.

She had no energy to argue when he suggested they check her carry-on, so she tucked her gloves and hat into an outside pocket and nodded.

"What of the shawl?" Jean-Luc asked.

No. She shook her head. It made her feel like Marko was with her.

"That's okay," he assured. "Let me pack your coat. The shawl will keep you warm enough, and you won't need to carry that much stuff."

She shrugged out of her coat and he took care of fitting it in the case. The attendant marked the luggage and handed him the boarding pass. "*Merci, monsieur*," she said, lowering her gaze and smiling demurely. "Have a pleasant trip, *mademoiselle*."

"*Merci*," Jean-Luc replied, smiling at the young woman. He placed the boarding pass inside the passport, then handed them to Kat and waited for her to secure them in her laptop bag. "Very nice," he said approvingly, and once again took her hand. "You only have your computer, the phones, the documents, and your identification. That should be comfortable."

"First class is pretty comfortable," she noted, smiling for the first time since Jean-Luc had arrived to pick her up.

"That it is," he replied, and for the first time ever, she heard him laugh.

Relaxed and comfortable, she walked beside him and didn't bother to read the signs or check for gate information. The man at her side would take care of details.

"Don't think too much, *ma petite*. Just trust in what you feel and all will be good. Marko will finish as quickly as he can, and he'll explain this turn of events. The only thing you need to do is trust him," Jean-Luc said, closing his hand around hers and giving it a reassuring squeeze.

"Are you reading my mind or something?" Kat looked up and found him grinning.

"*Non, mademoiselle.* I know your nature."

Were all French men so arrogant? He was as sure of himself as Marko was. The weird thing was that she didn't mind the cavalier attitude. She actually appreciated the reprieve it gave her from worrying. "You're almost as bad as Marko."

"Thank you," he said, swinging her hand in a cheerful way. In just one day, Jean-Luc had become a trusted friend. "We have some time before you need to pass through security. Are you hungry?"

"No. But what about the car?"

"My problem, not yours." He guided them into a café and held up two fingers. They were seated, and he ordered in rapid-fire French.

She missed the whole conversation, but smiled when the server returned with two tall glasses of orange juice.

What was it with these men and their juice?

Once the plane had reached cruising altitude, Kat powered on her laptop and connected to the Internet. There was nothing new from Marko, so she typed out at quick message.

I hope you're well and things are working out with your family. Jean-Luc took good care of me and got me on the flight. We're in the air and headed to New York. I should be home around nine EST.

His reply flashed on the screen within seconds.

Do you still consider New York a forever home?

She sighed and thought about the question. Home? What was a home? But before she could complete the thought and reply, a second message flashed.

Need to go.

And he was gone. No explanation, nothing to tell her why he'd sent her back to New York in such a hurry. *It must be a huge wine crisis to need me out of the way*, she thought. Nothing else made sense.

She leaned her head back and took a deep breath. She was going to stay in the little Pollyanna world Jean-Luc had suggested and just wait for Marko to take care of things. It was so much easier on her psyche and her heart. It hurt too much to think that he'd changed his mind and didn't want her any longer. Maybe his family emergency had to do with the outrage they'd expressed when he'd announced he was bringing her home?

No. She shook her head and closed her eyes. Marko loved her, and he'd make everything all right. She knew it. She trusted him. She loved him.

Pollyanna land worked just fine. By the time the crew started with dinner service, she'd finished the rough draft of the article and was proud of her work. Napping with the laptop on and open on the snack tray, just in case Marko texted again, she woke to a dead battery. Disappointed, she stowed the computer and snuggled up with the soft cashmere. She slept until the flight attendant tapped her shoulder and asked her to prepare for landing.

The plane touched down, and as they taxied to the gate, she called her mom and left a message for them to get together in the morning. She couldn't wait to tell her all about the trip, and most importantly, she wanted to tell her about reconnecting with Marko. Her mom had always loved Marko.

Welcome home, Kittykat. Exit door & on the left at arrivals.

Paul had given up his Saturday night out to pick her up at the airport. That was the only thing that worried her. Why would Marko send Paul? Had something bad happened?

She hurried off the plane, zoomed past immigration, and was one of the first at baggage claim. Having nothing to declare, she was done with customs in no time. Gate to arrivals accomplished in under half an hour. She pulled the carry-on, loaded with designer clothes, from baggage claim and pasted on a winning smile. Life was good.

She'd accomplished what she'd set out to do and had returned with a story and love in her heart. She'd done it all in just over a day.

"Kittykat," Paul called, as she rounded the security barriers and walked into his open arms. He placed a big kiss on the side of her head and squeezed her tight. "You look beautifully fucked."

"Cut it out," Justin said, pulling her out of Paul's embrace and into his. "You look wonderfully in love."

"Yes," she said, looking at her friends with real joy. "On both counts."

"*Excellenté,*" Paul cried, pumping his right fist into the air and bending his knee up to meet it.

"Is that even a word?" Justin asked.

"Who the fuck cares," Paul replied, still grinning. "I'm just glad she's finally come to her senses."

Paul took her luggage and Justin carried her tote, the two of them sandwiching her in a welcome-home hug. They wanted all the details before they walked to the car, but Kat couldn't get past the way she'd left Paris.

"I was going to stay and add a few days to the trip. We were supposed to fly to Provence and meet his family tonight," Kat explained, still feeling confused. "I don't know what happened or why he didn't want me there, but Jean-Luc said to just trust Marko to take care of things. Did he tell you what happened?"

"Hold on, Kathryn. Let's take this one question at a time," Justin said. "No need to get all worked up over something that could be nothing. I'm sure there is a good explanation for it."

"What did he tell you?" Kat asked.

"He didn't," Paul said. "He texted. Said something came up, and then asked if we could meet the plane. When I texted back yes, he said to check email for your flight information. That's it. I had no clue you were planning on extending the trip."

"Maybe he didn't want me to meet his family," she said, her earlier sassiness gone. "I'm not exactly the kind of woman they would have picked for their son."

"Are you for fucking real?" Paul hissed. "That man has been so in love with you for years. He'd do anything for you."

"Sorry, sweetie. Paul's right. Stop jumping to stupid conclusions," Justin agreed. "Now, put that smile back on your face and give us all the romantic and sordid details."

"Not unless you bribe me with a drink first," she said, letting go of the doubt. She'd had a wonderful time with Marko—the best day of her life—and she wasn't going to run this time. She was determined to give them a shot.

"The bottle is in the car," Justin said. "In honor of this momentous occasion, we picked up an eighty-dollar bottle of French wine to drink at your place. You can thank me later. *After* you dish out the whole scoop." He opened the car door and offered her shotgun position. "Only because you've had a long trip."

She gave him a quick peck and hopped in, snapping her seat belt in place before he could change his mind. "I'm not saying a word about Marko until I've had that wine."

Paul laughed and slipped into the driver's seat. He turned on the ignition and pulled out of the parking spot. "So, spill. Who is this Jean-Luc character you mentioned?"

"Jean-Luc is Marko's hot driver. The man is wicked," she cooed, making a show of loosening her wrap and fluffing her hair.

"How hot?" Paul and Justin asked at the same time.

"Very, very, very, very hot," Kat replied, fanning the heat creeping over her skin. Her friends would die if they knew all she knew about the man, but there was no way she was sharing detailed information.

"Holy cow," Justin exclaimed, jamming his shoulders between the seats and touching the blush spreading up her neck. "She has a crush on Marko's driver."

"I do not. I don't. Just because a man is hot doesn't mean I drool over him. However, he is drool worthy." She placed a hand in the center of Justin's chest and pushed him back against the seat. "Anyway, he's a great guy. He's the one that met me when Marko couldn't make it. He took me to the airport and got me on the flight."

"Go on," Paul said, rolling his hand for more. Her friend knew her too well, had known her too long, to believe that was all there was to Jean-Luc.

"That's it," she said. "He's a good guy that gets things done." She stared out the front windshield and scraped her teeth over her lower lip. It seemed like Marko chose friends that got things done. From Jean-Luc to Antoine, to Cyril, each one of them got things done. She liked that. But she liked everything about Marko more. She *loved* everything about Marko. "Did you know French guys are seriously into juice?"

"What?" Paul shook his head and threw her a searing glance. Justin scooted forward and turned questioning eyes on her, a perturbed look on his face.

"Seriously. They drink a lot of fresh squeezed juice in Paris."

"Fermented grape juice." Justin snorted.

"That too." She raised her shoulder and winked.

"Fuck. Drive faster, damn it," Justin swore, pushing on Paul's arm. "We have to hear what really happened in Paris. You need to tell us about everything and everyone, but mostly, we want the Marko details."

She threw back her head and laughed. It was great having friends who shared her joy. Maybe they were just a little over the top with exuberance about a possible hookup, but there was no doubt they were genuinely happy for her. After all, they'd given up their Saturday night out to get the information fresh off the plane. They were excited for her, not concerned that something had gone terribly wrong and had ended her fairy tale.

"Don't you want to know what happened with the feature?" Kat settled in her seat, determined to follow her friends' lead and enjoy the moment. "Don't you want details on what a spectacular researcher and writer I am?"

"Sure," Paul drawled. "We'll get to that. Keep going on the other tidbits for now."

She started with how meeting Cyril on the flight had set the mood for romantic possibilities, and then described how Marko had surprised her at the airport, but neither one of her friends tried to pretend shock. "Those smug grins are because you knew all about it."

"Sue us for being good fairy godbrothers," Justin said, chuckling at her observation. "Of course we knew. Did you really think Paul would splurge on upgrading you to first class?"

"Looking back on it, I guess not," she agreed, continuing with the story. She reserved the Marko details for wine time, but did get a huge reaction from her friends when she mentioned the other café patrons and their exhibitionist qualities.

"Holy shit. I think we need to plan an excursion to Paris," Justin exclaimed. "This keeps getting better with every hour of the trip."

They parked and made it up the stairs, excited about plans for an upcoming trip. But the moment they were inside and their coats were on the hooks, Paul turned to Kat and pushed her onto the couch. "Spill."

Only too happy to share, she accepted a glass from Justin and started with how good time had been to Marko. They had finished the expensive bottle of wine and had started on the seven-dollar reserve she'd splurged on last week, as she moved from the Eiffel Tower to the ideal microcosm of Île Saint-Louis, her favorite spot being the private rooftop. Negative thoughts fled from her mind, and her body relaxed.

She gave in to the urge to rest her eyes for a few minutes, then opened them and found herself being carried to bed by Justin. He tucked her in and kissed her good night. Paul leaned over her, swept her hair back from her forehead, and brushed a chaste kiss on her lips.

"Marko's a lucky man. Sweet dreams, Kittykat." Those were the words that sent her to dreamland, until a ringing from the living room jostled her from sleep.

Getting to the phone on time wasn't in the cards. It stopped ringing before she'd even found her bag. Her regular cell showed no missed calls, but then she remembered the phone from Marko and checked the display. Sure enough, she'd missed his call.

She tapped the screen and returned the call. It went to voicemail, but a chirp sounded that she'd received a voicemail. The recording was pure static. An incoming call came through.

"Hello? Marko?"

"Kathryn, I needed to know you're home." He sounded anxious, as if there was a reason she wouldn't make it home.

"Of course. I was sleeping. Paul and Justin left about two hours ago. You okay?"

"*Oui, mai non*, be—" Static buzzed over the line. "Hotel." More static. "American." Static. "Paris."

"Marko, I can't understand. There's too much interference. Let me call you back."

"*Non, c'est ma connexion,*" he said, sounding clearer. "Is that better?"

"Yes," she breathed, holding the phone tight. "I miss you terribly."

"I miss you, *bella*. I feel there is nothing I can do. Nothing." She could hear the frustration, perhaps anguish, in his voice, and she, too, felt helpless. Static . . . horrible static grated on her nerves. ". . . soon. I've got to go. I love you."

"I love you," she repeated into the static, and then her knees folded beneath her and she dropped to the couch. He'd ended the distressed call with *I love you*.

Chapter Twenty-Four

Kat had no energy for clothes and makeup on Sunday. So rather than meeting her mother and Ralph for lunch, she took a long bath and babbled on the phone until the water had gone cold and she needed to get out. Her mom got an earful about the perfect man who had made Paris more romantic than she'd ever thought possible.

Wrapped in her bathrobe, she sat on the couch, slurping delivery miso soup and watching a full season of *Grace and Frankie* on Netflix. She wished Charlie would come home already, but her roomie wasn't due into Penn Station until late Tuesday afternoon. The stubborn woman refused to fly. She had to get over that fear of airplanes if they were going to visit Paris soon.

Kat had plenty of time to work on her story, which was totally awesome and definitely getting her that byline, so she spent the night with a pint of ice cream and waited for Marko to call.

He didn't. He also didn't call on Monday or Tuesday. She'd tried calling him, but each time it went directly to voicemail. He'd sent three texts asking how she was and explaining he'd call soon. But the texts weren't enough. She needed to hear his voice. Her bubble of bliss deflated as the time went on. When she couldn't take it any longer, she called his office line.

"I'm sorry, Mademoiselle Taylor. Monsieur Renard is not available at this time," a female voice announced. "He is not accepting any calls."

Not that Kat was jealous, but she was bothered. The other woman had more information than she had on Marko's schedule, and she also seemed to know why he wasn't accepting calls. Unfortunately, the sultry female voice wasn't willing to share.

"Thank you," Kat said, aiming for professional courtesy. "I'll try his cellular."

"*Non, je suis désolé, mais. . . .* I do not believe that will work. Would you like me to relay a message?"

She declined and disconnected. She'd wait it out. Marko would call. He had to.

Excited to see Charlie, Kat made a point of meeting her friend's train. She wanted to be the first to get the cruise news and hear how she'd done in the romance department. Arriving at Penn Station, Kat texted Charlie. Head down, she paced before the agreed-upon news-stand when her new French phone vibrated in her pocket.

"Marko?"

"*Bella* . . . Kathryn . . . I . . ." Damn, there was that static again. "American." Same damn word. "Paris."

"Wait. Please wait. Don't hang up," she pleaded. "I'm at the train station. I'm running up the stairs as we speak. I can't hear you again." Her heart pounded against her rib cage as she weaved between the nightly commuters and up the stairs. She was out of breath, doubled over on Seventh Avenue, and holding her side. "I'm here." She gulped frigid air into her lungs and spoke into the phone. "I'm outside. Try now."

"I . . ." Fuck, fuck, fuck. Static. ". . . back. They're . . ."

"Marko?"

Nothing.

"Marko?"

Frustration barreled over her like a rogue eighteen-wheeler on a Tennessee mountain road, throwing her into an isolating pain like none she'd ever experienced. She stomped her foot and wiped at the tears streaming down her cheeks.

An incoming text chimed.

Don't cry. Pls, don't cry. I need you strong.

Kat looked over her shoulder, turned on her heels, and searched the wide sidewalk. He wasn't there. But he knew she was crying. There was a plea in his words.

I'm fine. Waiting to hear back from you. She added a <3, then hit send.

Realizing he wasn't going to call, she went back underground and got out of the chilly evening weather. He said to be strong. Actually, he said he *needed* her strong. She'd be strong. She squared her shoulders, and with her head held high, she returned to the newsstand.

She tried calling Marko again; then she called the *boulangerie*. It was nearly midnight there, so the fact that Antoine didn't answer at the bakery was no surprise. She contemplated calling his direct line, but didn't want to overreact and jump to conclusions. She would have called Jean-Luc, regardless of the time, but she didn't have his number. Instead, she dialed Paul's number and left him a voicemail to call her as soon as possible.

She needed help.

It was nearing the end of rush hour, but the train was half an hour behind schedule, and Penn Station was Penn Station. It never stopped bustling with activity. She bought a gossip magazine and leaned against a wide cement column, making herself as small as possible. Her shoulder ached from knocking against the concrete as she'd tried to avoid running over a little old lady during her dash upstairs earlier, so the less physical contact, the better.

Charlie didn't seem to think so. She raced up the stairs and wrapped her arms around Kat. "Oh. My. God. What an amazing trip."

Forgetting about the shoulder pain, Kat returned her friend's excited hug and then looked her over in earnest. Lightweight jeans, a really low-cut shirt, and a pair of Converse shoes. "You'd better get some clothes on before you freeze that gorgeous tan off. Are you even wearing socks?"

"Yes, I'm wearing socks. They're no-shows." Charlie dropped the suitcase on its side and unzipped the main compartment. The woman positively glowed. No regretful eyes or telling hair bun. No pink electronic cigarette in sight, either. Just a glowing Charlie, who had clearly been *beautifully fucked*—as Paul would have put it.

"Please tell me you're wonderfully in love," Kat said, squatting and helping Charlie search through her open suitcase for her coat.

"Got them," Charlie said, pulling out a long white jacket and a scarf. "I had amazing, earth-shattering, bone-rattling sex. The best sex of my life."

"Obviously," Kat replied, rolling her eyes. She closed the suitcase as Charlie got into her jacket. "What's his name?"

"I'm not saying," Charlie snapped, zipping up the jacket.

"What?" Kat couldn't believe her roommate's refusal to talk. The other woman was bursting with sexual energy, but she wasn't talking. "Why won't you tell me?"

"Because my personal activities don't relate with the article. I'm not writing about what I did, but the opportunity to find love on a cruise." Taking hold of the suitcase handle, Charlie hooked her arm through Kat's and started walking.

"Seriously? You're going to leave me hanging like this?" Kat should have enlisted Paul and Justin for the inquisition. Screw their Tuesday-night handball games. They would have gotten Charlie to talk.

"For now," Charlie replied. "We're still figuring things out. I'll tell you all about him when things are settled."

"I don't get it. Why are you so cryptic with all of this?" Why was everyone in her life so cryptic? Was the universe trying to tell her something? Was it trying to let her down easy so her heart didn't shatter into thousands of little pieces at her feet? "Is it possible to find love on a cruise ship or not?"

"It definitely is," Charlie confirmed, blushing under her tan. "Did you find love in Paris, my friend?"

"I did," she breathed, fearing that love would remain there. Once again, uncertainty welled in her throat. She looked down the street for a cab and stepped off the sidewalk. She was way too vulnerable to explain. "It's obvious why Paris is always listed as one of the most romantic cities in the world. The history, the flavor, and the zest for romance are everywhere."

They hailed a taxi and settled into the back seat. Kat told Charlie about the architecture of the buildings, the beautiful streets, the unique life of the river, the delicious food, and especially the allure of the café life.

"And where did you find love?" Charlie asked.

"At the airport." Actually, love had found her and sucked her down like an undertow beneath a serene sea. She would have kept running, blind to what it meant to be in love and to feel someone's love, if Marko hadn't shown up and negated her friendship rules. "Marko was waiting for me when I landed."

"Marko? School Marko?" Charlie tugged on her seat belt and turned in her seat. "Did Paul have anything to do with that?"

"Of course," Kat said, snorting and shaking her head. "But it's okay. I still love him. They had the whole thing planned before you or I knew about the assignment. Everything. When Marko learned about what had happened with the jackass and the company's expense account, he and Paul brainstormed the premise of the feature. Marko paid for everything. Both of our trips. You were right, such expensive research wasn't in *City Wings'* budget."

"I knew it." Charlie clapped her hands and laughed hard. "There was no way Paul would have paid for my cabin. No fucking way." She placed a hand on her hip and gave Kat a searing stare. "Why didn't you tell me Marko was loaded?"

"It's not about the money." Kathryn sank against her seat and closed her eyes. It really had nothing to do with money. She was over that, but money was presently her biggest obstacle in returning to Marko. "Marko is more that a damn bank account."

"You're preaching to the choir, Kathryn. I get it," Charlie said, pointing a finger to her chest. "I really do."

"You of all people should," Kat agreed.

Charlie was a trust fund girl. It made no difference that she never touched the money. The woman was loaded.

"I'm sorry. I'm a bit on edge," Kat admitted, as the taxi pulled up to their building. "I may have found love in Paris, but I think I may have lost it there, too."

Chapter Twenty-Five

Kathryn sat on the floor, her back against the couch and a water bottle dangling between her knees. She didn't know if she was feeling sorry for herself or if she was just losing her mind.

The logical side of her brain told her that his family had rejected her and he was alienating himself from her. Her heart said it wasn't possible. He loved her and he wouldn't run—that was her MO, exclusively a Kat.

Opening the only bottle of wine left in the house, Charlie grabbed two glasses and came to sit beside her. "Tell me everything. Start from the beginning. The good and the bad. Don't leave anything out."

Kat told her about being upgraded to first class, receiving the iMessage while she was on the plane, and almost everything that had happened until the call had dropped outside of Penn Station.

"It doesn't add up, though," Kat said. "A few months ago—shit, a few days ago—I would have believed that the Renard family didn't think I was good enough for him."

"Today?" Charlie asked.

Kat considered every detail, everything they'd experienced over the years, and everything that made Marko the man she loved. "Today, I know that Marko loves his family dearly, and no matter if I come from the right gene pool or not, he loves me. Marko wouldn't run from us. He never has."

Charlie was nodding, but the questions still remained and hung between the friends like a huge wrecking ball. "Why are you here?"

Kat considered the question, really thought about it and wondered why she was acting like a bystander in her own life. Why wasn't she with him when he'd said he needed her? Needed her to be strong. He needed her.

"I think he 'sent' me away on purpose. He's a bit of a lovable tyrant, but he's also arrogant enough to think he always knows best. I'm afraid that something bad has happened. He thinks he can protect me if I'm away from it."

"Like all that talk about going to Provence and eating his mom's Sunday dinner meant nothing," Charlie added. "Not."

"Exactly." Kat placed her glass on the coffee table and stood. "I have to get back to Paris. He needs me."

"What time is the flight?" Charlie hopped up and carried their glasses to the sink.

Kat checked her phone. It was only twenty after seven. Paul was on the courts till eight. "I'm waiting on Paul to call. I need to ask if he'll purchase the ticket with his charge card for me. I maxed out my card and I have twenty bucks until payday."

"You're shitting me," Charlie said, reaching for her bag and pulling out her computer. "Why didn't you ask the minute I came off the track?"

"I know what you make. You're as broke as I am," she reminded her friend, reaching into the closet for the vacuum cleaner. Kat was about to crawl out of her skin. She had to find something to keep herself busy until Paul called. "Paul will spot me. And don't tell me I know better. You have a rule."

Charlie fixed her with a disgusted stare and parked her hands on her hips. "Get your ass over here, Kathryn Taylor." Charlie patted the space beside her on the couch. "Rules are made to be broken. We have a ticket to buy."

"Okay." She returned the vacuum to the closet and walked to her friend. "That just means you need to vacuum later."

"I will," Charlie replied, typing into the address bar. "Toss me your passport and go pack."

"Don't need to," she said, grabbing her purse and verifying that the passport was still in there. "There's a closet full of gorgeous clothes waiting for me in Paris."

Suddenly, Charlie turned solemn. She twirled her finger in her hair and reached for the missing e-cig. "Do you think he's hurt? I mean physically hurt?"

"I spoke with him." Kat worried her lower lip, but shook her head. "No. And Jean-Luc assured me he was fine. He wouldn't lie. I can't explain it, but I knew something was very off from the moment he sent his driver. At first, I thought it was related to the vineyard. Then, I slipped into an old way of thinking and took it personally—"

"But you said you never believed that," Charlie reminded her.

"I didn't. It was dumb of me to go there." Old habits were hard to break, and a sense of shame filled her for falling back on them. She knew better. She knew him.

"When he called today, I actually had chills racing down my spine." She rubbed her hands up her arms, trying to chase away the fear. "He sounded so bad. I've never heard him sound like that, and it had nothing to do with the static."

There were no direct flights until Wednesday, so they picked one with a layover in Dublin. It departed at a little after ten. Kat would be in Paris Wednesday afternoon. Charlie booked directly with the airline while Kat spoke with Paul.

She washed her face, pulled her hair into a ponytail, and collected the red cashmere off her pillow. It was her turn to be strong. Love was a two-way street.

"I'm so blessed to have you guys," Kat said, fifteen minutes later. "Thank you." Hugging Charlie, she climbed into Paul's car and headed to JFK.

"I wish you would have told us earlier, Kittykat," Paul said, changing lanes and laying a heavy hand on the horn. "One of us could have gone with you. We don't need you upset and on your own. Justin is beside himself and super pissed off that I didn't see this coming. So am I. I'm powerless in all of this."

"This isn't about you being the patriarch of our group. It's about me doing what I need to do and being there for him." When she'd needed Marko, he was there. A shoulder to lean on, a hand to hold, he'd been there. She wasn't going to run or hide from him. "If I could make what he's going through a little more bearable for him, I will. I have a lot to offer."

"It's about time you realized that." Her oldest friend took her hand in his and squeezed it tight. "You've always had a lot to offer, and you did. You just didn't see the value of it before."

Hoping she offered enough to make a difference, she read Marko's last text and pointed out the word need. "It's really my turn."

"It is," he agreed. "You can do this." When they pulled up at the departure area, Paul turned on the hazard lights and turned off the ignition. He placed eight hundred-dollar bills in her hand. "This is all the ATM allowed me to withdraw for the day. Justin has your account information, so we'll transfer funds first thing in the morning. Let me know if you need anything else."

"This is more than enough. Thank you." She folded the cash into her wallet, checked for her passport, and stepped from the car feeling truly lucky to have such friends. When Paul came around and adjusted the wrap on her shoulders, she walked into the comfort of their two-decade-long friendship and wrapped her arms around him. "I'll admit that my idea of financial success has stood in the way of me doing what was right, but having generous and rich friends does make it easier to deal with." She pinched his muscled abs and kissed his cheek. "Thank you. I promise to pay every penny back as soon as possible."

"Stop thanking me for the money. Money doesn't mean anything to me, and you know it. We're on this ride together, Kittykat. You'd hold my hand if I needed you." He swatted her backside, and turned her toward the doors. "Go find your man."

Money really didn't mean anything. Some people had more than others, but it didn't make the person. She glanced over her shoulder and waved good-bye. "Check your email for the feature."

"Forget it," he called. "I'm not publishing it."

"It's done. You can use the pictures I'll attach if you like."

Sitting at the gate, she repeatedly checked both phones for text messages. Each time she called Marko, she reached his voicemail. As they announced the flight to board she typed out a text.

I love you, bello. Everything will be okay.

During the flight, she read through the feature and attached her pictures. The caption on one of Marko standing at by the window read: *Paris may be the perfect place for romance, but the perfect place for love is anywhere with your person. This is my person, the man who holds my heart and future, my Marko.*

Owning what lived in her heart, she hit send and lowered the cover of the laptop.

"I brought two this time," Antoine said, handing Marko the new cell phone he'd requested. "Try not to slam these into the wall."

"I don't use them in here." Marko raised his head from his hands and acknowledged his friend. He glanced at the unrecognizable woman lying in the bed, checking the monitors to make sure the lines moved and the images pulsed. "The signals interfere with the machinery. I have them powered off and only turn them on when I leave the unit."

"Turn this one on when you exit the building and are across the street," Antoine said, releasing a long breath. He stood before the glass, his shoulders dropping in defeat. "She's so small. So fragile. I wish there was some way I could help."

"You gave her your blood. That helped." Marko walked up to the other man and placed a hand on his shoulder. "I'm forever in your debt."

"There has to be more we can do." Antoine wiped a large hand down his worried face. "Can I give more blood?"

"No. Thankfully, she doesn't require more transfusions. The doctors said her levels are stable. She's responded to the therapy and the edema has gone down. They're going to wake her from the coma today." Marko had to believe she would be okay. She was too good for this, too young, too beautiful. Their world would crumble if she didn't wake up. Martine was a fighter. She would open her eyes and bring sunshine to the world.

"What time?" Antoine asked, stuffing his hands in his pockets.

"The doctors are checking on her in the morning. They'll let us know when around eight." Time was moving too slowly. Too many things they couldn't determine. For the first time in his life, Marko was at the mercy of someone else's expertise. It grated on his nerves. "Maynard doesn't know which way to turn. He must focus on Martine, but my aunt Laurel is having a very difficult time dealing with the uncertainty. Cecile has been good to her, holding her hand and reassuring her that Martine will make it."

"But you are the one who has not left the hospital," Antoine insisted. "You look like shit, my friend. Go home, take a shower, and get some sleep. You have seven hours before the doctors come to speak with you."

"I can't leave her alone," he said, pushing his fingers through his hair. He sat on the metal chair and returned his head into his hands. "If she wakes up on her own, she'll be terrified. She can't be alone."

"I'll stay with her. I won't leave that sweet angel alone."

"Thank you, but I can't go until I know she's awake. I can't." Marko was tired. Fighting to remain calm, he managed a few minutes of sleep during each night, but he hadn't left the hospital once. Antoine had insisted on visiting every day, multiple times a day to be exact. He'd been the first one to offer blood. The man was as good as his word. He wouldn't leave Martine alone.

Marko stood and walked back to the window. "On second thought, I'll take you up on your offer to stay, but only for a few minutes. I want to try and reach Kathryn. I need to hear her voice."

"You could use one of her big smiles and soft hugs right about now—she'd . . . Why did you send her away?" Antoine asked, his brows knitting in confusion.

She'd accepted him, accepted them. She was about to meet his family, and he'd spent time after his meeting buying her a ring. "I've waited a long time to make her mine. I was sure that things had finally come together for us." But just like the first time he had been about to offer her a ring, a fucking asshole had wreaked havoc on their lives.

"Her father was killed by a drunk driver. It tore her apart to see him hooked up to those machines." Marko pointed through the glass. Kat had to make the decision to take her dad off life support. All he could do was hold her shattered heart and accept her wish for time to heal. "I won't make her relive that time in her life."

"I understand," Antoine agreed. "Go. I'm here. I won't let anything happen to Martine." He handed him a paper bag. "Brought you a shirt from your place. Take a minute and wash up in the lavatory. You're scaring the family looking like that."

Marko nodded in agreement. He looked really bad. A fresh shirt was greatly welcomed. "Thank you."

"There is an all-night café across the street. Order something to eat and drink, and call your woman from there. The connection will be normal."

"Normal," Marko repeated, shaking his head and turning to go. "I'll be back in ten minutes."

He walked past the unit's doors and dialed Kat.

Chapter Twenty-Six

Relief flooded over Kat when she saw Antoine's large frame behind the counter at the *boulangerie*. He offered a cookie to a toddler and wrapped a baguette for the young woman accompanying the little boy. Kat tossed too much cash at the driver, thanked him, and bounded out of the taxi and into the bakery.

"I'm so happy you're still here," she called, pushing on the glass door and storming into the fragrant shop. Practically hurdling over the young boy, Kat walked around the counter and didn't give a shit about observing local tradition. She wrapped her arms around the big man and buried her face in his chest.

"Kathryn, everything will be okay," Antoine assured, cupping the back of her head and holding her close. "Welcome home, *ma chère*."

"Marko isn't answering his phone. All calls go directly to voice-mail. I tried texting when we landed, but he hasn't even read it yet."

"Shhh, *chère*. He is all right. Look at me." He cupped her face and lifted her chin. "You are the best medicine for him—"

"Is he hurt?" Sobs clogged her throat and tears marked her cheeks.

"*Non*." Antoine shook his head, a cautious look in his eyes. "Not physically. However, his cousin Martine has been hurt. He has been with her since Saturday."

"Take me to them." Her voice was demanding. She regretted her abrupt tone, lowered her gaze, and apologized for being rude. "I'm sorry, Antoine. Please. I need to be with him. You must take me to him immediately. If Martine is hurt, Marko is hurting. He must be devastated. He loves her."

"I know," Antoine agreed, removing his apron and hanging it on a peg. He spoke to the counter girl, gave her permission to close early, then tossed her a set of keys and asked for her to lock up behind them. "*Allons-y, Kathryn*," he said, much to her relief. "Martine is at the American Hospital of Paris. Her condition is critical, but she has the country's best doctors working on her. Marko has not left the hospital, other than for ten minutes last night when he called you." Antoine spoke in a low and deliberately calming voice.

There was more to it and she knew it. Antoine was sharing information with extreme caution, and Kat was hesitant to press him further, but she needed the facts. "What is wrong with Martine?"

He drew air between his teeth, and his fingers gripped the steering wheel so hard, the tips went white. His Adam's apple bobbed, and his eyes gleamed with moisture. Tension sucked the oxygen from the air. She wanted to cover her ears and drown out all the bad in the world. Blinking back more tears, she closed her hands into determined fists, digging her fingernails into her palms.

"Please, Antoine. I must know what is happening. Please."

Nodding, he raised his left hand to his eye and made to rub the corner. "Martine was in a very bad accident. As I said, her condition is critical. She is a strong girl, and she is fighting hard. The injuries are severe."

A sense of déjà vu washed over Kat. Her skin prickled with remembrance. Her eyes stung and her vision blurred, but she swallowed hard and cleared her throat. "What kind of injuries?"

"She has numerous broken bones and fractures. Her liver was damaged, and she lost a lot of blood. A long surgery stopped the internal bleeding. She's had five blood transfusions so far. Her face is so bruised and swollen you can't recognize her. *Martine, une jolie petite ange, est tellement mal.*"

"Her brain?" Kat asked in a tiny whisper.

"Cerebral edema," he confirmed solemnly. "The doctors placed her in an induced coma—"

"No," she cried, covering her face and shaking her head. Her face burned and her chest ached. Not again. This couldn't happen to Martine. "No, no, no."

Antoine pulled the car to the side of the road. Engaging the hand brake, he rubbed a soothing hand over her shaking shoulders and down her spine as she sobbed. "This is not your papa, *ma chère*. Martine is improving. The little angel has responded well to the therapy. The doctors are gathering at this very moment and considering waking her."

"When?" She looked up at him, biting her lip and praying.

"It could be at any time. The whole family is there. No one has called yet."

She pressed a palm to her chest and took a deep breath. "Just give me two minutes to compose myself. I need to be there for Marko. He's been exposed to such trauma before, and seeing his cousin like this must be torture for him. He was there when my daddy passed. He saw it all."

"That is why he wanted to protect you from this tragedy," Antoine explained.

"I don't want his protection. I want to support him. To let him know I'm there for him, no matter what." She lifted her chin and dried her tears. Rummaging in her bag, she retrieved her computer and stowed it under the seat, pulling the floor mat over it. She also pulled out eye drops and a pack of gum. "Two minutes," she repeated, leaning her head back and holding the drops over her eyes.

The crisp scent of antiseptic turned her stomach, but Kat squared her shoulders walked down the white corridor toward a family gathered at the end. She saw him before he spotted her, and her heart ached for the man who turned from shaking the doctor's hand to wrapping his arms around the weeping family huddled beside him. He was nodding, speaking to them, and holding the family together. The support he offered was visible.

Marko looked up and met her gaze. Alarm flashed in his eyes. Shaking his head, he said something to the two older men and walked to meet her before she could make it to the end of the corridor.

Dark circles rimmed eyes that appeared sunken. Stress stretched over his forehead and marked his jaw. His hair was messed and his overall disheveled appearance attested to his lack of sleep. Reaching them, he pulled Kat into his arms and held her tight. Placing a kiss on the side of her head, he turned to Antoine. "Why did you bring her here?"

"Because I asked him to," Kat answered, spreading her fingers over the side of his face and turning him to look at her. "I'm here now." She leaned up and kissed his cheek. Bringing her mouth to his ear, she whispered, for only him to hear, "Lean on me, my love. Trust me, Marko."

He inhaled and his chest rose against her, filling her with encouragement and reassurance. Cupping her face, he sealed his mouth to hers, and she shared her strength and love with ardor and dedication. Color tinged his pale features, and she smiled up at him as he stared at her as if she were a ghost. "*Je t'aime, bella.*"

"I love you, too, *bello.*"

"How is Martine?" Antoine asked, his stance anxious.

"They weaned her off the ventilator and medicines this morning. She did very well. They removed the tube, and she's been breathing on her own since noon. They stopped the coma-inducing medication, too. She has not woken up yet, but the doctor I just spoke with is confident she will be awake soon. His team has been observing Martine all day. Her mother and father are with her now." He looked back over his shoulder, then took Kat's hand. "Come. We need to be with the family."

Determined to be his rock, she laced her fingers in his and pressed her shoulder along his arm. Marko leaned on her. She released a long breath.

An elegantly dressed woman wiped a handkerchief across her cheeks and watched them approach. She stretched her arms out to Kat, and when she walked into them, the woman kissed her lovingly on both cheeks.

"I am Angelique and this is Marcel." She reached for the hand of a very handsome gentleman, a vision of what she imagined Marko would look like in the future, with more salt than pepper hair. She placed Kat's hand in Marcel's big palm. Kissing her gently on the cheek, he closed his fingers around her hand and pulled it to his heart. "This is not how we wanted to meet you, my dear girl, but family comes together in good and bad. I welcome you with all my love."

"Thank you, madame—

"*Non. Je suis maman.*" She held up a dainty hand and tossed the objection to the air, making it a fact.

Kat glanced at Marko, and he was actually smiling, with more color in his handsome face than before. Her heart swelled with love, and in spite of the circumstances, she met his smile.

"*Oui. Maman,*" Kat agreed.

"*Et je suis papa*," Marcel said, gathering her in an embrace and kissing the top of her head. "*Merci, mon fils.*" He thanked his son. "I have always wanted a daughter."

"Maman is right. This is not the setting I would have chosen to introduce Kathryn, but I am very glad she came." Marko placed his hands on her shoulders, and she reached up and took one in her hand. No matter how loved and welcomed she felt, this moment wasn't about her and she couldn't relax yet. It was time for her to help her man with this heavy load. She was there to offer him the support he needed.

"From what I've heard, Martine is a fighter. She will surprise everyone with how fast she gets well." Kat glanced at Antoine, who was standing alone and looking through the window. His shoulders were tense and his jaw hard. He didn't take his eyes off the sleeping woman.

"With Kathryn here, Martine will wake twice as fast. That meddling little cousin of mine wouldn't want to miss any of the action," Marko added, gaining a soft laugh from his mother and father.

"*C'est vrai,*" his mom said.

"Very true," his dad repeated.

The family filtered in and out of Martine's room, taking turns speaking to her. When Marko had gone in to Martine, Kat asked Antoine if he wanted to go with her to bring back some coffee and juice. He shook his head and lowered to whisper in her ear. "I'm sorry, Kathryn. I want to be here when she wakes up."

"I understand," she replied, giving him a knowing smile, then turned to the family. "I'm going downstairs to get some drinks. Any special requests?"

"We will go together, my child," Marcel insisted, collecting everyone's order and offering her his arm. As they walked down the long corridor, he covered her hand and curled it over his forearm. "We will have a proper celebration for you and Marko when Martine is well. The whole family together."

Marko rested his elbows on his knees, watching for his father to return with Kat. When he saw the red wrap at the end of the hall, he exhaled in relief. He needed to know she was okay and near. He didn't know how, but his strong and beautiful Kat had come to this place, a place he knew she hated with a passion, for him. He was so tired, so worried, and he couldn't do anything to make things better.

Wake up, Martine. I have someone for you to meet, you noisy little brat. Wake up, he thought, massaging his fingers over his forehead.

The family was sitting on the Spartan metal chairs, sipping their drinks and sharing colorful stories of Martine's spunk, and Antoine sat guard at her bedside. Then, suddenly, Martine opened her eyes.

Chapter Twenty-Seven

The elevator stopped and Kat followed Marko to the bedroom. The toll of the last few days was evident in his stride, but he held his shoulders and chin high in a gallant display of strength. She ached to tell him that he could lean on her, let her help, but words appeared so insignificant in the big scheme of things.

The T-shirt she'd worn while lazing around on Saturday morning was still lying on the chair, and everything else also seemed exactly the same.

"I gave the housekeeper the week off," Marko said, taking her coat and tossing it over the T-shirt. Considering how meticulous he was in all aspects of his life, his coat landing atop hers surprised her. She walked up to Marko, who was sitting on the ottoman removing his shoes. "I wanted to keep everything like it was last weekend—when you were here."

"When was the last time you were home?" Kat asked. She instinctively knew his answer, but logic said it couldn't be.

"With you," he replied. "I couldn't leave Martine alone until I knew she would make it." His shoulders fell a little, and suddenly the confident and self-assured man looked exhausted. The stress carved on his face was easy to read. She wanted to wipe it away and start over. To see the proud fire in his eyes and the determined set of his mouth. Instead, he sat before her tired and vulnerable, exposed to the hurt and trauma he'd had to pull his family through. And he had. Marko had been a pillar of reason and strength for the family, consulting with the doctors, relaying the family's wishes, and doing everything in his power to see his cousin recover.

Without fail, Marko did what was needed, regardless of the personal cost.

Reaching down, she cupped his face and brushed her lips over his mouth. "I wish I could wave a magic wand and make everything okay. I want to press rewind and go back to Friday, then start all over again so we could stop Martine from coming to Paris."

"No one could have stopped Martine from doing what she wanted. Ever. She insisted on visiting. She wanted to meet me at the café on Saturday before you arrived so she could pump me for information. We had a rendezvous for three o'clock. Her curiosity was piqued. She wanted to know every detail about our personal life and where the relationship was going. She wanted to meet you before the rest of the family." He shook his head, smiling and caressing the side of her thigh. "As for Friday, it was perfect. Friday, you arrived. I would never change that."

"Friday was amazing—even if you orchestrated the whole event," she admitted.

"Sue me," he said, echoing their friends' words as a smile cracked his features. "The truth is, I'd planned to come to you earlier, but the work situation kept spiraling out of control. The timeline was altered, and I needed to make a decision earlier than anticipated. I wanted to make that decision with you. I want my future with *you*."

His words melted her heart. She smoothed her fingers over his temple and through his hair, needing to show him that their relationship was a two-way street. "I also want my future with you. But I don't ever want you to send me away like that again."

"I had to," he said, standing and turning his back to her. He shucked off his shirt and unbuckled his belt. "The last thing I wanted was you with me."

"Marko," she gasped, hurt pulsing inside her. He didn't want her when he needed her. He'd sent her away, like a disposable inconvenience.

"You don't understand," he insisted, jamming his fingers through his hair and staring at her with a desperate look. "It was all happening again. The same exact thing. A drunk driver. Martine's life hanging by a thread. She was rushed into surgery to stop the internal bleeding. We all gave blood, but that wasn't enough. Her brain kept swelling, and they had to place her in a coma. She was on life support, just like your dad."

Her legs went limp, but she managed to drop to the ottoman. She hid her face in her hands, and struggled to take in air.

"That's right. A fucking machine needed to breathe for her," he rasped, resurrecting images of her father being hooked up to machines and tubes she'd long buried. Her father had not woken up. They'd taken him off life support and the monitors had stopped.

"You needed me," she said in a strained voice, no longer the girl who had fallen apart after the last beep had sounded. She stood and reached for him, placing a hand on his forearm. "I should have been with you."

"I couldn't let you relive the painful memories of your father's death. And I couldn't relive the pain of you running from me."

She'd done exactly that, and because of her past, he didn't trust her.

"You lost your father. Your mom lost her husband. The world lost a good man too early." Marko pulled away, shutting his eyes and closing her out. "*I lost you*. I can't lose you again. Instead of giving you the opportunity to run, I sent you away with the intention of coming for you when it was over. You shouldn't have come back. But now you're here. I'm not letting you run again."

He turned and walked toward the en suite bathroom, leaving her chilled and angry. "This isn't going to work if you don't trust me," she called to his back. "You can't protect me from living life."

"It's not you I don't trust," he answered, not looking back.

Fuck! She was so damn stupid. He needed her and all she did was whine about her needs. That strong and beautiful man had chinks in his armor.

He turned on the shower and the mirrors steamed. Kat entered the room and watched as Marko stepped into the oversized glass shower. He rested his chin on his chest, and rubbed the back of his neck as the water beat down on it. He stood there, not moving, not washing, just standing.

Shedding her clothes, she stepped in behind him and ran her hands over his back. "I'm not running."

His shoulders rose as he took a deep breath, and she wrapped her arms around his chest and pressed her cheek to his wet skin. "I need you as much as you need me. You'll never send me away again, and I'll never run again. I'm done running, *bello*."

He turned in silent acknowledgement and cupped her face. His dark gaze studied her face as desire built between them. His hard chest heaved against her soft breasts, and he pressed his erection against her belly. "Those are my favorite words, ever."

"Okay," she cooed, stretching around him and reaching for the shower gel. "Let me care for you."

She squeezed the soap onto a sponge and he closed his eyes. She caressed over his shoulders and down his chest, feeling the tension ebb from his muscles with each lathered touch of her fingertips on the edge of the sponge. Taking her time, she washed every inch of his gorgeous body, and dropped lingering kisses on the sculpted perfection.

The flavor of her man and the way his skin prickled beneath her lips had her yearning to claim him as hers immediately. But the feel of his fingers sinking into her flesh and the roll of the guttural groans from his chest steeled her resolve to make the moment last. She didn't want the feelings to end.

Prolonging the agony, her aching nipples brushed over his chest as she stretched up and washed his hair. Working the shampoo into a sudsy crown, she massaged his scalp and kissed the lids of his closed eyes. Pleasure spread through her while Marko simply stood and accepted what she offered. He didn't try to control her movements, didn't alter her pace, just waited for her to act.

She eventually guided his head back and swept the suds away from his forehead and down his back. A smile eased the stress lines on his face. Running a finger over the stubble on his jaw, she smiled back. She smoothed down the corded lines over the side of his neck and settled a kiss above his collarbone. Trailing her tongue to his chest, she made small circles around one nipple and licked at the flat, dark sphere until it pebbled and she sucked it into her mouth.

Relishing the bumps beneath her fingertips, she moved her mouth to the other nipple and nipped at the edges until she burned with the need to taste all of him. She lapped at the water sluicing over his chest and followed the rivulets that flowed into the dark trail of hair below his belly button.

"You're killing me," he rasped.

"I need you," she replied, her giving turning into possession.

She knelt between his legs, suckling gently along the heavy shaft. With one hand, she cupped his balls and stroked her thumb over the base of his erection. With the other, she pumped the smooth hardness of his length, following her grip with her lips until she licked at the intoxicating drop at the very tip.

Fitting her lips around the erect cock, she circled her tongue over the smooth head and felt, swelling within her chest, the pang of desire to take everything he had to give her, to have him lose control and take his pleasure in her mouth like he never had before. She sucked hard, stealing his ability to insist on a shared release as he had last time. The power of staking her claim on him rushed over her, burning in her body and pulsing between her legs.

Alternating between stroking and licking up his shaft, she rose to the right height to take him further into her mouth. Relaxing her lips, she curled her hands around his hips and buried her fingers in the taut flesh of his ass. She pulled and sucked him deep, moaning in pleasure as he stroked the back of her throat.

Marko's fingers tangled in her hair. He cupped the back of her head and thrust into her mouth, sliding over her tongue, taking her mouth like nothing else mattered. "Fuck, Kat. I can't. I can't fight it. I'm going to come."

Triumph thrummed through her. She increased the pressure of her lips and squeezed his ass. His cock swelled and jerked, spilling his release down her throat as she swallowed furiously to take every drop. He was hers. All of him. Claimed and possessed. Marko was hers. Everything he had to offer.

He released his hold on her hair and leaned a hand on the wall. His other hand cupped her faced and tilted it up. He didn't speak, but she saw everything he had to say.

She licked his taste from her lips, then placed a soft kiss on the side of his groin. "I love you," she breathed. "Thank you."

He groaned and somehow managed to pull her up and against his body. He lifted her off her feet and wrapped her legs around his waist. Turning off the water, he grabbed a towel and draped it over her curved back. He dried them off as much as possible, considering she kept her face nestled in the crook of his neck and their wet bodies remained linked the whole time, and then he carried her to bed.

Placing her gently on the mattress, he detached himself from her grasp, and swept her wet hair off her face. Tapping the towel on her front, he smiled down at her. "I lost control in there."

"I know," she acknowledged impishly. "I loved it."

He laughed and brushed his mouth over her lips. "I love you."

Sweeping the towel quickly over his torso, he dropped it on the floor and climbed into bed beside her. She turned her back to him and fit her body against his.

He gathered her against his chest and closed his lips on her neck in a long, wet kiss. With an arm across her breast and a hand between the juncture of her legs, he slid two fingers between her swollen folds and plunged them into her pulsing core. He pressed his palm tight against her and rubbed her clit.

"I'm not done yet," he breathed against her ear.

Chapter Twenty-Eight

Marko woke and reached for Kat. She wasn't in bed, but the delicious smell of bacon drifting up from the kitchen announced her location. He pulled on a pair of jeans and went to find her.

There she was, standing by the sink, wearing a pair of his boxer shorts, dark dress socks, and a well-worn sweater. Grinning, he lowered himself onto a bar stool and shook his head. He cleared his throat to let her know he was there. She turned and gave him a big smile, immediately popping a small piece of crispy bacon between his lips.

"You're so beautiful in the morning," he said, between chewing and pulling her into his arms for a kiss. "The best-looking breakfast cook I've ever seen." He didn't bother to hide his appreciation as his gaze traveled down, then up, her body. "And to think, you're all mine."

"All yours," she agreed, returning his kiss and folding her body into his lap. "Did you sleep well?"

"Very well," he replied, searching for a nonexistent clock. "What time is it?"

"It's almost noon." A conspiratorial smile bloomed on her face, and she glanced at the phones on the counter. "Your papa called the house around nine o'clock. Good thing I had brought the handset downstairs with me to call Antoine for breakfast fixings, because you slept right through that ring. You needed your sleep. It was your papa who suggested I also find your cell phone and bring that down here, too."

"What did Papa say?" Marko had slept all morning. Irresponsible. What if he was needed at the hospital? How could he let his guard down like that? "How is Martine?"

"She's doing well. She spoke with her mom and dad this morning for fifteen minutes, without needing a break. Cecile fed her a few spoonfuls of custard. Antoine said he could see her 'pretty eyes' today." Kat hooked her fingers into quotation signs in the air and raised her finely shaped brows in amusement. "Your papa said she's sleeping now. We spoke ten minutes ago."

Relieved, he squeezed Kat's waist and placed a kiss on her neck. He'd slept and the world hadn't gone to pieces. As a matter of fact, the world was looking and smelling pretty good. He wanted this forever. Every morning waking up to her in his life, hopefully wearing his clothes, her cheeks wonderfully pink from a night of lovemaking, and sweet words from her lips.

"Make it official, *bella*," he said, looking into her eyes.

She traced his jaw and kissed his lips. "Make what official?"

"Marry me," he said, covering her hand with his and bringing it to his heart. "Be mine and make me yours, officially."

Her breath caught and her cheeks flushed. "Where will we live? How are we going to make it work?"

"Together. We'll make it work together," he insisted. "We'll figure out the logistics later. We could live in New York or we could live here. I don't care where or how, as long as we're together. Marry me, *bella*."

"Yes," she breathed. "Yes." She crushed her lips to his and cried in delight.

Kat's heart overflowed with love, more love than she'd known existed.

He raised her hand to his mouth, and placed a kiss in the center. "At last. I keep you forever."

"You're stuck with me," she said, laughter bubbling in her voice. "I'm yours and you're mine. We'll figure the rest out together."

"I can't wait," he breathed, and claimed her mouth.

He was carrying her to bed when the phone rang. He stopped midstride and looked at her.

"Go get it," she said, secretly hoping it was her mom. "We have forever."

He placed her on her feet and backtracked to the kitchen. Approaching the counter, he called to her to come back. "It's your phone, sweetheart. Paul's calling."

"Pick it up," she said, skipping across the living room.

By the time Kat joined him, he had given Paul a quick synopsis and had already told him that his cousin was out of danger. He held the phone away from his ear, so she could she hear Paul's explanation about how he had searched Paris accident reports and used news connections to learn of what had happened. "Happy to hear she's awake and doing better, Marko. I'm sorry we weren't there for you. We didn't know, or we would have come back with Kat."

"I appreciate it," Marko replied. "Thank you so much. We were about to leave for the hospital in a few minutes, but became a little sidetracked. We have more good   "

Kat placed a finger across his lips, guessing that he was going to share the news of their engagement. *Moms and dad, first*, she mouthed silently.

"Hold on, Paul. Here's Kat. She's pining for the phone." Marko handed her the phone, and snaked his arms around her waist. She settled against him, feeling complete.

"Hello?"

"You're still pining for me, Kittykat?"

"Always, Paul, always," she said, shimmying seductively up Marko's body and tangling her fingers in the hair at his nape. "I heard Marko fill you in on Martine's condition. Isn't it wonderful that she woke up and is making remarkable strides?"

"Yes, it is." Paul paused, a note of hesitation in his breathing. He seemed to be choosing his next words carefully. "Kathryn, are you doing okay? Do you need me to come over?"

"No. I'm fine, my friend," she said in a soft voice. "Thank you."

Paul cared. When he'd looked into the accident reports, he had understood the similarities between her dad's accident and Martine's. Her friend had seen what she'd gone through and who she'd become afterward. Paul was rightfully concerned. Most importantly, he really cared. She was blessed to have such good friends.

"Are you sure, Kittykat? Justin and I can take the afternoon flight and be there by morning. We know this is hard for you."

"She's stronger than we think," Marko interjected. "Kat has been my rock since she walked into the hospital. She's good, Paul. She really is."

Like a beautiful rose, Kat's confidence bloomed in her chest. Marko had referred to her as his rock. He trusted her. "Thank you for being a good friend."

"That's my job," Paul said, his relief audible. "And now that we've established that our Kathryn is okay and that you're together, do you want some more good news?"

Perplexed, Kat and Marko looked at each other. A peculiar angst twisted in her stomach and she nervously closed her fingers on Marko's arm.

"Sure. Go on," Marko said.

"We're listening," Kat added.

"The Valentine's feature is yours, Kittykat. Good job. You've got your byline."

Kat squealed with glee. She jumped in the air and threw her hands over her head. Dancing around the room, she swung her arms in the air and tossed her hair around like a mad woman.

Marko laughed. "She's dancing," he explained to Paul. "She's real happy."

"And you, my friend, are one lucky bastard."

"I know it," Marko agreed, and let their friend go. He wrapped his arms around the waist of the still-dancing Kat and twirled her off her feet. "Congratulations, *bella.* I knew you could do it. You could do anything you set your mind to."

She covered her face with her hands and basked in pure bliss.

Passing on breakfast, they celebrated the happy day by making love in the shower—to save time. Dressed and ready to share their news with the family, they walked hand in hand downstairs and into Antoine's for croissants. He made them coffees, as well, and then handed her a little box with almond cookies for the family.

Jean-Luc stood at the curb. "Monsieur Renard." He tipped his hat. "Bonjour, Mademoiselle Taylor."

"Seriously, Jean-Luc?" She crossed her arms over her chest and tapped her toe, fixing him with a steely look. "I thought we settled this last time."

The driver fidgeted and glanced at Marko, whose smirk was easy to notice. He was more than enjoying her display of annoyance. Marko cocked his head and raised his hands in surrender.

Jean-Luc stepped forward and wrapped his arms around a conquering Kat. "*Bonjour, Kathryn.*"

"Better," she said, going up on her toes and planting a loud kiss on his cheek.

Once in the car, she folded her hands in her lap and turned to Marko. "Do you think your parents will approve?"

"Of us?" He nodded emphatically. "Absolutely. They already love you." Then he covered her hand with his. "They won't be happy about me going to New York, but they'll get used to it. They'll just need to make more trips across the Atlantic."

"Marko, you're not coming to New York," she said, confused by his assumption. She hadn't asked him to move to New York. He had responsibilities and duties only he could see to, and she knew it. "It isn't logical."

He tightened his hold on her hand, but didn't say a word.

"I spoke with your papa three times this morning. Once, when he told me to get your cell phone out of the bedroom and let you sleep. The second time about everything Martine needs to go through during recovery." She looked past the window and tried to hide her sadness. "And the last time was right before you came downstairs."

"I don't get it. Papa speaks to you for hours, but I can't even get reception in the hospital."

"He wasn't at the hospital," Kat said. "He called when he stepped out to clear his head." *And to share the burden with someone he didn't need to be strong for*, she thought. Marko and his dad had so much in common. They took care of the family. Made the decisions. Shouldered the responsibilities.

"For the long conversation, he was at the café across the street."

"It figures," Marko grumbled. "I didn't know about the café until two nights ago. Well, at least he managed to find a way to speak with you."

She wasn't sure it was her place to share what his papa had told her, but Marko needed to know. He couldn't be surprised with something so important. Worrying her lower lip, she hoped his father hadn't discussed the family's situation in confidence.

"Marko, I know it's difficult to think of what lies ahead for your cousin, but we can't leave. With Martine facing such a long recovery, they need you. Your papa is planning on asking you to take the reigns at the vineyard." She placed her free hand over his, and rubbed her thumb over his knuckles. "At least for the time being, we need to stay between Paris and Provence. I'll speak with Paul about making accommodations for an overseas writer. With the right slant, I can write from anywhere. For now, you need to be here. We need to be here."

"You said we. We." He curved his palm at her nape and kissed her. "I love you, Kathryn Taylor. I love you so much."

With the bakery box hanging from one hand and Marko swinging the other, Kat walked into the arms of his *maman* for a consuming hug and a flurry of kisses. "*Bonjour, mes chers. Comment allez-vous?*"

"We are well," Marko answered, swooping in and placing more kisses on his mother's cheeks. "How is our girl?"

"Beautiful." The matriarch's face beamed with delight and her eyes twinkled with joy. "Marceau and Maynard have seen to all the details, and the doctor is preparing Martine to be moved to a new room—one where her brothers will be allowed to visit."

"*Pardon,*" Marko said, giving his mother another kiss and striding toward his father and uncle, creating a tight testosterone huddle as they discussed the new development.

"You are glowing, *ma chère.*" Angelique took Kat's hand and pulled her toward the corner of the waiting room. "You have good news to share?"

Unaccustomed to the keen observation and forwardness, Kat inhaled sharply. She and Marko had discussed how they were going to announce their news, and it wasn't at the hospital. With her mom on FaceTime, they intended to tell all three parents—four, including Ralph—at the same time. Heat infused her cheeks and she nodded, incapable of dismissing the woman. "We do. Good things have been happening all day."

"*Oui?*" Angelique held Kat's hands in her lap and leaned forward. "Of course. These things happen in threes. I am listening, *ma chère.*"

Kat giggled and rubbed Angelique's hand. "Well, there is much to tell. Marko would like to visit with Martine, and then perhaps you and his papa will join us across the street for the news."

"*Bien.* I will not ruin the surprise for Marcel." She pinched her thumb and finger at her lips, twisted them, and threw away the symbolic key.

"I can't . . . well, actually, I can, just a little," Kat whispered conspiratorially, leaning closer to the other woman. "Do you remember the research that brought me to Paris?"

"*Oui, oui,*" Angelique said, rolling her hand for Kat to continue. "It was about finding love in Paris."

"Well, my boss called and informed us the piece will be published in the Valentine's Day edition of the magazine." Confident the news would satisfy Angelique in the interim, Kat braced for the onslaught of congratulations. They didn't come.

"I expected that, Kathryn. That is very nice. Now, tell me the real news," Angelique prompted. "How did my son propose? Where?"

Stunned, Kat withdrew her hands, sat pin straight, and glanced nervously at Marko. Her gaze must have burned a hole in his back, because he glanced at her and immediately came to her side.

"Why do you women always find a way to sabotage my schedule and plans?" Marko asked, lovingly cupping his mother's face and shaking his head in amusement.

"Because you take too long," his mother replied. "Now tell me everything."

The threesome's laughter drew the remainder of the family to their circle, and Marko announced that Kat had agreed to marry him.

This time, there was an absolute onslaught of congratulations and cheers. His mother spoke of a spring wedding at the château, and the men reviewed a mental list of trusted contractors that needed to be contacted to start work immediately on a proper home.

"Mademoiselle Renard is ready for you," a nurse said, interrupting the celebration. She indicated for Kat to follow.

"At least there is still one woman who adheres to my schedule," Marko joked, taking Kat's hand and leading her to his cousin's room. He pushed on the door and stepped next to Martine's bed. "Perfect timing, *chérie.*"

Marko entered the code into the keypad and fit his gloves in his coat pocket. His fingers skimmed over the box he'd placed there for safekeeping. He laughed aloud, realizing he'd skipped tradition and gone straight for what his heart wanted. Her. The ring was an after-thought. And to think he'd stressed over the right diamond and proper setting, when he already had the most valuable jewel in the world.

"What's so funny?" Kat asked, walking into the foyer.

"I am," he said, chuckling and pulling her back toward the eleva-tor. "Indulge me with a quick ride to the rooftop. Please."

Wide eyed, she obliged his request. He knew he must have looked like a lunatic, hurrying up the iron staircase, but he wanted to add a little romance to his proposal.

"This is my favorite spot in Paris," she breathed, intertwining her fingers in his.

"I hoped you'd say that. This is your view." He brought their hands to his chest and lowered to his knee. "I never considered a fu-ture without you, *bella*. By now, you must know I only let you go in order to give you the space you said you needed to accept me. I al-ways planned to come for you."

"Always?" The wind swept her hair off her pretty face and her cheeks flushed.

"Always," he repeated. "The plan was to seduce you with the ro-mantic allure of Paris and my wonderful charm, then drag you back into my life. What I didn't plan on was realizing that I'd follow you anywhere. You are my life. I may have chosen and refurbished this house so Paris could win your heart, but, sweetheart, Paris is no longer a player. I want you and only you."

"You have me, Marko." She tugged on his hand and tried to make him stand. "I told you, you're stuck with me."

"Give me a chance, my impatient woman. From the moment you stepped off that plane, you continuously altered my seduction strategy."

"Are you saying I screwed up your plans?"

"Most definitely." A sense of pure delight flashed through his body. Only Kat could make him so eager that he'd do things out of order, and that was something extra he loved about her. Regardless of how, he was happiest with her.

Pretty white teeth scraped over her lower lip, and she squeezed his hand in understanding.

He reached into his jacket, and with happiness pounding in his heart, he opened the small blue box. "*Bella*, will you wear this ring as a token of my love?"

"Yes," she breathed, then her gaze settled on the princess-cut diamond ring, her mouth dropped open, and her hands flitted to her chest. "Yes. Oh, Marko. You did have plans."

"I most definitely did, but I much prefer the way things happen with you." He slipped the ring onto her finger and lowered his lips to her knuckles. "*Je t'aime, bella. Je t'aime.*"

Chapter Twenty-Nine

Three weeks later, life had settled into a comfortable routine. With around-the-clock medical supervision, Martine had returned to Provence and was improving rapidly. Kathryn's mother had also arrived, and she and Angelique were planning a dream wedding for May. Ralph and the Renard men claimed to spend their days supervising the laborers at the beautiful house, which sat at the top of the mountain, but in reality they spent their time sampling the potential wedding food and deciding which wine went best with each course.

Marko spent business hours between Château de M's operational headquarters in Provence and the satellite office in Paris. Often Kat would accompany him, her MacBook in tow, and she'd managed to rewrite the ending of her novel. She planned on revisions with a literary agent, and was looking forward to the submission of the finished manuscript to publishers.

Sitting at her desk, in her new office at Château de M's luxurious Paris headquarters, she admired the view of the Eiffel Tower outside her window. As requested, Paul had worked an overseas staff writer into *City Wings'* masthead. He had assigned her a series of articles about the most romantic day trips available to honeymooners in Paris. She was finishing the last paragraph of a piece about the Eurostar train between Paris and London when there was a knock at the door.

"*Ciao, bella.*" Marko strode in, brushing a kiss over her hair and placing a priority-mail package on her desk. "This just arrived from New York. Want to take a break and tear into it?"

"That's an advance copy of the magazine," she cried, excitement racing through her. She fanned her face with her hand and looked at

Marko. "You open it. I'm too nervous." She held out a trembling hand as proof.

"No way, Kat. This is your baby. I'm just along for the ride." Marko chose a bottle from the wine cooler and uncorked what Kat recognized as one of his favorite vintages. He arranged it on the desk with a wine glass on either side. "I'm ready for the celebratory drink."

She took a deep breath and picked up the package. Tearing the perforated seam on the back, she closed her eyes and reached inside. The feel of the cover's glossy paper slipped under her fingers, and she gripped the spine and pulled out the latest edition of *City Wings*. The edition with her very first professional byline.

She exhaled and opened her eyes. On the cover was her picture of Marko, the one she'd taken of him looking out over the city.

The headline read PARIS, with a subtitle beneath: *The perfect place for love.*

A caption scrolled across the bottom in italicized font was a quote from the article. *"Paris may be the perfect place for romance, but the perfect place for love is anywhere with your person. This is my person, the man that holds my heart and future, Marko."* By Kathryn Taylor.

"Paul has it right," Kat breathed, removing the sticky note scribbled with Paul's writing and holding it up for Marko to read.

You're probably reading this over her shoulder you lucky bastard. Take good care of her—or else! P

"You wrote this before you came back to Paris?" Marko turned her in his arms and looked down at her. He held her face in his hands and feathered his thumbs over her cheekbones.

"I did," she admitted.

Her heart filled with love as he lowered his head and brought his mouth to hers. "I guess my charming seduction worked after all."

"I guess it did," she replied, opening to his kiss and losing herself in her man.

Keep reading for a sneak peek at Charlie's take on the perfect place to find love in the next International Affairs romance, *Four Nights at Sea*, coming in December . . .

Chapter One

Charlie debated whether to kiss her boss or kick him in the balls. Paul was off his rocker with this one.

"That's right, ladies. This is your chance. We're going to feature the winning article in the Valentine's issue," Paul said, puffing out his mouth-watering chest and grinning haughtily. "The selected piece will join 'Aphrodisiac Foods from Around the World' and 'How to Say I Love You in Twenty Languages' in *City Wings*' Valentine's edition."

Holy shit! This was it. This was the chance Charlie had been waiting for. It was the break she needed.

"Our readers devour anything and everything having to do with international desires," he continued. "It's a way to escape the daily grind and dream of possibilities. Who would have thought New Yorkers were so romantic?"

Yes, Charlene—Charlie—Stanton wanted her writing to win. She wanted to publish a real feature, with her own byline, in one of the trendiest travel magazines for New Yorkers. No, she didn't want to compete against her friend and roommate, Kathryn Taylor, though. They'd worked together at *City Wings* for over two years, worked well together, and Paul was pitting them against each other. It was so messed up. A disastrous idea.

"Get out there. Do your research," Paul said, circling his hand above his head like he was a Texas rancher. "Lasso someone that makes your body hum, and write about the perfect place to find love, ladies."

"Seriously, Paul? Lasso someone that makes our bodies hum?" Kathryn rolled her eyes, then smacked her forehead with the back of her hand. "Wait. Hold on a minute. Wait . . . wait. I'm seeing a handsome man, in a far off and romantic place like Paris, sweeping me off my feet."

Paris. Kat had to go and mention Paris. Like, why? Did it really matter if Paris was the most romantic place on Earth if neither of them wanted to fly over and find out?

Charlie didn't travel well and wasn't in the mood for a trip to the doctor in order to get a prescription so she could get on a flight. Kathryn had to stop speaking about the perfect place to find love on the other side of the Atlantic. How did one argue the romance of Paris?

Wondering why she'd ever picked up the stupid vape stick when she'd never even smoked, Charlie reached for her pink sixty-dollar vaporizer, and twirled it in her fingers. She answered the silent question in her mind. The thing was a crutch. Something to keep her grounded when thoughts crowded her mind and she wanted to scream at the world. Screaming and throwing temper tantrums was not allowed in the grownup world. Puffing on vanilla-flavored vapor kept her mouth occupied. It kept her from engaging in the unladylike behavior.

"I think we can take a small detour from the publication's travel angle on this," Charlie said. After all, living in New York did have its benefits when it came to an abundance of male prospects for the feature. "Why can't a woman find love in her neighborhood, and *then* sail off into a foreign and exotic land with the love of her life?"

"If it's done properly, I can see it working. However, any featured lovers must take off in the end for a foreign destination." Paul nodded, tapping his fingers on the table as he considered her argument.

Maybe, just maybe, Charlie could convince the sexy tyrant to see things her way? Hope spread in her chest and she leaned forward in her seat.

"There is a pragmatic benefit, too," Paul added. "If we concentrate on finding love locally, more of our readers will relate to the accessibility of that goal and can dream of escaping to a romantic place with their loves."

"Exactly," Charlie said, breathing with relief.

Paul encouraged her to continue, so Charlie barreled on. "The dating scene has evolved so much over the past few years. There's always the chance of meeting someone at a bar or a club. Online sites host a bunch of events in this city. And let's not forget the old-fashioned way of being introduced by common friends."

"Great options." Kathryn looked doubtful. Charlie and Kathryn had exhausted all those options, but neither had found Prince Charming at a neighborhood hangout. Her friend was even more disillusioned than she was. Kat didn't believe that love could last. Yet, she was blabbering about far-off and exotic locations. Maybe because Kat loved to travel and Paul was willing to tag along?

Doubtful. Charlie was screwed. Kat angled for Charlie to write about Paris. What was up with that? Why couldn't they keep it in New York? Considering how many people lived and worked in Manhattan, if you couldn't find love in the Big Apple, you couldn't find it anywhere.

"How are those local options working for you?" Kat asked, snapping her fingers before Charlie's eyes.

Kat continued on her Paris Romance 101 introduction, but if Charlie was honest with herself, she had to admit she was just as disillusioned as her friend with the local love options. She couldn't truly get behind any romance for herself. Sometimes things weren't fair. Like maybe it wasn't about the location. Maybe it was about the fact that Charlie hadn't let any guy in since her divorce. She simply couldn't. It was too difficult to decipher their intentions. Did they like her for her? Or did they like her for her trust fund?

"Not fair. Maybe it's been bad timing for me. I really haven't tried too hard. It's been difficult to trust anyone since my divorce, so maybe I'm the problem and the scene is just fine."

Paul cleared his throat and held up a hand. "You're not the problem, Charlie," he said, covering her hand with his own. "Your asshole ex is. So let's take jerks like him out of the equation for the benefit of this piece."

Whatever. She needed to relax. And just flirt. Like Kat and Paul were doing.

"This is a very incestuous organization," Charlie said, pointing from Paul to Kathryn to the door. "Between you two and the accounting department, a tree house should be the official headquarters of *City Wings*. You're all too tight."

The conference room filled with laughter. Paul and Kathryn had known each other forever, so they had no problem teasing or hitting below the belt. When it came to Charlie, they treated her with kid gloves. As if her divorce had been the end of her life. It hadn't. It had actually opened her eyes to what she really wanted. More than anything, she was so over the money-grubbing scumbags of the world.

Charlie was ready to move on from sitting-duck status. She was doubly ready for a real sex life—something she hadn't had with the ex—but she needed to learn how to compartmentalize physical and emotional.

Shit. Shit. Triple shit. She had to stop thinking so hard. Every-thing she wanted would come, after she had her byline. First, she had to prove herself as a competent and successful writer to her family. It was a matter of professional and personal honor.

"We're looking for love, not sexy interludes," Charlie said, an idea sparking in her mind. "Sexy interludes. But. Fine. Okay. Got it." She placed her palms flat on the table and stood. "If we're really looking for the perfect place to find love, why not a cruise ship? It's textbook romance. What about one designated for singles? Passengers board with an agenda. Just think how much fun we'll have writing about a cruise, Kathryn."

"Nope. There is no 'we.' You can sail away on a Love Boat, and Kathryn will fly off and take her chances in Paris," Paul announced. Kathryn tried to argue he reverse the assignments because she was nervous about running into a past fling, but thankfully he didn't budge. Charlie got the cruise. She sent up a silent prayer of gratitude. She didn't need the added stress of flying if she was going to con-centrate on her feature.

"Good," Paul said. "Time for you ladies to bring out the claws and get down to work. You each have your assignment. Your ex-pense accounts will be adjusted and ready to go by noon. See Justin for the details. Get me your stories by next Wednesday. I'll decide which one gets published in the Valentine's issue."

"On what criteria will the winner be chosen?" Kathryn asked.

"Whatever I want," he said with a devilish grin. "I'm the boss."

Two thousand dollars was more than enough money for round-trip bus or train fare and a reservation on Lovers Sail Tours. Just over a day on the bus, then she'd sail out from Miami on Thursday. Then off to romantic Cozumel. Add the singles on board and she was sure to get enough material for a winning feature.

Charlie reserved an inside cabin on the sixth deck and booked an excursion port. Lovers Sail recommended the "romantic" experiences, and was even willing to pair them up if needed. Partners would be determined once on board.

Clearing her immediate departure from the office with Paul, Charlie went home to pack.

With her expandable carry-on-size suitcase and leather backpack ready by the door, Charlie grabbed her cell and called for dinner. She ordered shrimp pad Thai, red curry beef, and two orders of the crab Rangoon appetizer, hanging up just as the front door crashed open.

"Charlie, I'm home," Kathryn called, her forehead wrinkling as she took in the packed bags.

"Aowww." Charlie pretended to rush and hide the luggage in the closet. Relieving her friend of the large brown bag, she peaked inside and squealed. "Fuck-me boots! Way to go, babe."

"Got you something, too." Her friend dangled a smaller bag, stuffed with tissue paper, and dropped onto the couch. Kathryn patted the cushion at her side.

Charlie sat and clasped her hands between her knees. She watched her roommate pluck tissue after tissue from the bag and fling them extravagantly over her shoulder. Amused with Katherine's stripper imitation, Charlie covered her mouth with her hand and made her eyes extra big with excitement. "Should I blush before or after the big reveal?"

"I'm sure you blushed enough while you were packing," Kathryn said, pulling out a package of batteries and waving them in the air.

Charlie burst out laughing and grabbed the batteries. "Thank you. These are much appreciated and will be put to good use."

"I hope not," Kathryn said, lifting a red lace thong from the bag. "I think you should get more use out of these." Next came the black lace and, lastly, the silk.

"You're too much," Charlie said. "You do know this is a work trip?"

"So what?" Kathryn replied, shaking her head. "A good reporter explores all avenues. *All.* Figured you could wear the granny panties the first night, but you'll need these for the next three."

Kathryn had assumed correctly. She had packed nothing but cotton underwear. Shaking her head, she stood and reached for the new lingerie. "For your information, I don't wear granny panties. They're cotton bikini panties. Practical. Pretty and sexy, too."

"Sure. If you're in high school." Kathryn scrunched her nose. "I take that back. Have you seen what those girls wear?"

"These are adorable," Charlie said. "Thank you." She walked the few steps to her suitcase and folded the new underwear into the outside pocket.

"Wait. One more thing," Kathryn said, dangling a skimpy pink string bikini from her fingers as she walked toward closet. "Pack this."

"No way," Charlie protested, sliding palms over hips. "Have you seen *these*?"

"I certainly have. You have a rockin' bod. You're not covering it with that stuffy one-piece you've had forever." She fit the bikini into the same pocket Charlie had placed the underwear in, then propped one hand on her hip and held out the other. "Give me that fugly suit."

"I like my fugly suit," Charlie replied, laughing and waving a dismissive hand through the air. The intercom buzzed. "Saved by food delivery. If you want dinner, you'd best be nice to me."

"I am nice," Kathryn insisted. "Didn't I just give you a sexy bikini and killer panties? Do I need to deliver a ripped man to your bed?"

"That would work," Charlie answered, plucking a five from her wallet for a tip and sashaying to the door.

Once they'd devoured the appetizers, finished half of each entrée, and switched dinners, Charlie confessed to packing mostly conservative outfits.

"My cruise-appropriate clothing is pre-divorce," she explained. "They're a little traditional, considering my mother had a hand in selecting my honeymoon trousseau, but it's fine. I'm not cruising as a participant. I'm cruising as a professional observer."

"Seriously? You packed *those* clothes?" Kathryn placed the red curry beef on the coffee table and stood. She disappeared into the bedroom, clearly on a mission, leaving Charlie cringing on the couch from the noise of the massive storage bins being dragged out of the closet.

"I can't fit into your clothes," Charlie called, imagining her friend tossing short and skimpy dresses over her shoulder. "Don't bother. Even if I could get your miniskirts over my hips, they'd reach my knees."

"I'll admit we have different shapes. You're blessed with knockout curves, I have more height, but we're almost the same size," Kathryn said, emerging with her arms full of casual, bright-colored clothes.

"They still have tags on them," Charlie said.

"I picked them off the clearance racks at the end of the season and haven't had a chance to wear them yet." Kathryn held up a neon-green tank top that said something about giving her coffee before speaking. "These will help with getting people to talk openly with you. They invite conversation." She placed a pink one over her chest. It read, *Ask Me*. "If being a non-intimidating professional is your goal, these will work in a casual setting. You could wear them by the pool bar."

"Yes," Charlie conceded, reaching for the tanks. "They're good, non-intimidating, and cute. If you don't mind me being the first to wear them, I'll take them."

"I don't mind," Kathryn replied, holding the bright-colored shirts high. "On the condition that you agree to take these dresses with you." She held up a barely there little black number. The plunging halter matched the nonexistent back, which matched the tiny skirt.

"That's not enough material to cover my hips." Charlie held up a hand in protest. "Even if I'm five inches shorter than you, it's barely going to reach past my underwear."

"Don't wear any." Kat handed her the items in order. Colorful tanks. Miniskirts. Skimpy and fun sun dresses.

Letting out a long sigh, Charlie stuffed them in her case and returned to the couch. "You need to look at it from my point of view, Kat. This assignment means something different to me than it does to you."

"What are you talking about?" Her friend gave her a sobering look and sat beside her. "It means a byline to me and to you. We've worked hard for our own features. Plus, it's an opportunity to break out of our loveless ruts."

"Kind of." Charlie reached for the e-cig and took a long drag. "I'll admit that what you're saying is mostly on target. However, there's never been a doubt in your ability to make it as a writer. Your parents supported your career goals—maybe not financially so much, because they couldn't, but they always cheered you on. Paul hired you because he knew you were a capable writer. He had proof from your school days." She puffed on the pink stick and chased the vanilla-scented vapor with a waving hand.

"You're a great writer," Kathryn insisted.

"Thank you," Charlie said, folding her hands between her knees. "I like to believe that, but my family doesn't. According to them, the only reason for me to attend Columbia Journalism School was to find the right husband, which I recklessly overlooked during my undergraduate education. I was there for my M-R-S degree."

"You are so much more than pretty wifey material," Kathryn said, her pitch a bit higher than typical. "You're such a talented writer, not to mention someone that I would always want at my side. Dependable, smart, hardworking, stable—"

"It doesn't matter. None of that matters to my family. From the time I was in sixth grade, my parents made my life's ambition very clear. My only job was to find the proper husband I was bred for, blend the families, and bow my head as he grew my inheritance." Her shoulders dropped in defeat, but her determination rose in opposition. "*I* can grow my own fortune. I don't need an inheritance and a man to validate me."

"You don't touch your trust account."

"No. I don't," Charlie agreed. "There are too many conditions and repercussions. I don't want to be played like a marionette. I'd rather live within the means I earn."

"Okay. Let's talk about how this week will make a difference." Kathryn covered Charlie's hand and squeezed in support. "I'm here for you. Let's brainstorm the best avenues to proving that you are more than a pretty face."

Relief and gratitude flooded Charlie. She was so lucky to have a friend who believed in her. "I'm going back to the basics. Starting with the five W's every investigative reporter asks. Who, what, when, where, why . . . I'm going forward with my intentions from the moment I embark. I'm going to interview all of my fellow passengers that are willing to share."

"Don't forget the how," Kathryn added, folding her feet under her bum. "I got it. Let's brainstorm all your key questions over a bottle of wine. That way, you're guaranteed not to miss anything you could use."

"Can't," Charlie said, checking the time on her phone. "I need to get to the Port Authority. My bus leaves in a little over an hour."

"Bus?" Kat shrieked. "Are you out of your mind? That's going to take forever."

"Twenty-six hours, to be exact. The same amount of time you'll have on the ground in Paris." Charlie winked and stood. She carried the dinner containers to the kitchen and set them on the counter. "If I take a flight, I'll arrive totally wrecked and the first two days of the cruise will be ruined. I hate flying and need loads of meds to get my butt on a plane. It would take a huge toll on my body. I'll bus it."

Shaking her head, Kat gazed at the floor. "You're going to regret getting stuck—wait!" She looked up, excitement playing in her eyes.

Charlie looked at her friend, wondering what exactly the massive brainstorm was. "You know I'm on a tight schedule, right?"

"I got it," Kat said, holding an index finger in the air. "I have twenty-six hours in Paris. You have twenty-six hours on the bus. So you need twenty-six interview questions for the cruisers." She clasped her hands together and rolled her shoulders. "Trust me. It's our lucky number. Twenty-six! Everything twenty-six."

"Okay. If you insist." Charlie stretched up and wrapped her arms around Kat's shoulders. "I really have to go. I'll work on the questions while someone else drives. You never know who may be on that bus."

"You never know," Kat agreed.

About the Author

Demi Alex writes steamy romances, blending emotional fulfillments of the heart and carnal desires in her work. Born in Athens, Greece, and raised in her own version of a big fat Greek life in New York, Demi was infected with book and travel bugs early, and currently admits the only therapy for this condition is to combine the two in fictional stories that allow her characters to let loose and experience all they crave. She attended SUNY at Stony Brook, and after changing her major numerous times, graduated with a degree in public policy and international studies. Her characters are loosely inspired by people she encounters while she travels or during the time she spends matching homes to owners as a Realtor. She simply has a passion for matchmaking that can't be put to rest. Readers can visit her online at www.demialex.com, on Facebook, and at @DemiAlex2U on Twitter.

www.ingramcontent.com/pod-product-compliance
Lightning Source LLC
Chambersburg PA
CBHW021242260626
47155CB00004BA/1263